BORIS KARLOFF as THE INVISIBLE MAN

Books by
Philip J Riley

CLASSIC HORROR FILMS
Frankenstein, the original 1931 shooting script
Bride of Frankenstein, the original 1935 shooting script
Son of Frankenstein, the original 1939 shooting script
Ghost of Frankenstein, the original 1942 shooting script
Frankenstein Meets the Wolf Man, the original 1943 shooting script
House of Frankenstein, the original 1944 shooting script
The Mummy, the original 1932 shooting script
The Mummy's Curse the original 1944 shooting script (as Editor in Chief)
The Wolf Man, the original 1941 shooting script
Dracula, the original 1931 shooting script
House of Dracula, the original 1945 shooting script

CLASSIC COMEDY FILMS
Abbott & Costello Meet Frankenstein, the original 1948 shooting script

CLASSIC SCIENCE FICTION
This Island Earth, the original 1955 shooting script
The Creature from the Black Lagoon, the original 1953 shooting script (editor-in-chief)

THE ACKERMAN ARCHIVES SERIES - LOST FILMS
The Reconstruction of London After Midnight, the original 1927 shooting script
The Reconstruction of A Blind Bargain, the original 1922 shooting script
The Reconstruction of The Hunchback of Notre Dame, the original 1923 shooting script

CLASSIC SILENT FILMS
The Reconstruction of The Phantom of the Opera, the original 1925 shooting script
The Reconstruction of "London After Midnight" the original 1927 hooting script (2nd edition)

FILMONSTER SERIES - LOST SCRIPTS
James Whale's Dracula's Daughter, 1934
Cagliostro, The King of the Dead, 1932
Wolf Man vs. Dracula 1944
Lon Chaney as Dracula/Nosferatu
Robert Florey's Frankenstein 1931
Frankenstein - A play, 1931 (editor)
War Eagles (as editor)
Karloff as The Invisible Man 1932

AS EDITOR
Countess Dracula by Carroll Borland
My Hollywood, when both of us were young by Patsy Ruth Miller
Mr. Technicolor - Herbert Kalmus
Famous Monster of Filmland #2 by Forrest J Ackerman
FILM DOCUMENTARIES
A Thousand Faces - as contributor (Photoplay Productions)
Universal Horrors - as contributor (Photoplay Productions)
Mr. Riley has also contributed to 12 film related books by various authors
as well as numerous magazine articles and received the Count Dracula Society Award
and was inducted into Universal's Horror Hall of Fame

James Whale with screen writer Robert Cedric Sherriff

BORIS KARLOFF
AS
THE INVISIBLE MAN

An Alternate History for Classic Film Monsters

by

Philip J. Riley

Hollywood Publishing Archives

BearManor Media

BearManor Media
P.O. Box 1129
Duncan, OK 73534-1129

Phone: 580-252-3547
Fax: 814-690-1559

Boris Karloff name and likeness are trademarks of Karloff Enterprises

Cover Art - ©2009 By Philip J Riley - Since none of the scripts in this series
were thought to exist and were never produced, we have created mock-up posters in the
vintage style of the period.
All photographs are from the Author's collection
Certain documents were reset in LoveLetter font since the microfilm was not clear enough.
The script *The Invisible Man* by R. C. Sherriff is reproduced from the original document.
Chapter on the writing of The Invisible man from R.C. Sherriff's autobiograhy "No Leading
Lady", London: Victor Gollancz, 1968

Note: You will notice a change in the size of the type on some pages. The reason for this is that
most of the early Universal scripts were printed on 11x13 legal size paper and needed to be
reduced to fit on this books 8.24x11 paper.

The Author would like to thank the following individuals who contributed and helped make
this series possible. Carl Laemmle Jr., R.C.Sherriff, Stanley Bergerman, Gloria Holden, Jane
Wyatt, Otto Kruger, Marcel Delgado, Robert Florey, Paul Ivano (Cinematographer), Paul
Malvern (producer), Elsa Lanchester, Merion C Cooper, Patric Leroux, Bette Davis, Bela G.
Lugosi, Technicolor Corporation, John Balderston III, Loeb and Loeb Attorneys, David Stanley
Horsley ASC.
Author's Note: I interviewed the producers, directors, stars, cast and crew in the early to late
1970s. They were recalling events that happened 35-45 years previous and sometimes memory
fades or events are recalled from their perspective point of view.

First Edition
10 9 8 7 6 5 4 3 2 1

The purpose of this series is the preservation of the art of writing for the screen. Rare books
have long been a source of enjoyment and an investment for the serious collector, and even in
limited editions there are thousands printed. Scripts, however, numbered only 50 at the most.
In the history of American Literature, the screenwriter was being lost in time. It is my hope that
my efforts bring about a renewed history and preservation of a great American Literary form,
The Screenplay, by preserving them for study by future generations.

Recommended reading: *James Whale a New World of Gods and Monsters* University of Minnesota
Press 1998 edition by James Curtis; *City of Dreams* by Bernard F. Dick, 1997 University of Ken-
tucky: *James Whale A Biography or The Would-be Gentleman* by Mark Gatiss, Cassell Wellingon
House 1995; Excerpts from R. C. Sherriff's *No Leading Ladies* (London: Golancz 1968) reproduced with permission of R.C. Sherriff.

Boris Karloff, circa 1932

This volume is more of a portfolio in the development of Universal's *The Invisible Man*. It is different from the other volumes in the series in that, after attempts by many writers, Carl Laemmle Jr. was not satisfied with any of the treatments until James Whale got R.C. Sheriff to write the final shooting script. As you will see even Whale himself wrote a treatment.

Many projects were announced for Boris Karloff, now Universal's top monster film star; they ranged from the supernatural *Cagliostro*, the classic monster film *The Wolf Man* to the science fiction projects *A Trip to Mars* and *The Invisible Man*.

Cagliostro had morphed into *The Mummy*, 1932. A *Trip to Mars* , which, to the best of my knowledge, at

7

least a treatment was prepared and a shooting script completed by R.C.. Sherriff, but nothing was found in the Universal Vaults or microfilm on the title.

The following is from James Curtis' ultimate biography of James Whale.

"A *Trip to Mars* remains the most intriguing of all of Whale's unfilmed projects. Its basis was a 27 page story written by Henry Hoyt during his brief stint as a staff writer at Universal in 1932. Hoyt had been more prominently known as a director for First National, where he had presided over half a dozen silent features, most notably *The Lost World*. With *A Trip to Mars,* Hoyt proposed a fantastic yarn about a group of humans stuck on a planet where "strange half-mechanical creatures" battled "giant insects with almost human intelligence." Making the film would require the same combination of live action and stop-motion animation that had so convincingly brought Conan's Doyle's literary dinosaurs to life.

Whale injected a liberal dose of humor into Hoyt's original story, making Professor von Saxmar more hard-up than insane and adding the character of a henpecked millionaire who bankrolls the professor's expedition as a way of escaping his wife. Still, Hoyt had concocted much that appealed to Whale's sense of whimsy. For instance, the professor's pet Irish terrier learns to talk on Mars and dies during a climatic attack of giant ants with a cheerful wisecrack on his lips. Whale compared it to *The Invisible Man* and promised it would "soar higher still into the realms of trick photography, than the earlier film. He also said that the studio had established a special "trick department" to enlarge their knowledge of stunt photography."

The final shooting script was completed by R.C. Sherriff in late December of 1932. Even the creator of stop motion effects, Willis O'Brien applied for a position at Universal around this time period after *King Kong*. Perhaps in hopes of making this film

The Wolf Man, with Robert Florey as director, was shelved. (To be revived in 1941, starting Lon Chaney Jr.'s success as Universal's leading horror attraction all through the 1940s.)

But *The Invisible Man* starring Karloff was announced in the Universal Exhibitor's Book for 1932-33.

And Carl Laemmle Jr., wanted James Whale to direct it. Whale opted to do *The Road Back* but he still turned in a short treatment for *The Invisible Man* on January 3rd, 1932.

So Robert Florey was assigned to write and direct and he and Garrett Fort turned in a first draft on April 9, 1932.

H.G. Wells rejected the Florey/Fort adaptation (Wells had script approval as part of his contract).

Next it went to John Balderston who used many of the elements of the Fort script, but that was also rejected.

Over the next few months treatments were written by Gouveneur Morris, John Huston and Richard Schayer (All included in this volume)

Again from James Curtis' Whale biography:

"When the road back was shelved in November 1932 Whale was once again assigned to the project, Preston Sturges was composing his own fanciful version of the book.

Sturges, the celebrated author of *Strictly Dishonorable,* turned *The Invisible Man* into an elaborate revenge scenario incorporating aspects of the Frankenstein legend. Dr. Sarkov, a Russian chemistry professor who lost his family at the hands of the Bolsheviks, devises a way to make the maniacal Boris Karloff invisible. Sarkov uses him to murder the Soviet official responsible for the crime, but loses control of his creation. The Invisible Man begins a reign of terror, culminating in an attempt to kill both Sarkov and his fiancee before he himself is destroyed."

The next author was John Weld wrote a treatment based more on the novel and he was assigned to write the shooting script which was completed on February 9, 1933.

Whale was just finishing another film, *A Kiss Before the Mirror* when he was again to direct based on the acceptance by Wells of the Weld version.

However final approval ended up with R.C. Sherriff, who actually knew H.G. Wells.

It was Sherriff's version that evolved into the final shooting script, however at this time Karloff refused to do the picture due to a salary dispute with Carl Laemmle Jr.

Sherriff described the working condition at Universal Pictures during the writing of the screenplay.

"Universal was a boom town. Everything was fresh and vigorous and light-hearted, and everything they touched was turning into gold.

Later on the studios got jaded and sophisticated. They grew too fast, spent too much and had spectacular failures that ran them into financial troubles they weren't prepared to cope with. Producers and directors got too big for the boots. There were feuds and jealousies, intrigues and plots behind the scenes. Men rose and fell from power with astonishing rapidity. "Always be polite to the gatekeeper," people said. "He may be head of the studio next week." But in those golden years of the early 1930s there wasn't any time for petty quarrels. There was work for all, and the studios couldn't keep pace with the tremendous demand for talkies.

Universal was one of the best. They had recently made *The Phantom of the Opera, King of Jazz,* and a string of spectacular Westerns that earned fabulous money. The star of the cowboy pictures used to arrive at the studio in an all-white Rolls-Royce dressed to match in an all-white cowboy out-rig with golden spurs. The studio was laid out in streets of huts and bungalows, with the big stages looming out like aircraft hangars. The important people had bungalows with trim lawns and flower-beds round them, and their offices sported think carpets and carved oak desks, but for the rest it was rough and ready, with the dry brown desert grass round their huts still waiting to be cleaned away.

The studio was presided over by Carl Laemmle: "Uncle Carl" to everybody, and everybody loved him. He was called the Grand Old Man of Hollywood, although he couldn't have been much over sixty. But sixty was venerable in that young up and coming business , and he was no doubt the oldest man then at it. Whale too me to meet him. He was a little beaming goblin of a man, a Jew from Germany who worked his way up, they said, from running nickelodeons in small amusement arks. He wasn't much good, I was told, at reading or writing but he had the gift of picking good men and the sense to leave them alone to do their jobs.

He was friendly and affable, but didn't have much to say and didn't ask me any questions. He took it for granted that an English writer was a creature from another world who didn't talk his language, and being a shrewd, sensible little man he couldn't see the point of wasting time trying to make contact.

"Take him round to meet Junior," he said to Whale.

Junior Laemmle was a young edition of his father who had recently come from college to be productions manager of the studio. It was a family business, and that's what made it friendly and intimate. Junior with good schooling and his years at college, brought to the studio the things his father hadn't got. He mightn't have been so shrewd and tough, be he was equipped to make easy contact with everybody who came to work there. He was genuine and sincere and liable. "This *Invisible Man* story," he said, "we reckon it's fine stuff for the screen, but we haven't hit on the right approach. Jimmy Whale's got a hunch that you're the feller to do it, and if you go along to the story department they'll give you everything we've had done."

The story department was in considerable confusion, which wasn't to be wondered at when you allowed for what they had to try to do.

I always thought story departments ought to be segregated from the hurly-burly of the studios. They ought to have had a quiet place away from the noise and hurry where they could work peacefully, with leisure to read and think. It never happened that way.

Producers and directors wanted them close at hand to make emergency running repairs to shooting scripts that had broken down in the middle of production, or to give split-second advice on scripts they'd got to start shooting without delay because expensive stars were being kept waiting. The result was that they never had time to read anything in peace. It was their job to see a story through from the raw material to the finished screenplay, but they were swamped with stuff sent in to them by agents. Piles of it arrived each morning. It was dished out to readers who prepared brief outlines, and as most of the readers were paid per outline they read the book as quick as they could and made the outlines at hot speed. No outline done like that could possibly do justice to a novel with any depth or quality in it, so it rested on pur chance, hit or miss, whether anything went farther than an outline.

The story editor was working in his shirt sleeves, his collar undone and his tie hanging loose. His desk and whole office were stacked with books and scripts. He was a big, fat, cheerful man who seemed to be enjoying it. Every few minutes the telephone rang and he broke off midway though what he was telling me to answer it. He'd say: "Yes Bert, I'll see about that. No, we haven't read it yet; it's the hell of a big book, so we'll have to call you back this afternoon.

He told me, in greater detail, what Whale and Junior Laemmle had already told me about the fate, so far, of *The Invisible Man*.

On his desk stood a pile of scripts, a dozen or so of them, about a foot high. They were screen adaptations of Well's book, all by different writers, but the story editor said a lot of people had read them and they'd all come to the same conclusion. "There's good stuff in them," he told me, "but we don't reckon that any of them quite hits the bull's-eye. It's a swell story with a great idea in it, and it ought to make a world beater on the screen. It'll be terrific if we get a real good job, and Jimmy Whale reckons you're the man to do it. So we want you to take all these scripts away with you and sift them out, and get the best stuff into shape for a real good screenplay."

Having trouble working at the studio Whale came up with a plan to help him out. "Come in and watch me shooting *The Old Dark House* and pack up after lunch." [All Sherriff had to do was show up in the morning and then drive to his hotel where he could work in peace. He started reading the pile of previously written scripts.]

". . . I sorted them out and began with the first that had been written.

The man who had turned it out no doubt had the original H.G. Wells book beside him, but to justify his employment he had got to improve on it. If he had stuck to the original story and made a faithful adaptation the studio would probably have said he hadn't got any initiative or imagination of his own; that they weren't paying him good money merely to copy out what Wells had written. So he set aside the original story and given the invisible man adventures from his own imagination. The studio had no doubt felt there were good ideas in it but not enough, and it was passed on to another writer. The second writer had got to go one better and invent a lot more new ideas. The third writer had to trump the one before, and so it went on, each new effort becoming more extravagant and fantastic and ridiculous. One writer took the scene to Tsarist Russia at the time of the Revolution and turned the hero into a sort of invisible Scarlet Pimpernel. Another made him into a man from Mars who threatened to flood the world with invisible Martians, and all of them envisaged him as a figure of indescribable peril to the world, threatening to use his unique invisibility to reform it or destroy it, as he felt inclined..

One thing stood out clearly in every page I read. The charm and the humour and the fascination that had established the original Wells story as a classic had been utterly destroyed, and there wasn't a word in all that massive pile of scripts that I could use without throwing aside my own respect for a story that had enraptured me since boyhood.

I was in a quandary. I didn't want to go to the story editor and pose as a superior person by saying that the stuff I'd read was rubbish. I'd brought a certain amount of prestige with me from England: my opinion might be listened to and respected. I couldn't say anything that might undermine the careers of young writers when for all I knew they might be right in the way they'd gone about adapting *The Invisible Man*. Maybe the original Wells novel wasn't the sort of stuff that people wanted on the screen; maybe it had got to be blown out and exaggerated in the way these writers had done it. I didn't know. I didn't know enough about the picture business to be certain, and that was my quandary. I'd never even written a screenplay myself. Playwriting and screen-writing were as different as chalk from cheese, and it would be sheer vanity to go along to the story editor and tell him that all these other writers didn't know their job.

The more I thought about it the more certain I felt that the original Wells story would never have become a classic if it hadn't had something in it far better than all this tripe I had been reading. But I couldn't get anywhere without a copy of the book. I only had the memory of its fascination to me as a boy. I had a copy at home but hadn't re-read it before I left. It hadn't worried me when I discovered I'd forgotten it, because I took it for granted that there would

be plenty of copies in the studio. But the studio had long since lost their only copy."

"Some way or other I'd got to get hold of one, so I went round the few bookshops that existed in Hollywood. Some had vaguely head about it, but that was all. One book seller told me it had been out of print for years. He might get a second-hand copy if he advertised for it, but he was rather doubtful. I couldn't wait for that, so I got the car out and drove down to Los Angeles. I didn't rekon it was a city that went in much for classics, and the calls I made on the bookshops in the main streets confirmed it. Their shelves were full of the latest best-sellers, stacks of paper-backed Westerns, lurid sex romances and crime stories, but for the book I was looking for I got the same dead-pan answer that I got in Hollywood.

I began to wander down the squalid side streets. There were lots of second-hand junk shops selling garish ornaments, decorated Indian pottery, fusty Mexican rugs and framed pictures made of sea-shells and beads. Most of them had a box of old discarded book, but they were merely tattered copies of the stuff I'd seen before. I wandered on until I came into the Chinese quarter. It was colourful here, but smelly. I came .into a sort of market with open stalls that sold everything from jewelry to cabbages. In one still there was a box of old breasy magazines mixed up with stuff that looked like hair out of a mattress. I didn't like touching it: it might have been discarded Chinese pigtails. But pushing the magazines aside I came upon an assortment of small books in faded brown cloth covers. Apparently they all belonged to a uniform edition, and must have come at some time in the past from the library of somebody who read the classics. There were volumes of Scott and Dickens, strange things to find in a Chinese market. Probing deeper I found Kipling, then *Kipps* by H.G. Wells. I was so excited that I could hardly keep my hands steady as I rummaged on. There were more Dickens, more Scott, then more Wells. I began to fear that the vital, all-important book was missing, but there at last it was: The Invisible Man. It was an incredible piece of luck. I wouldn't have looked in a hundred years in that musty old box if I hadn't been at my wits' end and practically given up hope.

It cost me fifteen cents, but was worth a gold mine. The smiling Chinese stall-holder suggested that I might also like a pickled cabbage? Possibly a crayfish or a small pork pie? But I was more than satisfied.

When I got back to the Château Elysée I opened the precious little volume and put it out in the sunlight on the balcony. It had the musty, sickly smell of the Chinese market, and I wished there had been some way of fumigating it. It had been, I imagined, in that old box of junk for years, and every sort and condition of people had picked it up and pawed it. I had left it out to air until after dinner, and it didn't smell so bad when I brought it in.

I began to read: "The stranger came early in February one wintry day, through a biting wind and a driving snow, the last snowfall of the year, over the down, walking as it seemed from Bramblehurst railway station and carrying a little black portmanteau in his thickly gloved hand . . ." And with those opening lines all the memories came flooding back of that fascinating first chapter which had gripped me as a boy and held me entranced until the end. I read on through the night and when near dawn I finished I knew very clearly why Wells had been acknowledged as a master.

His secret was a simple one. To give reality to a fantastic story, he knew that it had to be told through the eyes of ordinary, plain spoken people. If you tried to fasten extraordinary people to extraordinary events the whole thing fell to pieces, and that's what the writers of that massive pile of screenplays had done. They had invented fabulous events and surrounded them with unreal characters.

Having read the novel I was up against a problem that would need a lot of guile and subterfuge to overcome. The story editor rang up next morning to know what I thought about the scripts he'd given me, and I went across to see him at his office. I told him I thought the scripts were fine, brimful of clever inventions and exciting scenes; but if I were to extract the best material and try to put it together as a coherent script I couldn't hope to produce more than a patchwork that would never hold together on the screen.

In the circumstances I asked whether he would agree to my setting aside the other scripts and making my own adaptation of the story. I didn't say a word about the original novel I'd unearthed in the Chinese market. If I'd told him I was scrapping all the stuff they'd paid good money for, and was going to adapt the story, chapter by chapter, exactly as Wells had written it, then I was fairly sure he would have been upset and disillusioned. They were paying me $1,500 a week for my own original ideas, not to copy out an old book they'd given up as useless.

The story editor welcomed the idea. The more new stuff they got the better. It was in his mind, no doubt, that an extra script would add weight to the enterprise; they might then get an even bigger writer, at $2,000 a week, to boil down the whole bundle and make a super screenplay of it.

"How long will it take you?" he asked.

Whale had warned me that they always wanted things in a hurry, but if you stood out they'd give you the time you needed. There wasn't any desperate rush. Whale couldn't get around to a new assignment for at least three months, and I promised the story editor I'd have my script finished for when he was ready to begin work on it.

So everything was satisfactorily arranged. In was to go right ahead with my own screen version of *The Invisible Man*, and the story editor told me to come in and see him if I ran into any problem he could help me over. I said I certainly would, but all I wanted was to be left alone.

We didn't stay long at the Château Elysée. Summer was coming, and the night in Hollywood were hot and airless, so one evening we drove down to the coast at Santa Monica and found an old timber-framed hotel on the palisades overlooking the Pacific.

There was a bungalow in the garden that we rented for the rest of our stay. We were very happy. My mother like it because she got to know some pleasant Americans who lived there in retirement. Every morning when I'd gone off to the studio she would take a walk on the palisades or sit in the gardens talking to her new friends, or go into Santa Monica to do her shipping. There was a little kitchen where she cooked our Sunday lunch, and she found a butcher in Santa Monica who had come from England, and he cut the joints in the way she wanted them.

I soon got to know what a boon it was, in Hollywood, to have a home to go back to in the evenings. If I'd been alone I couldn't have avoided going out to parties, and even the best of them were so exhausting that I wouldn't have been fit for my night's work when I got back.

I had to go to some, because the glamour of *Journey's End* had followed me out there and invitations came from people I couldn't refuse and didn't want to refuse. Charlie Chaplin asked me round for dinner. An invitation to dine in Hollywood with Chaplin was like an invitation in London from the Prime Minister. It was a lovely house with nothing flamboyant about it, and Chaplin reminded me of Kipling in his boyish zest for life and disarming enjoyment of his success. It was a small party, not more than half-a-dozen, all from the Hollywood aristocracy. Sam Goldwyn was there: he talked about Douglas Fairbanks and the dialogue went like this:

Goldwyn: The trouble with Doug is that you can't get him down to serious work because he's always making love.

Chaplin: He can't make love *all* the time. What does he do when he's not making love?

Goldwyn: Then I guess he just practises.

The dinner party was enlivened by Charlie Chaplin, who had recently been to Japan. He got up half-way through the meal and gave an imitation of a Japanese wrestler facing his opponent. He stood there crouching down and doing nothing beyond making little threatening movements with his hands and screwing up his face into fierce little snarls, and I was sorry when the butler said, "Your dinner's getting cold, Mr. Chaplin".

The "wild parties" that Hollywood was famous for never came my way, and from what I heard about them I didn't miss anything. The real people, the established stars and producers and directors, lived quietly and spent their evenings at home. They were too busy at their work and to go to dinner with Ronald Colman or Boris Karloff or Norma Shearer was like dining with friends in a quiet house at home.

For our own part we settled down to the sort of life that suited us. Every morning I would go to the studio. It was an invigorating sunlit drive across the hills: the morning air was clear and cool, and you smelt the wild honeysuckle and forgot about the movies until you came round a bend in the road and saw Universal Studios lying on the plain beneath you. I would give my secretary the script I'd written overnight, then wander around watching anything that was going on. Sometimes I'd meet the story editor hurrying along with a pile of scripts under his arm. He'd say, "How's the screenplay going?", and I'd say "Fine", and he'd say, "Keep at it, boy!" and hurry on.

By this time the whole area outside my window surrounding the crashed aeroplane had been covered with artificial snow: the aeroplane was supposed to have crashed in the Arctic wilds of Alaska. When everything was ready to shoot the scene a machine was set in motion to blow imitation snow in all directions to provide the necessary blizzard. The snow was made out of a certain brand of breakfast flakes that were light and realistic. It attracted the butterflies, and once some little brightly coloured birds swooped down and started to eat it.

Soon it was full summer, and at weekends the beaches beneath the palisades were crowded with people who drove out from Los Angeles for a day by the sea. Sometimes we took a picnic lunch and drove along the coastal highway to Santa Barbara or Palos Verdes. Other times we drove inland: over the hills and through the orange groves and away into the desert.

After dinner we would walk on the palisades in the sunset. There was no lingering twilight that followed the setting of the sun, as at home. The sun would drop down behind the rim of the ocean, and the glow it left behind quickly faded into night. It would be quite dark by the time we got back to our bungalow. My mother would go to bed, and I would settle down in the sitting room to work on the script of *The Invisible Man*.

A screenplay, to my way of thinking, lay about halfway between a stage play and a novel. You were free from the narrow boundaries of the stage, but had to keep from wandering down the bye-lanes open to the novelist. People might take a week or more to read a novel, putting it down and taking it up again when they felt inclined. There were intervals between acts in the theatre when the audience got up and relaxed, strolled around outside and talked to their friends. But when a film began there wasn't a break until it was finished. The audience never left their seats or took their eyes off the screen, so you couldn't afford to let go of them for a moment. You had to prune away the side-shoots and keep to the main stem, and every line of dialogue was there to drive the story on.

I took that line with *The Invisible Man*, but Wells had paved the way for me. He never drifted away into anything that wasn't essential to the story, so it wasn't difficult to stick to the novel as he had written it. I dramatized it chapter by chapter, and it was mainly a matter of turning narrative into dialogue. I had to add ingredients here and there to tighten up the drama, and condense a lot to pack a novel of two hundred pages into a film designed to play for a hundred minutes, but when it was finished I felt reasonable sure that this was the genuine unadulterated story which Wells himself had conceived.

When she had got it all typed out my secretary said it was too long. In the way they set them out at the studio a script played to an average of a page a minute, and there were ten pages to many.

This was a shock, because there wasn't a scene in it that I hadn't already cut to the bone.

"But you don't have to worry," she said. "The story department has had a lot of experience in cutting scripts down. If you leave it to them they'll soon get ten pages out of it.

But I didn't want that to happen at any price, because I was reasonably sure they'd go at it with a carving knife and slice out big chunks anyhow and anywhere, mutilating scenes vital to the story. The only thing was to start afresh and write the screenplay over again. It was an exhausting job, but good practice in dramatic economy, and I soon began to find lines of twenty words that could be spoken just as effective in ten.

I sweated over it for a week, working most of the nights, for time was running short. But it came out all right in the end. When my secretary typed out then new version it was down to a hundred pages, so I gave the whole thing a final polish and sent it round to the story editor.

What would happen next I didn't know.

My main anxiety was that the studio might by now have come across their long-lost copy of the original novel. If they had, and compared it to the script, they'd probably say to each other, "This guy's pulled a fast one on us. He's copied the whole damn thing out of the book—just like Wells wrote it. He hasn't thought up anything of his own, and all the good money we've paid him has gone down the drain"

When a week had gone by without a word I began to fear the worst. I needn't have worried, because the silence was merely due to their having copies made for handling round to all concerned, and the first word came from Whale, who drove down one evening to see me in Santa Monica.

He had got the script, he said, the previous evening. He had sat up reading it most of the night, and thought it was magnificent. It was so simple and straightforward, so free from affectation: the characters sprang to life in the first words they spoke: the suspense was tremendous and breathlessly exciting. It knocked all those other adaptations into a cocked hat. They can't hold a candle to it, and he was delighted.

Whale was an old friend. We understood each other so well that it had been in my mind to confide in him that everything I had written was pure and simple Wells, Wells from start to finish: that all I had done was to dramatize and condense the story to fit the screen. But on second thoughts I decided to keep quiet about it. The script put me so high in his estimation that there wasn't any point in watering it down. He had obviously forgotten the original novel: all that concerned him was that I'd produced a work of genius, and he was the happier because I had been his protégé,

There was a further reason for his enthusiasm. The studio had just told him to forget about *The Invisible Man* and make a sequel to *Frankenstein* next. *Frankenstein* had been his first picture for Universal. It had been a big money-spinner and had established his name as a film director, but the idea of making a sequel to it repelled him.

"They're always like that," he said. "If they score a hit with a picture they always want to do it again. They've got a perfectly sound commercial reason. Frankenstein was a gold-mine at the box office, and a sequel to it is bound to win, however rotten it is. They've had a script made for a sequel and it stinks to heaven. In any case I squeezed the idea dry on the original picture, and never want to work on it again."

But it had put him in an quandary. He was under contract to make another picture, and had turned down all the *Invisible Man* scripts as useless. They were pressing him for a decision, and he was facing up to the miserable ordeal of the *Frankenstein* sequel when my script had come life a gift from heaven.

"I'm not just using your script as a way of getting out of this horrible *Frankenstein* sequel," he said. "It's a lovely job, and I'd do it if I had a hundred scripts to choose from"

Whale was one of the studio's top directors, but I knew that the final word must come from Junior Laemmle, the production manager, and I asked Whale what Junior was likely to thing about it.

"You leave Junior to me," he said. "I'm fairly sure he hasn't looked at the script yet. If I know the studio, nobody's read it. That puts me one up on the others, so I'm going to see Junior in the morning and move heaven and earth."

At oen time Whale had been an actor, and he told me afterwards about the performance he put up in Junior Laemmle's office on the morning after he came to see me.

Hollywood, at that time, was suffering from a run-away inflation in verbal superlatives. Men had to work hard to persuade a studio tha the things thay wanted to do were worth the money. They were always searching for bigger and more impressive words, because the old ones had long since been worn out. To say that a story was "good" or "interesting" didn't mean a thing. To capture a studio's attention it had to be "epic", "Terrific", "stupendous". They dearched the dictionary for superlatives, but even so the most extravagant words soon lost effect and came to nothing.

Whale was well aware of this. He knew that if you'd got something you honestly and genuinely believed in, it was impossible to say so in verbal currency that would have the necessary purchase value. So he took a different line. He cut it all out. He walked into Junior Laemmle's office with the script and laid it on the desk. 'Have you read this new screenplay for *The Invisible Man?*' he asked. As Whale expected, Junior hadn't—which was all to the good. It gave Whale a flying start.

"I haven't had a chance to get around to it yet, Jimmy," Junior replied. "But I'll have a look at it this morning."

"Then *don't!*" said Whale. "Don't read a word of it in this office with all the distractions of the studio going on around you!:

Junior began to be intrigued. Nobody had ever before demanded that he was not to read a script in his office. He was accustomed to people pushing sccripts beneath his nose and saying, "Read it now, Junior—read it now."

"Tell your secretary to call off anything you've got on tonight," said Whale. "Take the script home and don't look at it till you've had your supper. Then tell them you not to be disturbed for the rest of the evening. I needn't tell you not to go to bed till you've finished it, because once you begin reading it nothing on God's earth will make you put it down till you've finished it."

By this time Junior Laemmle was so impressed that he forgot all the bombastic superlatives he was accustomed to and said, "You mean it's good, Jimmy?"

Whale then went round to the story editor, who also hadn't yet had time to read the script. "Junior has cancelled all his engagements tonight to read it," said Whale, and I want you to do the same." The story editor rarely took scripts home to read: he had a belly full of them in his office all day. But the news that Junior was going to read it overnight put him on his mettle. If Junior rang him up in the morning about it he couldn't tell him that he hadn't read the stuff. So he said "Okay, Jimmy, if you say it's worth giving up the evening for, then that's good enough for me."

And so the two key men who held the fate of a story in their hands took the script home and read it before they went to bed. If it hadn't been for Whale they probably wouldn't have look at it for weeks.

How much came out of the way Whale had played upon their curiosity and how much was their own genuine opinion I didn't know, but the next morning Laemmle Junior and the story editor arrived at the studio bursting with enthusiasm. The script was terrific, stupendous, the best they'd read in years. The word went round: by mid-day everybody that mattered in the studio was reading it. Even old man Laemmle had it read to him aloud.

Next day I was invited to lunch in the executive's private dining-room. All the departmental chiefs were there, and all agreed that the script was epic. How many had actually read it was anybody's guess. Pretending you'd read a script was a fine art in Hollywood. Some people got so good at it that they could offer lengthy and discerning criticisms without even knowing what the story was about. The departmental chiefs were busy men. They had their work cut out to keep abreast of their jobs, and didn't get much chance to sit down undisturbed to read a screenplay. But they had to know enough about the script of the important pictures to talk about them when required, so they usually gave them to their wives or secretaries who told them enough about the story to put them wise.

But when both Laemmle Junior and the story editor proclaimed their enthusiasm for a script, and a lunch was announced next day to talk about it, the executives had to act quickly, and some might even have taken it home to read themselves.

In any case, when we sat down to lunch they all seemed to have the thing at their finger-tips, and all had worked up some stuff to give them a talking point. One had apparently read *The Fortnight in September*, and said that the screenplay for *The Invisible Man* combined the simplicity and naturalness of that best-seller novel with the dramatic impact of the world renowned Journey's End. The other enthusiastically agreed.

They'd probably hadn't read the novel or seen the play, but were glad to hear that I had wrapped up the money-making potentials of both in *The Invisible Man*. For that morning at least I was the golden boy of the studio.

For one thing I was devoutly thankful. It was clear that their long-lost copy of the original Wells novel had not turned up. Nobody even mentioned it, and with such acclaim ringing in my ears it would have be professional suicide to tell them that the whole screenplay, from start to finish, had come straight from Wells and not from me. Hollywood was young, ambitious, basking in the glory of breaking into untilled golden land. If they bought and old book like *The Invisible Man* it was only because it had in it a germ that they could fertilize and make grow into something far beyond the imagination of its creator, and that's why I knew was disastrous it would be to tell them what I had done. When they asked what had inspired me to write such a wonderful script I told them that it was all due to them for giving me a free hand, and that I was very happy to have given them something in return.

Before lunch was over everything was settled. The sequel to Frankenstein was put on the shelf and Whale was to begin *The Invisible Man* as soon as he was ready. The publicity manager went back to his office to announce it to the press, and the others went back to their offices convinced that they had a money-spinner in their hands.

R.C. Sherriff, 1968

You will note that in the Schayer version Karloff's name changed from Honan to Horan (This was probably due to different typist of Schayer's original hand written manuscirpt) and Colin Clive is mentioned as the doctor who creates the invisibility ray.

(The chemical "Monocaine" was drempt up by Sherriff - thus making it unnecessary to use the elaborate electrical devises used in *Frankenstein*

Carl Laemmle Sr. President of Universal Pictures

Carl Laemmle Jr., Production Manager

Claude Rains, who took over the lead after Karloff turned it down - LEFT Director James Whale

Colin Clive was originally plaanned as the scientist who invents an invisible ray in a loboratory that resembled Frankenstein's lab. Karloff's part was the lab assistant Honan, whom is made invisible in an experiment (See the Richard Schayer treatment on page 91)

THE INVISIBLE MAN

By

James Whale

(Star - Karloff)

Jan. 3 1932

An important personage lies dying in a magnificent bed-chamber. Priests, doctors and relatives group themselves, grimly mourning, so deeply we possibly suspect treachery.

Hope is abandoned, priest is about to administer last sacrament, when one of the servants rushes in, breaks through the group and says if only his master would permit his doctor he know he could cure him. The mourners are outraged, and start to bully him out, when the dying old man notices the commotion, demands to know what it is. An evil looking doctor tells the dying man it is only a poor, crazed servant who wants to bring some quack doctor into his presence. Upon further insistence the servant is brought to the foot of the bed, in much the same manner as an early martyr, surrounded by priests, etcetera. The of man motions for them to let him speak. The servant tells his tale. He doesn't know who he is, but a strange, tall, thin man whose face no one has ever seen tends all the poor of the village, and refuses payment. He is surrounded by mystery. They think he is expiating some dreadful sin, and the villagers call him the invisible man.

Horror and consternation in the bed chamber! They are about to fall on him and drag him from the room, when the old man in a weak voice orders that the doctor be brought.

They drag the servant out of the room, pull him down the stairs, throw him on the floor of the hall, and bully him more than ever. The peasant now having the backing of his master, suddenly takes on a new authority, and makes his own conditions. He must be driven alone to a spot he will point out, and no one will be permitted to go to the doctor's abode. A conveyance and driver are brought and they clatter off into the night.

A few shots of weird aspect brings us to a lonely spot on the outskirts of the town.

The servant suddenly cries, "Stop!" The driver pulls up suddenly, and is about to get down, but is mysteriously prevented from doing so by the servant who says: "Everything depends on your being blind and deaf - stay here and do nothing until I return."

We follow the servant through weird gates past shadowy trees, expecting to come upon a strange house, but instead he hops over a wall into a queer bleak churchyard with gleaming crosses, and grim ghostly monuments.

He comes at length to a dark family vault with iron railings, in which is a little gate, which he opens and passes through, looking round however furtively before doing so. Standing in the middle of the enclosure is a monument, somewhat like an upturned sarcophagus, tall and grim, an exquisitely carved angel's head with spreading wings is at the top. Taking up a heavy stone the servant knocks three times on the grave, making a horrid sickening noise. There is silence for a moment, and we then hear a slight subterraneous rumble, followed by a a voice from nowhere. "Who are you?"

Servant mumbles his name accompanied by two rapid knocks and we hear more rumblings coming up from the earth. The servant now stands upright in front of the monument expectantly.

CAMERA FOCUSES on the angel's beautiful face, which slowly hinges outward, revealing a dim, vague, but horrid shape in the aperture, framed on either side by the two delicate angel's wings.

The face in the aperture is very startling. It is wrapped entirely in bandages, rather like a mummy, and wears a pair of heavy dark glasses. It moves and speaks: "Well, William, what is it?"

Whereupon the servant begs him to come and see his master, adding, it is a matter of life and death. The voice which is very beautiful, sardonically replies:

"It is always a matter of life and death. - Come in"

We now have the thrill of introducing a mysterious BEING of the Dracula and Frankenstein order, but with the difference of meeting what is obviously a delightful person behind that cryptic makeup.

The lid of the sarcophagus opens mysteriously and both the stranger and the servant disappear into the bowels of the earth. The lid of the sarcophagus closes and the CAMERA PANS up to the smiling expression on the angel's sweet face as the picture FADES. . .

AS AN ALTERNATIVE SUGGEST INSTEAD OF A FADE WE
COULD GO ON IN. The stranger switches on an electric
torch, leads the way followed closely by the servant, both
disappearing into the bowels of the earth.

THE CAMERA anticipates their entrance into what is obviously an old family vault. The walls of the interior are
lined with coffins, resting on marble slabs. In the center
of the chamber lies another casket, on which are strewn a few
magazines and papers, and which serves as seat and table.

The stranger gracefully indicates for his visitor to
be seated, apologizing for lack of modern comforts, and for
the magazines which are slightly out of date. There is a
very short scene, and with charming manners, which however
have a firm authority behind them as he asks to what he
owes the pleasure of this visit. The peasant tells of his
master, who is a good man, lying at the point of death, being
slowly murdered by poison, or starvation, and we learn
that the servant's wife and child were miraculously cured
by the mysterious stranger, who leaves the peasant for a
moment and disappears behind another door, into what will
ultimately be the laboratory of invisibility, but which we
do not see now.

He reappears however, very shortly, with hat, stick and
a small bag, and as they exit. . . we DISSOLVE BACK into
the sick bedchamber.

There is much commotion in the house. The doctors and
relatives are all there insisting the old man take further
doses of their medicine, but he weakly waves them away.

They are just about to overcome his reluctance however when
the priest says"

"Listen!"

There is silence and we hear the rumble of the carriage
wheels. They rush to the window and there is considerable
suspense, as the carriage stops, and the servant alights,
alone, shutting the door after him. We watch him from above
coming up the steps of the house, and disappearing under
the lens of the camera.

The crowd all rush to the door of the bedroom and after
a little suspense it opens, and the servant enters. He gives
some instructions from the invisible man which are, they
must all leave the room and passages quite clear. After some
protest this is done.

The stranger is now brought in to the house by the servant. His entrance if full of mystery and we avoid shots of
his face. The CAMERA being either behind, or at such an angle
it accentuates the weirdness of the mysterious figure. They
cross the hall, mount the great staircase, stand for a moment outside the bedchamber. The stranger asks if his instructions
are carried out, and they enter.

THE CAMERA still following them into the huge bedroom. The
firelight is flickering with ghostly effect. No sound is heard except perhaps the ticking of a clock, or the bark of a dog.

The CAMERA moves swiftly to a CLOSE-UP of the old man, and
we discover he has been blindfolded. Into the shot the stranger's
expressive hands, feel pulse, take temperature, etcetera.
As we hold on the old man the hands go out of the shot, and mix

certain medicines. The old man's breathing is very labored
and somewhat ghastly, one of the stranger's hands gently
raises the old man's head, and with the other gives him the
mixture. Hands go out of the picture, puts down the glass,
and and gently lays the head back on the pillow. After
a moment's sympathetic caress the hands undo the bandages,
and we discover the old man's eyes have closed, his breathing
has become easier, and he peacefully sleeps.

Still keeping the stranger's back to the camera we see
him collect his props and prepare to leave, before he does so
however, something dramatic must happen to the invisible man,
and our story must develop. It might be that the daughter
who has remained, concealed in the room, rushes forward
dramatically, and tearing off the stranger's cloak and hat,
demands to know who he is.

It is child's play to snatch a tense moment here, as the
gruesome face savagely turns upon her and looks into the
CAMERA.

In a weirdly tender scene the girl might here discover
her lover, who had mysteriously disappeared, because of a
horrible disfigurement to his face during scientific experiments for the good of the poor sick. After a heartbreaking
scene she enters the most exclusive order of nuns in a
convent, and banishes herself from the world.

The stranger returns to his tomb, and in an agony of
spirit, wrestles with God. His hands clasped in religious
fever, he prays:

"OH THOU WHO ART INVISIBLE

and to whom nothing is unseen,

who carest for the sick and fatherless,

who created the earth and all that is upon

it, to whom there is no mystery in man or

beast; THOU who gavest and takest away, hear

the prayer of thy Servant, and remove from

the eyes of mortal man the harmful sight of

this frightful face, that I may be allowed

to do thy will unseen."

At the end of the prayer, which is terrible in its intensity, the music, which has accompanied the entire picture
in the grand opera manner, swells into something like the
grim apparatus we lead up to the slow unwinding of his
bandages, revealing for the first time in his features a
horror so fantastic, so unbelievable hideous, that although
he deals with the devil himself, we sympathize with his
desire to become invisible. With the old servant as an
accomplice, and with all the arts of Camera and mystery
trickery, the stupendous achievement is complete, but our
horror grows as we discover that during the transition the
mind has completely changed, and now has only a longing
to kill those very people he had healed and befriended.

His first victim is the poor, crazed servant and we
FADE OUT on the delightful spectacle of his being slowly
strangled to death by invisible hands. As a crowning piece
of horror and before the death rattle of the victim announces
his demise, the stranger's horrible face, which now has the
added terror of a murderous mind, becomes visible in the victim's
last fleeting moment from this beautiful world. Having been
suspended in air the victim falls dead on the floor, with a face
frozen in horror. The corpse receives a violent kick from an

invisible foot, and our CAMERA panning down, traces footsteps
of naked feet, treading in blood, to the door. Coming up to the
door handle we hear a squeak, and the door opens of its own
accord, almost immediately however, closing to the accompaniment of soft laughter, dying away as the invisible
man FADES OUT into the lovely night.

If this is too mild the corpse could be lifted by invisible
hands, dragged swiftly out, and flung either on to a grave
in the churchyard, or into a still farther recess in case we
wish to pile future corpses into a funeral pyre.

A short series of diabolical murders is planned and
executed.

Meanwhile the lovelady is about to take her final vows
to enter the most exclusive order of Sisterhood. In this
scene which offers scope for magnificent production, the
splendor of the ceremony of consecration could be searched
for impressive details.

Knowing the invisible man is on her track, we
could build suspense by having the most elaborate presen-
tation. The acolytes could trim the altar, priests, processing
back and forth with all the ritual stressed. The procession
of nuns with swing censors, the novices prostrate in white
on the steps of the altar. The clanging of the bells, and the
peal of the organ. The CAMERA, which is now on the face of
the holy bride, exquisitely sad, and spiritually beautiful
PANS swiftly across the Cathedral to a door, which slowly
opens. A knife stealthily creeping towards the altar, accompanied by the soft footfalls of naked feet. The knife

furtively passes in and out pillars, and eventually comes
to a stop, setting high up in the great carved chair of
the Bishop.

We cut several items during the ceremony to this playful
knife, somewhat in the nature of the hand on the bannister
in "The Dark House", and as the lovely bride is receiving
 the sacrament, the knife raises and completes its bloody
work.

Our meal of horror is not yet complete, The liquer is
still to be served. Our eyes surely must pop completely out
as we watch the knife jerk itself free from the now unlovely
corpse, raise itself in mid-air, and plunge itself quivering
into the heart of the remorseful invisible man. Who, as his
life's blood ebbs swiftly away, becomes gradually visible,
revealing for an instant, a face so fantastically horrible that
even we who are used to such dishes, close our eyes, as the
sound of a dull flopping thud forces the sickening news
through our other senses, that the lovers are united at last

Finis

Gouveneur Morris, author - seen here with Lon Chaney on the Goldwyn Studios Lot

THE INVISIBLE MAN

By

H.G. Wells

Suggested picture treatment by James Whale and Gouverneur Morris

Latmos is a hill town. From a distance it resembles a patch of snow. The houses are the pur white of white-wash. The roofs red. But the cubic contents of all the dwellings, added together, would not equal that of any one of four great buildings which dominate the sky-line. The cathedral with its great towers of an equal white, the monastery of St. Martin, the convent of St. Ursula, of Latmos Castle. The convent and the monastery are out of all proportions to the community which they are designed to serve. Savory in design, rectangular, and of peculiar lime-stone which has turned black with age, they resemble the hulks of two sea-going ships stranded in a pond. Latmos castle is like that in which the Lady of Shalett wove her web: "Four gray walls and four gray towers." Between the castle and the church there has always been an amiable understanding. The church in Latmos is so rich that it has never had any designs on the wealth of the Counts Latmos. These Counts form a long, upright and God fearing line which emerges from the dark ages and in the great bed-room of Latmos Castle seems now to be drawing to and end.

The inhabitants of Latmos have never maintained any vivid contact with the outside world. They are superstitious rather than religious. But they are under the complete dominance of the church. Latmos is really two white cities. A city of the living and of the dead. The population of the latter is far more numerous than that of the former.

The habitations of the living are simple and direct. Plain walls, roofs steeply pitched because Latmos is in the rain belt, with doors and windows well spaced. But the habitations of the dead are often grotesque; mournful imaginations seemed to have gone mad in the creation of some of them. The ruined wall and arch of part Roman and part Saracen workmanship are evidence of earlier civilization. It would surprise no one to learn that under the medieval and modern burial ground were catacombs dating from the Roman conquest.

The room in which Count Charlemagne Latmos lay dying was of vast proportions. The ceiling was vaulted. The reveals of the windows showed the outer walls of the room to be twelve or fourteen feet in thickness. A fine chimney piece of renaissance design showed that the old feudal fortress had been "Done over," in that exuberant period. The vast four-poster bed in the midst of which the Count lay had the width of a double bed and a half. The covers severe strong walls were softened by magnificent tapestries. The floor was thickly carpeted with the skins of wild animals. The minutia of the room were of incredible beauty and value. In the gold candle sticks you suspected the cunning hand of Berrenuto Cellini. The fittings of the dressing table were of solid gold. So also the two great bowls filled with roses at the end of the center table. The Count himself, must at one time have been a tall and strong man. He was still handsome, or he would have been handsome if his head and face of a Roman Conqueror had been serene and tranquil. The eyes roamed and were restless and very wild. You had the feeling that this was either because of fear or pain or in that picture of both.

For many days, the nearest of kin had been assembled in the castle, waiting for the end. Through the door leading to an anti-chamber, these came and went, to keep abreast of the progress of which the disease was making. Count Latmos had give brothers and three sisters, all younger than himself, who would profit greatly by his death. Physically there was a strong family resemblance. They had aquiline faces. The youngest of the brothers, Count Pepin, was prematurely bald. He resembled a fine bird that has been conscientiously plucked. The brothers and sister have brought their families. The oldest of the Count's sisters struck a bird-like head into the room and in an eager whisper which must have been audible to the dying man, as his hearing was still active, asked

"How is he?"

This question was obviously addressed to the Doctor, who having taken the dying man's temperature, had stepped back from the bed and was angling his thermometer into a position into which it could be read. The five brothers grouped in the embrasure of one of the windows, stopped the whispering that was going on among themselves and turned their eyes with one accord upon the doctor.

Nobody could have looked at the doctor because they liked to look at him. He had a face at once cruel and drafty.

He did not at once answer, but beckoning to the woman, he moved closer to the five brothers.

"He cannot live until morning," he said.

After a long pause, the oldest brother said: "May we count on it?"

"Scientific men," said the doctor, his lips twisting in an evil sneer, "Do not guaranty anything, but you may count upon it. Nothing can save him now but a miracle."

"My brother," said the woman, no longer whispering, "Has had everything that he ought to have in this extreme hour. We must send at once for the Archbishop to take his dying confession and to administer extreme unction. I think that Pepin should have entire charge of the funeral arrangements. He is always such a capital master of ceremonies. Now I think. . ."

But the doctor interrupted her with a certain curtness.

"The Countess Esmerald," he said, "Has kept watch by her Father's bedside for forty-eight unbroken hours. He forced her to take an opiate and lie down. She made a condition and he promised to have her called at the approach of death.

"Poor, dear, beautiful Esmerald," said the dying man's sister, "How all this is going to hurt her and already she has been hurt more than any young woman out to be hurt. Do you really think that she is choosing wisely? Do you really think that she will be happier in a convent?"

"Undoubtedly," said the Doctor, "She thinks so at the moment. But, if she knew what I know of this world and the people in it, she would neither renounce a vast fortune in favor of her Father's brothers and sisters, nor go into a convent. If she knew what I know, she would go to Paris and she would let Old Father Time men her broken heart."

"It would be a pity," said the sister, "To disturb her mind with wordly suggestions. She has convinced herself that she has found a way to peace.

"Curious," observed the doctor," That one person's way to peace should be the way to wealth to so many others."

Lurking anxiously in a deep shadow near the head of Count Latmos' bed was an old and trusted personal servant, Lasca. But he had come out of this shadow and approached the group who were conversing close enough to hear what was being said, and when the oldest of the five brothers said:

"Now, who will go for the archbishop?" he at once offered his services.

"I will go with pleasure," he said eagerly and made a swift limping movement toward the door of the ante-room, but the bald headed Pepin, ceased him twistingly by the wrist and exclaimed fiercely"

"Oh no you don't!"

The eldest brother spoke, his voice was equally cruel but more calculated:

"You have persistently tried," he said, "To turn the natural and peaceful ending of a great and good life into a scandal. Because of your long and faithful services to my beloved brother, we have been lenient with you. Bit I have reached the limit of my patience and the next time you speak the word 'poison' I will wring your neck. Go back to the Master and stay by him until the end."

The doctor and the five brothers remained in the room. The nurse and Lasca watched the dying man at close range/ The Count's sister went to summon the Countess Esmerald and to send a message to the archbishop. But the Countess Esmerald cannot have been far off for she appeared almost immediately. Her dress was white and she herself was very pale. Her dress was so direct and simple that it was equally appropriate to the present year of grace or to the thirteenth century. She did not look out of place in a feudal castle. With a nod to the five, brothers, the doctor went gravely to meet her and accompanied her to her Father's bed-side. She spoke in soothing whispers to the dying man, but he did not seem to hear or understand and in his eyes was no light of recognition. Count Pepin, the bald head, appeared to be giving his attention to a whispered conversation with his brothers, but in reality his attention was concentrated on the servant Lasca, and when he saw that this one was trying to get the attention of the Countess Esmerald, he went swiftly to him and jerked him away from the bed-side and forced him into a far corner of the room.

"Even if I thought that you could save my brother's life," he said fiercely, "I would not let you try. This time there is not going to be any slip, twixt the cup and the lip.

"He is being murdered in his bed," said Lasca.

"Shut up!" said Count Pepin, You dog, you beast."

Her hand lying coolly on her Father's fevered brow, the Countess Esmerald turned her great, sad, lamenting eyes to the doctor.

"Can nothing more be done?"

"My dear child, " said the doctor, and for once, at least in his life, there was real sincerity in his voice, "I am very sorry for you."

"It is not easy for me," she said simply, "The man I loved with all my heart and soul disappeared. From that day to this there has been no word or sign from him. All that I have to remember him by is our great love for each other and a few words in his handwriting on a sheet of paper. "My dear dear love, you will never see me again. This is best for you. Forget. . ."

"And now I must stand helpless and see my dear Father go away
from me for ever."

"Perhaps," said the doctor impulsively, "Time will mend your
broken heart. Are you sure that the church will give you peace?
Money and time work miracles."

She smiled sadly and shook her head, "Not for me," she said.

At that moment there was a sudden sound of feet and chairs
moving in the ante-room. A man servant in a beautiful livery
stepped within the death chamber and announced in a clear voice.

"The Right, Reverend, Grace, The Archbishop of Latmos."

The Gothic doorway from the ante-chamber filled suddenly
and almost gayly with white and violet and crimson. Two acolytes,
beautiful as angels, proceeded the archbishop into the death
chamber. They carried the tears and the body of Christ in golden
vessels. A smell of incense at once accurate and sweet came into
the room with them. The archbishop himself stood at least six
feet three in his stockings. His face and hands had that transparent waxy look which is produced naturally by holiness and
scientifically by undertakers. He was a man perhaps seventy years
old, but his hollow face was not wrinkled. He had a look at once
of great force and great sweetness. He paused at the threshold
of the room and holding up his right hand with his first and second
fingers extended, (a huge amethyst gleaming on the first finger).
He said solemnly," Pax vobiscum,"

In that moment, it was probably that even the avaricious
and murderous brothers and sisters of Count Charlemagne Latmos
had a feeling of awe, reverence and perhaps, fear. It is certain.

that Count Pepin for a moment loosed his grip on the servant

Lasca, for this one wrenched suddenly loose from him and considering

his age and his lameness, darted the length of the room and flung

himself kneeling at the feet of the archbishop crying as he knelt

and wringing his hands and looked upward into the serene beautiful

face: "Sanctuary, sanctuary."

An effort, almost concerted between the doctor and the brothers

of Count Charlemagne to interrupt Lasca before he could have a say

with the archbishop was thwarted by the archbishop himself.

"Stand back," he said, "This old servant has claimed the

sanctuary of the church.

For a moment he held them with his eye. Finally Count Pepin

laughed and shrugged his shoulders.

"He is crazy," he said, "But by all means, hear what he has

to say, if it interests you."

The archbishop bent his head and spoke in a kind and tolerant

voice.

"What is it Lasca? he asked.

"They," said Lasca, and who was meant could not be mistaken,

"Are poisoning my master. He is not dying of natural causes. I

know a doctor who could save him, but they will not let me fetch

him. I am being held a prisoner."

The archbishop spoke now with more gravity.

"We shall not go into the accusation of poisoning, he said

"That is unthinkable, but if Dr. Buscot has given Count Charlemagne

up and declared him in extremist, it would seem fair enough to call

in some other doctor and give the Count a chance for his life.

What doctor is it Lasca, whom do you propose to fetch?"

"Sanctuary, sanctuary."

An effort, almost concerted between the doctor and the brothers

"In the last two years, your Grace," said Lasca, "There have been three miracles in the City of Latmos."

"That is true," said the archbishop, "Two honorable men, who had lead blameless lives were declared on the point of death. A doctor, a stranger to this place, was sent for. I do not know how , or by whom. He made it conditional that he be left alone with the dying man and that no one approach him or molest him. No man saw his face."

"And what?" cried Lasca in excitement, "Became of the two men who were dying?"

"They were brought back," said the archbishop solemnly, "From the valley of the shadow.

There was a third miracle, "insisted Lasca.

"The miracle," said the archbishop, Of Maria Tolusc, a woman so saintly that one of these days she will perhaps be canonized."

"And, was she also declared to be dying? asked Lasca, his eyes literally snapping with excitement.

"She," said the archbishop, "Was declared dead, but the strange doctor appeared and resurrected her from the dead."

"Your Grace," cried Lasca in a strong voice, On all three ocassions it was I alone who knew where to find him and who fetched him."

"Can you find him again?" asked the archbishop.

There is so little time," said Lasca, "And I am very lame."

"My carriage," said the archbishop, "is in the court-yard. It is at your disposal.

He turned to one of the acolytes. "Archmede," he said,
"Tell Pharos to drive this good man wherever he shall direct.

The archbishop turned to Lasca with a sudden energy said
to him:

"The faithful servant who loves his master is loved in turn
by the most High. Hurry!"

The exclamatory protests which arose as Lasca, proceeded by
the acolyte, hastened from the room, were instantly quelled by
the archbishop.

"If you do not wish the Miracle Worker to be fetched," he
said, "It is logical to believe that you wish the Count Charlemagne
to die so that as quickly as may be, you may inherit the vast
riches which the Countess Esmerald has renounced. The world
would believe that. I myself could not but believe. Furthermore,
It is my belief that the police would order the body of Count
Charlamagne to be examined and its contents analyzed for traces
of poison.

The court yard of Latmos castle, except for a delicate
renaissance gallery let into the thickness of the wall at the
height of the second story, a gallery i which there were groups
of flowering plants in ornamental pots, was a grim military well-
like construction of the Ninth Century. It was paved with cobble
stones. The Cardinal's carriage had entered the place through a
much flattened Gothic Arch. Here and there, in the grim granite
walls, fantastic crests and coats of arms carved in limestone had
been inlaid, making a straight line from shoulder to shoulder of the
Gothic archway, a row of savage spikes pointing downward, showed that
an ancient Port-cullis, if not operative, was still in place. The
Cardinal's carriage was of an old fashion. It resembled a little
the pumpkin coach in which Cinderella went to the ball. The body of
the coach was slung on a broad leather straps instead of springs. The
candle-lamps, huge and ornamental, appeared to be of solid silver.
Upon the door-panel there was in scribed in heraldic colors, the
broad flat hat of an archbishop conventionalized. There were two
smooth-shaven men on the box. These wore hats, not unlike that of
the archbishop, coats drawn smartly in at the waist, knee breeches,
silk stockings, square toed black brogans with large silver buckles.
Four handsome white geldings, in rich harnesses gleamed in the moonlight

As Lasca, preceded by the acolyte came into the scene, the
acolyte gave an order in Latin. The two men on the box touched their
hats. The lesser of them descended nimbly to the ground and held
open the door of the carriage so that Lasca might enter. Lasca, after
the door of the carriage so that Lasca might enter. Lasca, after the door was
closed upon him said:

"In the name of God, hurry."

The groom, the acolyte and the coachman on the box, crossed
themselves. The groom lept back to his place. The coachman

cracked his whip above the ears of the leaders. The coach jerked
forward. The courtyard offered exactly enough turning room, neither
more nor less. But the coachman was a man of art with his ribbons
and the turn was executed at speed. The coach and all disappeared
into the darkness of the flattened archway.

Lasca had asked that he be driven to the main gate of the
cemetery which was surrounded by a high stone wall. It crowned
the hilltop upon which the town was built. Clouds crossed the
heavens like puffs of smoke and there were glimpses of a distorted
moon. Against the sky-line could be seen crosses and other monuments of the dead which no longer stood squarely upon their bases.
Bidding the coachman to wait for him, Lasca passed through a narrow
arch and limped painfully up a flight of narrow stone steps, worn
hollow be generations of mourning feet. At the top of these steps
one on either side, were guardian angels. They were of the thirteenth century. Their wings broken; their crossed hands locking
many fingers, their noses worn flat by the same processes of
erosion which have gashed out of the living rock, the Grand Canyon
of the Colorado. Beyond the angels could be seen the highest
point of the cemetery, but Lasca's business took him over and beyond
this. In a fantastic and unexpected hollow, he came to a dark
corroded family vault with iron railings in which there was a
little gate. It appeared that he had a key with which to unlock
it, but before doing so, he looked about him furtively. The entrances
to the family vault resembled an upturned sarcophagus, wider at
the top than at the bottom. But instead of a Roman matron or an
Egyptian Pharaoh to crown a decorative arrangement of stone-bandages.

was suggested vaguely the human form and was the had of an angel
placed between two spreading wings. Within enclosure was a tombstone of a little child. From the couchant lamp upon the top of
this, the head had been knocked. Lasca picked this up and knocked
three times, horrid, sickening sounds upon the breast of the angel
mummy. After a pause there was what sounded like a subterraneous
rumble. A moment later a voice might have been heard. It did not
seem to come from anywhere in particular. The voice had in it a
quality of hurrying and impatience.

"It is you Lasca?"

"You must come at once," said Lasca.

Again there was that sound of subterraneous rumblings and all
of a sudden the beautiful carved face of the angel swing inward
until it could no longer be seen and in its place, and in the dark
aperture, which its withdrawal had made, was revealed a big and
horrid shape, framed on either side by the two delicate angel's wings.
Like a mummy, the face which had appeared in the aperture was wrapped
entirely in bandages. The eyes were completely hidden by a pair of
box-like dark glasses, such as are worn by chemists dealing with
dangerous chemicals or by steel workers to protect their eyes from
flying splinters.

"Why must I come at once?"

"Because," said Lasca, "A good man, perhaps the best man in
the whole world, except you, is dying and only you can save him"

"I might have saved him yesterday," said the voice, "I might
save him tomorrow if he is still living, but I cannot go to him
tonight.

"In the name of God." said Lasca.

"i am sorry," said the voice gently, "But my experiment, which
is more important than the life of many good men, cannot be left
to itself. I am sorry my old friend I cannot go with you."

"When I tell you who it is that is dying, you will have to come
with me!" cried Lasca.

"And who is it?" asked the voice. "That is dying."

Lasca lowered his voice almost to a whisper. "It is, said
he, "The Father of the Countess Esmerald."

"I will be with you in a few seconds," said the voice. Its
quality was altogether altered. It was eager, incisive.

While Lasca waited, he tried to fit the head of the lamb back
on its little stone-body but it would not stick.

Again there were sounds of subterraneous rumblings, stronger this
time and the whole mummy-like door, with the angel head in the top
of the wrappings, swung outward, revealing a black passage which
carried on the lines of the door and at an end of turning of which,
far, far off in the bowels of the earth, was an effect of light and
shadow, such as delighted the painter, Rembrandt. From the mouth of
the passage-way emerged a fantastic figure. The bandaged head a
goggles seen previously was surmounted by a broad brimmed high-crowned
felt hat, the broad brim of which was limp and droopy. The body that
belonged with the bandaged head was in loose black clothes. It was
a huge body by not symmetrical. You had the feeling that it was a
strong body which had survived some terrible accident. For the rest
the fantastic figure walked with a limp, carried a stout ivory cane
and the conventional black bag of a physician on call.

"Hurry," he said.

"Yes," said Lasca, "Hurry."

When the servant and the mysterious man in black came limping

down the cemetery steps to the waiting carriage, the groom, who stood
ready to open the door of the carriage, was almost overcome with
superstitious terror, crossed himself. But also, shifting his reins
so as to get his right hand free, did the coachman on the box.

Lasca was the first to enter the castle. The Countess Esmerald
was waiting impatiently for them. The castle seemed empty.

"Is the coast clear my lady?" asked the servant.

"Nobody will see him or disturb him."

"But, does that apply to me? I wish to speak with him and thank
him."

"That applies to you too my Lady." said Lasca -

"Very well," she said, and turning, she moved rapidly away.
Lasca turned and beckoned to the stranger, who remained hidden in
the shadow of the archway. He lead him hurriedly, through vast
luxurious halls and saloons in which there were no evidences of present
human occupancy, up a noble stairway, on which their limping feet
resounded, into a more ancient and narrower hall, through the ante-
chamber, now empty, and into the vast bedroom of Count Charlemagne
Latmos. After a brief examination and a taking of the sick man's
pulse, the stranger spoke.

:You are in a bad way, my old friend." he said, "But I have come
in time. Open the black bag Lasca."

From the black bag he made a selection of drugs and syringes.
He worked very swiftly. He bared the crook of the Count's left arm.
This he cleaned swiftly with alcohol.
"Clench his hand Lasca," he said, "He cannot do it for himself
and may God help me to locate a vein. Aha!

Skilfully inserting the syringe which he had chosen, into the
located vein he drove the piston home.

"They have built in his blood," he said, "A whole edifice of poison. This will burn it to nothing, and this. ." he held up a second syringe, "will begin to put back into him the life which has been slowly draining away."

In a part of the castle which was probably not very far from her father's room, Countess Esmerald paced slowly to and fro, her face was upturned. There was in it, commingled with the sadness, a look of hopefulness. As she paced, to and fro, her lips murmured prayers and her beautiful fingers told the beads in her rosary. The immediate relations and relations in law of Count Charlemagne had been herded into a vast saloon together with the doctor who had been in attendance. At the doors of this saloon were strong, rough, looking men, in a kind of rustic uniform. Each wore upon his breast an ornamental silver shield, upon which was engraved the word, "Forrester." Each of these men carried on his belt a wicked looking bore-knife in a handsome sheath, and each of them carried at attention, the high powered rifle. It was evident that the Countess Esmerald had given certain orders and that the wicked brothers and sisters of her Father had had their teeth pulled. They were gathered about the saloon in knots. Certain knots were belligerent, others apprehensive.

Once more the mysterious stranger located a vein, but this time in the right arm of Count Charlemagne and gave an injection. The wild, roving, insane eyes of the dying man, almost instantly became human and presently the eyelids closed down over them. He made a long sighing noise and then turning slightly and carefully, on his right side, went tranquilly to sleep. Lasca fell on his knees before the mysterious stranger and caught his hands in his and began to kiss them.

"Don't be an idiot Lasca," said the mysterious stranger, his voice gentle and tender, "Just because I happen to know a few things that other people don't know is no reason to make a God of me. Your master will live. He will be as well as ever. But I have lost Precious time. My experiments! If it is not to be done all over again from the beginning, I must have help. Will you come back with me to my - - workshop?"

"You don't have to ask," said Lasca.

The stranger laid his hand on the brow of the sleeping man.

"Like a child," he said.

Then, gathering up his stick and his black bag, he said;

"Let us go, but first tell your mistress that her Father will live. I will meet you at the postern.

The stranger had reached the narrow hallway opening off the ante-room and was passing rapidly through it, when the Countess Esmerald, stepping into it from a half hidden doorway, called after him;

"Doctor," she said, "Please let me thank you."

The stranger seemed to sink his head deeper into his shoulders and increased his speed, but she overtook him.

"I do thank you," she said.

His voice came back over his shoulder with contempt in it.

"Your word was given that I should not be spied on or molested," he said.

"It is the weight of my gratitude, said she, "Which has broken my word to you. I am sorry, but I do thank you and thank you."

The stranger hurried on for a few limping steps, but no longer hearing the sound of her pursuing feet, came to a sudden halt in a deep shadow. The corridor was lighted on one side by an occasional shot-window

It was in the dark, between two of these, that he had halted. But he did not turn toward her. His voice came to her over his shoulder and from beneath the broad brim of his hat.

"I am glad," he said, "That you broke your word. There is something that I wish to say to you."

She drew closer to him.

"Do you, he said, "Wish your father to live out his remaining years in peace and contentment?"

"How can you think otherwise?" she asked.

"The matter," said he, "Rests in your hands."

"What must I do? she asked.

"You must not," said he, "Renounce your heritage in favor of persons who are not worth it and you must not enter a convent and thwart your youth and beauty of their human destiny."

He jerked a sudden question at her.

"Why," said he, Do you wish to enter a convent?

"Because," she said, I lost the man I loved and I shall never love another."

"You lost him," said the stranger, "Did he die?"

"I think," said she, "That if he were not dead, he would have changed his mind and come back to me."

"Do you still love him☐" asked the stranger.

"You do not seem to me," said she, "The kind of man who asks foolish questions."

There was a sudden break in the stranger's voice.

"My dear, he said, "I am very sorry for you, but for your father's sake, you must promise me that you will reconsider what you have said that you would do."

"Is your interest in my father so deep?" she asked.

"In your father, yes." he said, "And all that belongs to him"

"I have a feeling," said she, "That I have known you. May I ask who you are?"

"You may ask," he said, "Of course, but I shall not tell you."

He moved on as if wishing to end the interview, but she followed him as if to insist upon an identification. He halted in the next shadow between two of the shot-windows.

"You do not have to tell me," she said, her voice suddenly exultant, "I know who you are. Your voice, your clear voice. Oh, my dear love."

"I am not your dear love," he said, in a choking voice, "I don't know you, I never saw you before."

She laid her hand on his shoulder, but he brushed it away savagely.

"Why tell me what is not true?" she said.

"Very well," said he, "And what if I am your love and you mine? I vanished out of your life for your own good."

"But", she said, "Enough water has passed under the bridges to show that it has not been for my good."

"My dear," he said, "If you could see me as I am, you would turn away in horror and loathing."

"You think so," she said, "Try me."

"That," said he, "I will not do. And now, everything is all over, all over, please don't talk to me any more, please don't follow me any further."

But, like fate, she followed him to the next shadow.

"Do you think, "said she," That I loved the visible man which you were? Oh, I loved that too of course, but what I loved was the invisible man which you still are."

"Oh my dear," he said, "I would give my soul to believe you."

"Then believe me," she said, "It is very simple, believe me for our love's sake."

"Come a little further," he said, "And look!" Then he halted in the strong fan of moonlight that came through a shot-window. He turned and straightened himself and took off his hat so that she could see clearly the hideous bandage and those grotesque dark goggles. He took off the goggles and held out his arms to her. She made a faltering step forward as if she would go into them, but she could not. Her head drooped, she made a little sound of moaning and fainted dead away on her feet. If he had not caught her in his strong arms, she must have fallen headlong on the stone pavement. He carried her then, the length of the corridor to the hallway at the head of the grand stair. All the time, he murmured over her, lover's words.

"My dear, my darling. Gracious, golden, beloved."

Near the head of the stair was a couch, covered with velvet. Here he laid her at length. His hands hovered a little over her face and shoulders, but did not touch her. With a groan, he stumbled himself from her side and began to descend the stair without looking backward. In the great hall below, he found Lasca waiting for him.

"Did you tell the young Countess that her father would live?" he asked.

"Yes," said Lasca, "Then I came here by the surret stair."

"You have waited longer than you expected," said the stranger.

"That is true," said the servant, "What delayed you?"

"A dream,: said the stranger, "From which I have waked. . .Let me go. . . I don't need you."

The stranger stumbled down into the court yard where the archbishop was waiting. The footman opened the door for him, but he passed on toward the broad entrance arch as if he had neither seen the carriage nor the footman.

His moment of high hope had failed him. The cup, brimming with sweetness had been dashed from his lips. He staggered like a drunken man. He did not know where he was going or why. He passed through narrow back streets in the oldest part of the city. A wind had risen and there were gusts of rain. The sky would cloud completely over and then would break and there would be ghastly sudden effects of moonlight. For the most part, he moved swiftly, but sometimes he came to a sudden halt, then he looked upward. At times he walked slowly with bowed head. He reminded one a little of Christ in the Garden of Gethsemane. He came to the place of punishment. Here upon a lonely black gibbet, hung the body of a man in chains. Upon the beam of the gibbet was a black cat.

The Countess Esmerald, having recovered from her swoon and remembered what had happened, sought despairingly for the stranger. That which had caused her to faint had not been so much revulsion as surprise and shock. If only she might have another chance, she could cherish that bandaged head in her breast and give consolation love and passion. At last she gave up her search. She encountered Lasca and he told her that the stranger had gone. She went then to the rich eight-sided room in which the archbishop and acolytes waited the turn of events. The archbishop stood tally with his back to an open fire. He had been told that his services would not be required that night by Count Latmos. Once more the

mysterious stranger had turned up in a nick of time and performed
a miracle. Upon perceiving that the young Countess was in some
catastrophic mental agony of some kind, he waved to his acolytes, who
withdrew out of ear-shot.

"My poor child," he said, "Your father is going to recover. He
is going to be himself again. What has happened to make you look as
if the world had come to an end?"

"I have seen him, Father." she said

"The man to whom you were to be married?" asked the archbishop.

"It was he," said she, "whom Lasca went to fetch and who saved
my father and now he has gone away again and it is my fault. He has
gone away because I hurt him."

"It is easily seen," she said, "I would give my soul
to undo what has been done. He met with some terrible accident; after-word he
felt that no woman could possibly bear to see his face. That
was why he vanished, but just now I told him that no matter what the
disfigurement, it did not matter to me. It was not the visible man
which I had fallen in love with, but the invisible man. I persuaded
him that this was true. I made him believe me. I knew from his voice
that he had found happiness again but he put me to a test. He stepped
into the moonlight that shown strongly through a shot-window in the
gallery. He took off his hat and turned his face so that I could see
it. Father, believe me. I was not repelled. I wanted only to be in
his arms and to say that it did not matter and to comfort him. But I
am a weak woman. I was shocked by what I saw beyond all reason and I
must have fainted. When I came to, he had vanished again. He is

nowhere in the castle and Lasca does not know where he has gone."

"Do you wish me," said the archbishop, " to try to find words with which to console you."

"No," she said, "I wish you to absolve me from the vow which I made to enter the church."

"You made that vow," said the archbishop "in the belief that the man you loved was dead. You know now that he is not. Surely the Good God would not wish you held to a promise that was made upon false premises. I myself was sorry when you made the vow. I thought that perhaps time and wealth would cure you of the agony of body and spirit in which you found yourself. I thought that you might be of more service to God in the secular than in the religious world. Hereby I absolve you from your vow." and he made the broad sign of the cross over her face.

At this moment Lasca limped quickly and happily into the room.

"Saving your presence your Grace," he said, "And saving the presence of my young mistress. Everything has turned out as I said it would. There has been another miracle. The good Count, my master, will recover. Already he has regained consciousness and he is asking for the Countess Esmerald."

The Countess Esmerald literally flew from the room and the face which she was able to show her father was cleared of all its agony and suffering. There was in it nothing but gladness and solicitude. She leaned over him and he was strong enough to bend his arms about her. The Countess Esmerald shed some tears.

"You mustn't cry," he said, "It is rather the time to eat and drink and to make merry. I only know that I was dead and that now I am alive. What happened?"

"A miracle."

"Did I dream," he said, "or did I see the face of my brothers and sisters gathered about me."

"You did not dream it." said she.

"And what has become of them?" he asked.

"They are in the golden drawing-room," she said, " under guard."

Her face had in it a cold finality.

"Because of the money," she said. "They did not wish you to live. Their trunks and valises are being packed. I have ordered carriages to take them to their homes or to the train."

"The miracle, I take it," said Count Chalemagne, "was a bitter disappointment to them."

"It was." said his daughter.

Count Charlemagne chuckled.

"Uncle Pepin," said she with a smile, "had already begun to make grandiose preparations for the funeral."

"I am not a harsh man." said Count Charlemagne, "but I hope that I may outlive the lot of them. I wish it were possible to peep into the Golden drawing-room and see their faces. Who performed the miracle which saved me?"

"Farralone." said she.

"Your Farralone!" he exclaimed. "Has he come back from the dead?"

"He wasn't dead Father, " she said, "He came back and now he has gone away again and although I am very happy about you, I am very unhappy about that and I shall be unhappy until I have found him and he is locked tight in my arms where he belongs."

Countess Esmerald sent Lasca into the night to see if he could not find her lover and persuade him that she still wanted him and bring him back to her. Lasca, supposing that Farralone had returned to his habitation in the cemetery, went there at once and

again knocked with the lamb's head upon the breast of the
mummy angel. Even after a second knocking there was so subterraneous response. It was then that he perceived that in
closing the tomb, Farralone in his haste had made an incomplete
work of it. The tomb was not tightly closed and Lasca was able
to swing open the swathed stone figure and to close it behind him.
He was evidently familiar with the place. He traversed narrow
twisting and complicated passages, all of them wider at the top
than at the bottom and palely lighted here and there by Roman lamps
set in niches. Here and there were fantastic fragments of frescoes.
These were mostly of an early Christian nature. Holy families
made trips to Egypt in the company of an absurd donkey. Mary
received her first intimations of pregnancy from a lop-sided angel.
Wise men followed a star. The passage lead eventually into a
large vaulted place that may have been a chapel. It seemed now a
master or a scholars study and of, an electrical laboratory and
a doctor's office. In a glass case were modern surgical instruments.
There were books, ancient and modern. In this chapel the frescoes
were better preserved. The subjects were religious, but as they
pertained almost entirely to the last judgement, they gave rather
an effect of devil worship. It is true that a bearded God the
Father, with one eye larger than the other, standing upon clouds
at a strategic point, was pointing upward with one hand and downward with the other. In obedience to the hand which pointed upward,
certain souls which had been saved, flew upward with silly smiles
of self-satisfaction into a conventional Heaven; but for one soul
that he saved, the Lord God with his downward pointing hand was
condemning the east nineteen to eternal hell fire. The damned

souls were being pitched headlong all over the place on to the
waiting pitchforks of demons. Every horrible torture by knives,
by boiling or by fire that can be imagined were here, graphically
and colorfully, represented. The frescoes might have been from the
hand of a remote ancestor of El Greco.

Upon what looked like an over-large gold-fish bowl with perpen-
dicular sides three parts full of a colorless liquid, curious beams
of light played. Lasca was wet and tired, but the peasant's blood
that flowed in his veins, told him that he must wait in patience.
Perceiving that a certain flame which heated a retort containing a
colored liquid through which passed the ray which fell upon the
goldfish bowl, was splitting and spluttering, he replenished its
supply of oil. It was while he was engaged upon this that Farralone
limped suddenly into the place.

HE was wet to the bone and he seemed a man at the limit of human endurances. But seeing that the flame still burned under the retort, his vitality seemed to renew itself and without a glance at Lasca, he dashed forward to examine into the state of his interrupted experiment.

"The lamp still burns." he said

"I got here in time to renew the oil." said Lasca.

But instead of thanking the old servant, Farralone turned on him savagely:

"What else have you done?" he asked.

"Nothing." said Lasca.

"Why are you here?"

"To find you and bring you back to the Countess Esmerald.

Farralone made a contemptuous sound.

"One look was enough for her." he said.

"You do her wrong." said the servant.

"I have never done wrong to any man, woman, or child." said Farralone.

His eye now sought that glass vessel which has been described as a gold fish bowl, half full of a colorless liquid.

"Good God," he said, "the tank is empty. What have you done with it?"

"Nothing." protested Lasca. "I have touched nothing."

Farralone bent over the tank and gazed fixedly at the surface of the liquid which it contained. His whole manner changed. When he spoke, his voice was softer. It was as if sudden excitement had made it husky.

"It must have climbed out," he said. "By itself. This time
if I had not been called off, I think that the experiment might have
succeeded. Now it is all to do over again, but I must have it back.
See if you can find it. It cannot have traveled far. I am sorry
that I spoke in anger. You must be exhausted my good Lasca. Find
yourself something to eat and dry your feet, then we will try again."

"It is my belief," said Lasca, "that even if the experiment
succeeds, no good will come of it."

"Why do you say that?"

"Because," said the servant solemnly, "anything that is against
nature is against God."

"Nonsense," said Farralone, "anything which increases by a
thousand fold a man's power to do good, to give comfort and to heal,
cannot be against God."

"Do you think that I lean all together upon science? To whom
do you think that I pray for the success of my experiment? God
helping me, I shall succeed.

Lasca, knowing that argument was of no avail against an intellect
which had ten times the strength over his own, shrugged his shoulders.
Taking a lamp from its niche, he began to search carefully for that
which had escaped from the tank. It was not to be found in the
scantily furnished chapel and he passed from there into a narrow
passage and for some time was not seen again. Farralone seemed once
more to be crushed with fatigue. He continued to look at the glass-
tank, but as if his thoughts were elsewhere. Presently his goggled
eyes began to rove among the frescoes until at last they came to rest
upon the figure of the Lord God, giving a salvation with one hand and
damnation with the other. Gradually the shoulders and spine of

Farralone straightened and stiffened all at once, lifting his hands to the Image of his Maker, and then clasped in an agony of spirit, he began to pray with a terrible, intensity of concentration and faith.

> OH THOU WHO ART INVISIBLE
> and to whom nothing is unseen,
> who carest for the sick and fatherless,
> who created the earth and all that is upon
> it, to whom there is no mystery in man or
> beast; THOU who gavest and takest away, hear
> the prayer of thy Servant, and remove from
> the eyes of mortal man the harmful sight of
> this frightful face, that I may be allowed
> to do thy will unseen.

For a time, his shoulders remained braced and strong as if in the hope that the prayer might be efficacious. But nothing happened. There was no answer, the was nothing but the silence of the catacomb and the empty tank upon which played the strange ray of light. Farralone's shoulders sank. He turned, and once more his eyes appeared to roam among the figures of the fresco without seeing them. He was a wholly dejected and disappointed man.

"I could, " he murmured, "have been the greatest agent for good that the world has ever known, but I have not been chosen."

He shrugged his shoulders and at that moment his eyes were arrested by a spirited rendition of Satan himself, high on a throne of Royal State, giving orders to demons. A sudden fancy took Farralone.

"Perhaps," he said with a certain sarcasm, "It is to you that I should have addressed my prayer. Perhaps my pathway to good lies through evil.

Could it have been the imagination of the half spent scientist?

It is certain, that to his eyes at least, the archaic and primitive painting of the devil, became more real, more rounded. It seemed also as if the eyes of the demon had rolled in their sockets and were now fixed upon the suppliant.

"Help me." cried Farralone in sudden ecstasy." Help me to go about the world unseen.

There was a sound of subterraneous rumblings which sounded like far off thunder. The flames in the Roman lamps became incandescently bright. Here and there from the floor of the chapel, rose sudden puffs of yellowish smoke. One of these suspended against the vaulted ceiling, completely obscured the image of the Lord God and His Blessed Angels. In that intense light, all the demonic figures and goings of the fresco came to life. The room became a fury of vengeance and torture. From before the eyes of Farralone, the last judgement was enacted. The place was filled with the groans, the screams and the shrieks of the damned and the old chapel gradually filled with the smoke from the hell fires. The figures of the torturers and their victims became obscure until at last even the figure of Farralone vanished in the smoke. The shrieks and screams of the damned however, persisted for sometime but in diminishing volume until at last there was silence. There must have been strong drafts of air in that place for the smoke cleared rapidly rushing hither and nither like armies of living things and being sucked furiously into the various passage ways which centered on the old chapel. Presently, and just before the smoke had cleared, the shrieks and screams of the damned changed suddenly to peals of vast satanic laughter. The laughter ceased

as the smoke cleared and all was as before, an ancient Christian
place of damaged frescoes and historic interests. Only Farralone
had changed. He was filled with an intense nervous energy. He
limped quickly to the glass tank, gazed for a moment fixedly into
the colorless liquid and then began to shout for Lasca.

"Come here." he said. "Do you see anything in the tank?
Do you see anything?"

"I think," said Lasca, "That I see what you see. A glass
tank half filled with what looks like water."

Farralone laughed a little madly.

"Perhaps." he said, " Your sense of touch is sharper than you
sight. Feel around in the tank and see if there is nothing there."

It did not even seem to Lasca to be any reason why he should not
dip his hand into the tank and feel about the bottom and the corners,
but his hand had no sooner reached half way to the bottom than the
spread fingers suddenly closed and with a piercing scream, Lasca
jerked back his hand. It may be said that Farralone also screamed,
but his scream was made up half of laughter and half of triumph.
Something not visible to the mortal eye seemed to have wound itself
tightly about Lasca's right hand. With his left hand he fought
to untangle himself. Farralone presently came to his rescue. Between them, by main force, the removed the invisible thing which
in seizing the servants immersed hand had so terrified him. Farralone
dropped the invisible thing back into the tank. It made a strong
splash.

Farralone's voice, if Lasca had had the ear to note it, had
lost its mellow qualities of human kindness. A tone of irony
and disdain had crept into it.

"You thought that the tank was empty." he said, "but if you

had had a pair of eyes in your head, you would have noticed that bubbles kept rising to the surface. And now you must help me. You must make me, like that thing in there. We must double the strength of the ray.

"I do not wish to help you." said the servant, "what I wish to do is against the laws of God."

Farralone's left hand was in the path of the mysterious ray which lighted the tank. It had been resting there for sometime and there it remained during the rest of his argument with the pious servant."

"I do not," he said, "wish you to go against your conscience, but if it can be done at all, it is a natural thing and a thing therefore which God himself has fore-ordained and made possible. You know better than another how I have been handicapped and harassed in my passion to do good and heal the sick. Think what we two could accomplish together old friend. You the visible partner and I the invisible. Now that I am on the point of success you will not be so cruel as to withhold your aid."

"I will not help you willingly, said Lasca, "But if you command me to help you, I have not the strength or the will to disobey you."

"Then, " said Farralone in a strong voice. "I command you."

He took the tank in his hands to make place for himself on the table where it lay. He lifted it clear off the table and then with a sudden scream, dropped it, crashing and splashing to the stone pavement.

"Look, look!" he cried, and he held up his left hand of which nothing remained or was visible but the extended thumb and fore-finger. It was as if the rest of it had been cut off upon a diagonal, the edge of which was as straight as the edge of a ruler.

Lasca recoiled as if he had been struck between the eyes. While Farallone, almost hideously elated by the apparent loss of three fingers and the half of a palm, advanced upon him, shaking the thumb and fore-finger and spluttering with triumph and laughter. But suddenly he stood still and with his right hand, felt for the missing members of his left. These apparently still existed, physical and solid, they hade only vanished.

"Hold still." he said. "Don't be such a ninny, my hand is just as good as ever it was. Hold still. I am going to touch you with the three fingers that you can no longer see."

Lasca shuddered while he was being touched.

"Please Sir." he said, "Don't go on with this."

"I must," said Farralone. "I have work to do. Good works and I cannot do them if people can see me. You have always trusted me, why don't you trust me now. I long to shake off this mortal evil which has become so horrible that no man can look upon it. But the ray must be stronger, there must be more pressure. It is easy enough to destroy refraction in a primitive form, but a man is a complicated thing. Think what we shall be able to accomplish, you and i, when i am invisible. We have an opportunity, you and I, which has never been given to any two human beings. Please don't abandon me now. We have both been good men all our lives long. Why should we change? Look!"

He pointed to the table on which the glass tank had stood.

"I will lie down here. You must play the ray upon me steadily increasing its compass and power until I have vanished utterly.

"I shall not have the heart to do it." said Lasca. "I think that what you wish to do is evil."

"Truly." said Farralone. "then look."

He took off his hat and his goggles and then swiftly unwound the bandages which covered the whole of his head and the most of his face. A face so mutilated and so horrible, that it is beyond description came into view.

"Look well," he said.

But Lasca could not look at all. He turned away from that horrible face, whimpering and Farralone laughed.

"Now, do you understand?" asked Faralone. "Suppose that I were ministering to a sick child and it saw this face. It would die. You yourself are fond of me. We have trusted each other for many years. Won't you help me now?"

"I will help you," said Lasca, "I see that I must help you."

With a sigh of gladness, Farralone laid himself down upon the experiment table. Lasca moved like a man in a dream toward the mysterious apparatus from which the refraction destroying ray emanated. A strong hissing sound and a brightening of the ray itself showed that he knew how to increase it efficiency and power.

"Is anything happening to me?" asked Farralone.

"Your face," said the servant, "is becoming indistinct."

Farralone laughed harshly.

"Blot me out." he said, "from the sight of human eyes. Blot me out. Make me invisible."

The hissing sounds increased and there was a sound of subterraneous thunder. Here and there in the chapel, puffs of sulphurous smoke arose. The diabolic frescoes once more came to life. The place filled with smoke, with demonic laughter and the shrieks and screams of the damned. The smoke cleared; the laughter and the screaming died. The hissing ceased. There was no longer any ray. Sitting upon the edge of the experiment table was Farralone's suit of clothes. The coat, the trousers. They appeared to be filled, but above the collar was no head. Below the wrist were no hands, but below the trousers were the socks and wet shoes in which he had limped through the events of that night.

On Lasca's face was a look of amazement and terror. He moved slow steps backward. The headless, handless figure perched on the edge of the table, lifted first one sleeve as if looking for the missing hands, then he stretched out his left foot and his invisible eyes must have seen that in its sock and shoe, it looked like a very usual foot. He crossed his left leg over his right and unlaced the shoe and took off the sock and when he saw that under these there was no foot to be seen, he laughed loudly with excitement and delight, then he took off his right shoe and sock. Then he slid to the floor, Lasca all the while watching him, open mouthed and horror stricken, darted to a corner in which it seemed was a large antique mirror in which a man could see himself full length. When Faralone stood before the mirror and saw himself full length, he saw only a well filled suit of clothes suspended a few inches from the floor with no visible means of support. Suddenly he laughed with a joyous laugh of a mischievous child and whistling an energetic jig, then for a moment or two, he danced prankishly in front of the mirror until he got laughing so, he could not dance anymore. Then he made a rush for Lasca and embraced him and seemed to kiss him of both cheeks. Lasca uttered a low moan of despair.

"We have don it man! We have don it!" exclaimed Farralone, "And now my friend, the world is our oyster."

His voice was no longer the voice of one who wishes to go up and down in the world, doing good deeds. It was the voice of the egoist, the self-seeker, the schemer who brooks no obstacles.

"But wait, wait," he said, "Perhaps I am not really invisible."

Then and there, with great haste and flinging his garments to right and left, he undressed himself and when he had finished undressing, you would have thought that there was no on in that place, but the anxious and terrified servant. Not knowing, perhaps, what he was doing, Lasca opened his shirt and produced a silver crucifix that was hung from his neck by a black cord. At that moment the invisible man's attention must have been on something else. Then he must have turned and for the first time seen that emblem against which, the powers of darkness cannot stand. He screamed at the top of his lungs and in the frenzy of fear.

"Don't do that." he screamed, "Damn you, don't do that; put that thing away."

Lasca hesitated, he seemed as one who has been suddenly bereft of will power. Slowly the invisible man became faintly visible. His horrible face was averted so that it could no longer see the cross. He was creeping toward Lasca with extended arms in a kind of side-wise, crab-like motion. His hands and his face were nearly visible to the rest of him. From the arm-pits down, nothing of him could be seen. But he moved on bare shadowy feet. It was only for a long moment of time that he was visible. Then the power which the cross had exerted upon him began to fail and once more it seemed as if Lasca was alone in the place. He had returned the cross to its place next to his breast and now he stood with clasped hands and upturned face. His lips moved and he prayed.

"Pater Noster Qui Est in Collis . . . "

He was not destined to speak any more of that prayer. In-stead, of stately Latin words, hideous choking sounds came from

his throat. His eyes seemed as if they were about to be forced
out of their sockets. It was just as if invisible hands had ceased
him by the throat from behind and were strangling him. With his
own hands he fought in vain to loosen the hold of the invisible
hands. Farralone's harsh laughter could be heard. There was in it
an exultant, demoniac quality. Las's tormented face was forced
upward until only the tips of his feet rested on the stone floor.
Soon, these could no longer find a hold. The old servant's arms
and legs and body went into a kind of horrible convulsion. He
could not have been better hanged with a rope. After some seconds,
except for the occasional twitch of a hand or foot, he hung still.
Then the choking hands suddenly loosed their hold and Lasca crumpled
dead to the floor where he looked like a pathetic heap of old clothes.

It wasn't likely that anyone would have been strolling about
the graveyard at that time of night. It is probable that no human
eye saw the door of the tombstone, in which Farralone had his
habitation, open slowly and thereafter close without any sign of
human agency. Nevertheless, that is what happened. And immediately
afterward, the little gate in the ornamental iron railing, unlatched
itself, opened, closed and latched itself again. The wind and rain
had been followed by a clear night of stars. In this the stars
were now beginning to grow dim and there was a hint of day. An
hour later, the earliest risers in Latmos became active. The
little town began to live. Carts of produce, which had come in
from the country on the preceding evening, were uncovered. The
arcaded market came to life. Peasant women chattered and scolded.
Their sons and husbands unloaded from the wagon, carts of live
chickens. There were also gagglings of live geese tied by the
feet, paddlings of ducks and even two or three whiteness of
swans. Wives, daughters, and maid servants of the burgers,
filtered into the market place, carrying baskets over their arms.
Here and there could be seen course sacks tied at the end which
seemed to contain things that struggled and rolled over. One of
those sacks came open somehow and a lively young shote made a mad
dash for liberty, venomously pursued by the old woman who owned
him. Laughter arose in the market place. One laugh, harsher and
more metallic than the others, seemed to come fro no one in
particular and was the dominant note. No sooner was the shote well
escaped from his sack, than a cart of lively chickens came open.
Ducks tied together by the feet got loose. Geese got loose and
presently it seemed as if all the available livestock was escaping.

To add to the confusion, farm dogs felt it their duty to join in the pursuit of the escaping pigs and fowls. In the rush to recover escaping profit, many people took unacceptable tumbles. They went down as if they had been tripped. There was less and less laughter, more and more angry cries. The uproar brought a constable. This one had no sooner shouldered his way into the midst of things, than his helmet was knocked from his head. He looked behind him savagely and there was no one there. He bent over to pick up his helmet and receiving from behind a sudden and insane impulse, sprawled on his face in the mud and slime. A stand, neatly piled with assorted vegetables, was overturned; eggs, began to fly and there were burst of triumphant metallic laughter. In the center of the market, was a deep pool of water, in the midst of which was an ancient stone fountain. Several persons, yielding to sudden impulses, tripped on the curb of this pool and fell in. It seemed as if the veritable spirit of mischief was abroad, and then it seemed as if this spirit of mischief had wearied and withdrawn from the scene. Stands were righted, chickens returned to their crates, ducks and geese retied by the legs until gradually the little market, jabbering and chattering, began to function. The policeman picked himself up and a nice old woman cleaned his face and his uniform for him.

In the outskirts of the town, near the single -track railroad which periodically connected Latmos with the outside world, in a sequestered dell, a small fire was burning and nearby lay a loaf of bread, a hunk of cheese and a live hen. The hen, all of a sudden

performed an astounding feat of gymnastics. She rose three feet
from the floor and her head remained stationary, whirled herself
round and round in the air like a fourth of July pin-wheel. Then
she dropped to the floor and lay still. Presently her feathers
split apart, flowering the line of the breast bone, and she appeared
to devest herself o their skin and feathers. A moment later, and
split from end to end, she laid herself upon the hot coals and began
to broil. The end of the loaf of bread broke itself off, rose to
a height of three feet from the ground, accompanied by a broken piece
of cheese and grew rapidly less and less, until it had vanished.
It wasn't long before all the bread and all the cheese, and all the
chicken, except the feathers, seemed to have vanished into the thin
air. The bushes at the back of the fire now parted and a dingy
weather-worn blanket, hitherto unseen, moved serpent like toward
this opening and disappeared into it. In a most secret place, the
blanket gave itself a toss and spread itself smoothly. When it
had settled down, the middle of it suggested the liens of a huge
human body. The blanket was just long enough to cover the feet
and the shoulders. Where the head and the neck of the body should
have stuck out, there was nothing but thin air. Presently there
arose in that place, a fainting buzzing sound. But it may have been a
bee.

A postern gate of Latmos castle opened on the moat which could
here be crossed by a narrow permanent stone bridge. At the near end
of the bridge, were a number of carriages. The postern opened and
the brothers and sisters of Count Charlemagne, with the families
filed out, accompanied by castle servants, carrying their baggage.

The expelled relatives fussed malicously as they crossed the
bridge and crowded into the waiting carriages. Count Pepin was the
last to cross the bridge. He turned, and standing on the edge of
the moat, shook his fist at the castle. Then he seemed to lose
his balance and fell into the moat. His infuriated wife, helped
to drag him out. She blamed him for his awkwardness and his
stupidity. He kept reiterating that someone had pushed him.

When the moon had been up for sometime, a beam of light fell
on the postern gate and its ornamental bronze knocker. The handle
of the knocker, began now to rise and fall with strong percussions
which reverberated loudly in the still night. The carriages with
the relatives had long since departed. There was no one in sight.
After sometime, there was a sound of bolts rasping and chains rattling.
The postern was opened and in the opening appeared a man, pale-
faced, and the trig uniformed body of one of the castle footman.
Seeing no one, he started to close the door, but could not. It
seemed to be resting at the bottom against an immovable obstacle.
Bending over to see what this was, he jerked suddenly backward, as
if he had been kicked in the face by a mule. He went over on his
back and would have screamed doubtless, if his air passages had
not been suddenly so compressed that he could not make any sound at
all. After a while, he lay still and the, his body sagging
between two fixed points, his head and shoulders and his bent knees,
he rose from the stone floor, came out on the bridge and seemed to
toss himself sideways into the moat. He sank. By the time the
concentric rings, occasioned by his sudden immersion had vanished,
the postern gate had closed to an accompaniment of slicing bolts
and rattling chains.

The bedroom occupied by the Countess Esmerald was tall and severe. Over the mantel there was the portrait of Farralone, before the disfigurement which had caused him to withdraw from the sight of man. The Countess, sided by her tirewoman, was getting ready for bed. The room was not in most ancient part of the castle. The outer wall was much thinner and was pierced by three french-windows which opened on a battlement. The Countess was seated in front of a dressing-table. The toilet articles were rich but of great simplicity. The Countess had covered her night-gown with a wrapper and her bare feet were thrust in white fur slippers. Her hair had been taken down and combed and brushed. Half of it had been rebraided, and the other half was half braided. The tirewoman's hands gently aside.

"I will finish it Griselda, " she said, "I shan't need you anymore. Goodnight and sleep well."

"It has been a long hard day," said the maid, "sleep will be good."

"I'm so happy about my father," said the Countess, "Already he seems almost like himself. Of course he is very weak, but his mind is active and he looks forward to man more years of contentment and usefulness."

"What has happened," said the maid," is a miracle."

"What happened, " said the Countess, "was because of skill and knowledge. There is nothing miraculous about them. When you come to me in the morning, if I should be asleep, don't wake me. Good night."

"Goodnight your Ladyship." said the maid and withdrew.

While she finished braiding her hair, the Countess Esmerald hummed and spoke, rather than sang a plaintive folk song that had to do with urns and willows and broken hearts and mourning doves. From that time until she was actually in bed, she broke off the song, only to take it up again. She stood for a long time in a grave contemplation of Farralone's portrait. She had hoped that Lasca would have succeeded in finding the mutilated original and bringing him back to her. She told herself that no disfigurement could effect her love for him or her wish to be with him. When she was in bed, her head was toward the windows and presently she turned even more away from them and lay with her face to the wall. She had blown out her candles but the room was bright with flooding moonlight. The ornamental bronze handle of the center window turned slowly downward. The window opened; a draft of air stirred the curtains; slowly the window closed and the handle turned up into place. Though the room itself was bright with moonlight, Countess and her bed were in deep shadow. When she heard Farralone's voice speaking to her, she thought for a moment that she was dreaming.

"I had to come back to you," he said, "I couldn't stay away."

She realized that she was awake and listening to a living voice.

"I am so glad," she said, "I hurt you and I didn't mean to hurt you."

"In the dark, "said Farralone," Men are much alike. You need never see me as I am. I shall only come to you at night."

"But my dear," she said, "I want you with me all the time."

"I am the best judge of that," said Farralone, "I am very cold."

She doesn't know quite what to answer, and he repeated.

"I said that I am very cold." he said, "Where you are it is

snug and warm."

An ugly quality had crept into his voice and for the first time she felt alarmed.

"Nobody will know," he said, "Don't you love me?"

"Of course I love you." she said, "Perhaps - -"

"Perhaps," he said, "You don't feel that we have waited long enough, but I do and I am not going to wait any longer."

There was a faint sound of struggling and the Countess raising her voice exclaimed:

"We musn't! We musn't!"

"Don't be a fool. he said; his voice trembled and was ugly.

Perceiving that he was determined to have her with her consent or without it, the Countess fought against him.

"You are not my Farralone." she said, "You are someone else. Where is all the tenderness and courtesy?"

He laughed in the dark and laid strong hands on her. She began to scream. Count Charlemagne, having slept for many restful hours, was wide awake. Hearing those screams and being a man of perfect courage, he felt, sick and weak as he was, that he must go to the rescue. He scrambled out of his bed with surprisingly alacrity and staggering from weakness, moved rapidly through a door near the head of his bed. This opened on a steep and narrow stair near the foot of which was his daughter's room, from which came the sounds of screaming. The Count's feeble hurried descent of the stair had a heroic quality. Over his nightshirt he wore a velvet wrapper, fastened by broad heavy frogs and embroidered with his coat of arms. His gray hair was tousled this way and that, but his eyes had in them the undaunted fire of an eagle. He pushed open the door of his

daughter's room and beheld her violently and convulsively trying
to open one of the french-windows, and screaming for help. She
was alone so far as he could see and his first thought was that she
had gone mad. She struck at the air with her hands and seemed to be
trying to twist loose from something that held her. The old man
hurried to the rescue. His idea was to take his daughter in his
arms and comfort her and soothe her. Instead he found that he had
grappled with something that felt like the powerful, naked, body
of a man. For the first time in his life, Count Chalemagne Latmos
knew the meaning of fear. Nevertheless, he clung valiantly and with
all his strength to that naked body and his efforts had one result.
The Countess succeeded in freeing herself, in tearing open the window
and rushing out on the battlement. Along this she fled, her long
garments' trailing after her. That which the Count Charlemagne had
grappled, jerked violently to free itself and was for following her,
but the Count, his battle blood up now, hung on like grim death
and with a surprising tenacity. Still clinging, he was dragged out
on the battlement. In the distance, the Countess Esmerald fled.
Born apparently, of the thin air with which he seemed to be struggling,
there was a sudden and hideous torrent of oaths and exclamations.
The invisible force no longer strove to free itself. It seemed
now determined to avenge itself on the feeble old man
who had, for a moment thwarted it. Count Charlemagne was suddenly
felled to the lead roof of the battlement by a dreadful blow. Then
he was caught up by one elbow and one knee and after swinging to
and fro twice, was tossed clean out over the battlement into the
night. After a considerable interval there was a distant sound of
a heavy splash. In his frantic and passionate pursuit of the

Countess Esmerald, the invisible man was handicapped by his lameness
As she fled along the battlement he gained on her, but whenever she
came to a flight of descending steps, he lost what he had gained;
furthermore, although she was in a state of panic, the terrain was
more familiar to her than to him.

She in turn was handicapped by her trailing garments and she was
out of breath with fright and the struggle to escape. The long
battlements, down steps and through arched galleries, she sled.
Across a formal garden, the gravel paths edged with Dwarf Myrtle
and the splash of waters audible; she came at last to a salley-port.
She had difficulty with the fastenings. Her fingers trembled so.
If the last bolt had resisted even a little longer, the invisible
man must have caught her. Seeing her as he though, trapped and at
his mercy, sounds which were not human came from him. He sounded
more like a pack of wolves than a man. But in the nick of time, the
pastern gate came open and she fled across the stone bridge which
traversed the moat. and thereafter downward through a park like
planting of trees until she cam to the outskirts of the city. She
could hear the uneven patting of the naked feet which pursued her.
She could hear the sharply drawn breaths of the man she had once
loved. She no longer made any sounds except those of quick breathing.
She needed every breath and every ounce of strength to keep her
distant from the pursuing horror. The good burgers of Latmos were all in
bed. The city lights were few and far between. She ran through a
slum and then through the chief business district, and then up
along the residential hill which was crowned by the dark bulk of
the convent of St. Ursula.

The Ursuline nuns maintained a small free clinic. Poor
persons who had been injured or taken sick, at any hour of the day
or night had ready access to skilled help. Within the great entrance
door, there was always a wakeful nun on watch so that when the
Countess Esmerald began to beat frantically upon the door with its
bronze knocker, it was a matter of seconds before the observation
grill in the midst of the strong door, swung open and the peaceful
charitable face of Sister Olga looked inquiringly out.

"In the name of Christ," cried the Countess, "Let me in."

The heave door swung open and she slipped through the
shints and helped to slam it shut, behind her, she could hear the
naked feet of the invisible man thudding up the convent steps. Sister
Olga had automatically closed the observation grill, but when the
invisible man, shouting like a beast, fell in turn upon the door with
a great thunder of knocking, she once more opened it and looked stead-
fastly out. From her neck swung and ivory Christ upon a cross of
black ebony. The beast-like shouting of the invisible man became a
kind of frightened whisper.

Sister Olga, looking into the night and seeing no one, and yet
hearing animal cries that had dwindled into whimperings, felt the need
of comfort and support and she began to make the sign of the cross. As
she did so, the face and hands of the invisible man became visible and
so the rest of him took on an illusive phosphorescent visibility. He
was turning his face away from the cross and the signs of the cross.
He was moaning like a man who has been cruelly hurt and maimed. As
he dragged his lame leg down the steps of the convent, he became less
visible and in a moment he had vanished. Muttering prayers, Sister Olga

closed and bolted the grill, then she turned and administered the Countess Esmerald, who had fainted dead away.

In the chapel like laboratory and workshop of Farralone, there was a block-front desk. The night, after the night which we have ventured to describe in which Count Charlemagne met his death and Countess Esmerald sought sanctuary in the convent of St. Ursula, a drawer of this desk suddenly opened. A sheet of white paper or parchment came out of this drawer and spread itself upon the blotter in the first position of being written upon. A small silver bowl stood on the desk, more than half filled with small lead-shot. Into this bed of shot and holding them erect, was stuck a number of white quill pens. One of these seemed to lift itself out of the shot to dip itself into a well containing ink, to shake off the surplus ink and forthwith to write upon the waiting parchment. When the quill had finished writing, it stood itself back among the shot. What looked to be a salt-shaker on a large scale, but which instead of salt contained fine sand, now shook itself over the wet writing on the parchment. Next the door of the glass case containing surgical instruments, opened, and a modern surgical knife with a blade nearly eight inches long, hideously sharp and curved, cam out of the case, moved through the air to the writing desk and laid itself down by the side of the sanded parchment. The parchment rose and the sand, with which it was liberally sprinkled was dispersed by a sudden sharp blowing, the knife and the parchment left the desk, side by side, and moved across the chapel, precisely as if each were held by an invisible hand and swung in time to the steps of the invisible man to whom they belonged. In this way they went swinging through the cemetery and through the darkness of the silent town. The moon had not yet risen. The knife and the parchment came at length to the main entrance

of the convent of St. Ursula. Here the parchment flattened itself
conveniently against the heavy door and with a sharp blow, the knife
pinned it in place. The sun was not yet up, but the abbess of
St. Ursula had risen, changed the hair shirt which she wore by night
to one which she wore by day, completed her ablutions, her private
prayers and penitences and dressed and was ready for the communistic
activities of the day. She was in her office. She had a business
like desk and a filing cabinet. There were also cold and grim paint-
ings of Saints and martyrs. There was a temptation of St. Anthony and
a St. Sebastian in whom there did not seem to be room for any more
arrows at all. In the corridor without the office, could be heard
suddenly a great brouhaha of female voices which drew nearer and nearer
and Sister Melanore, her dark doe eyes, wide and brilliant with
excitement, almost burst into the room.

"Mother," she cried, "Tintagal, the gardener, has something terrible
to show us. We don't know what to do. It is terrible; we are
terribly frightened. Other nuns older but no less agitated, followed
Malanore in the austere office. The abbess spoke sharply;

"You are behaving like a lot of hens who have had their heads
cut off." she said. "Tell me what has happened and don't all tell me
at once. Sister Olga, you look as if you had retained some vestiges
of common sense. What has happened?"

"When tintagal the gardener came to work," said Sister Olga. "he
found a writing pinned by a terrible knife to the door of the convent.
He will not let the things out of his hand until he has given the into yours.

"I will receive them with interest." said the abbess, "Bring him in.

Tintagal, it seemed, had been detained in the corridor without. He was a man too old to be regarded, even in the strictest nunnery as a man. He was therefore a privileged character and came and went much as he pleased. He was now brought into the office and thrust forward.

"It was a terrible knife, "he said, "and doubtless a terrible writing."

"He would not let any of us see the writing," said Sister Malnore in an excited querulous voice."

"He did well." said the abbess. "Lay the knife on my desk. It is indeed a terrible knife. And now let us see if the writing is also terrible.

The nuns were dying with curiosity to know what was written on the parchment, but the abbess had at that time no intention of gratifying their curiosity. She folded the parchment twice. Her mouth became a straight line. She stood for a few moments in thought. Then she said:

"Two of you prepare to accompany me. I must speak at once with his grace, the archbishop.

From the nunnery to the archbishop's palace was no great distance. The abbess, her mouth still a straight line, walked with quick deter- minded steps. She carried a parcel in which she had wrapped the knife and the parchment. Two of the older sisters walking side by side, followed in her steps at a respectful distance. The archbishop was feeding white doves in his high walled garden. The nuns, making little crunching sounds in the gravel and ushered by the archbishop's major-domo, approached him down one of the narrow paths. The arch- bishop looked up smiling and stepped forward from among his doves. The abbess advanced alone.

"What good fortune brings you at this hour?" said the archbishop.

The abbess slowly untied her parcel.

"May the fortune which brings me be good." she said, "But it smacks rather of evil. This," she said, extending the parchment to him, "was found nailed to the door of the convent with this." and she showed him the knife. "Tintagal, the gardener found this terrible writing nailed to the door of the convent with this terrible knife."

The archbishop took the parchment in his hand and read it. The smile left his face.

"It is probably." he said, "The work of a crazy person who imagines himself to be playing a clever practical joke. There is even a chance he may be dangerously mad. Ours are not the hands to deal with the matter. Give me a few moments and I shall be ready to go with you."

"Where are we going? asked the Abbess."

"We are going to see Baron Plydore," said the archbishop, "Our most excellent and efficient chief of police."

He raised his voice so that the major-domo could hear him and said:

"My carriage Andranark."

It was not long before the archbishop and the abbess with the two sisters facing them, were bolting and jolting through the streets of Latmos to a building in which the chief of police had his offices. His collection of weapons, his books of portraits, of thumb prints and handwritings.

Here, dear reader, the Whale/Morris treatment ends. Preceding, the treatment written by James Whale, alone, in which we get a hint of how this treatment ended. - (Ed.)

Notes on drafts "THE INVISIBLE MAN"

MEMORANDOM TO: FROM: John Balderston

Mr. Laemmle Jr.
Mr. Shayer
Mr. Gardener.

    1. This is almost a new story, and has been
written in ten days. For that reason I wish to establish
clarly what is being attempted. Firstly, please put
out of mind any thoughts of Frankenstein or other horror
films. This is essentially a fantastic melodrama. It
contains strong elements of horror, but also of humor,
and even of political satire.

    This picture falls naturally into four parts:

PART ONE: We see the man become invisible and go
forth into the world on his self-imposed mission to reform it by terror. Our object in this first part,
Sequences "A" and "B" , is to make our audience believe
in our major premise. (The invisiblity scene improves
on the creation scene in Frankenstein because the heroine
is the willing assistant of our "Menace" in hid experiment).

    PART TWO: (Sequences "C" , "D", "E" and "F") We
find the "Invisible Man" story treated as a joke in New
York, but the town is upset by two mystery murders, which
don't seem connected either with the Invisible Man or with
each other. We know our menace has done them, we "see"
him do them. But at the end of "H" , the newspaper murder
and the Invisible Man's proclamation to the public makes
the evidence overwhelming and convincing, creates a
situation in which the public will know and believe that
an Invisible Man is loose in their midst and has murdered
public enemies and proposes to murder more.

    PART THREE: At he beginning of Sequence "G" , it
follows, New York and the country know the truth and are
in turmoil, and our object here is to show through many
shots all the reactions that such a situation would create
in New York and Washington. We establish considerable
public sympathy for the Invisible Man so long as his
"executions" are those of public enemies, we show
how blood lust and mania have sent him completely crazy;
and by killing innocent people who were chasing him merely
out of curiosity, he forfeits all sympathy and becomes
merely a wild beast to be tracked down.

    PART FOUR: After the rising crescendo of excitement
in part three, we begin Part Four (Sequences "H" , "I" , "J")
quietly. The head of the Committee of Public Safety
explains to the President the man's cunning and the
failure of all his traps, and then plays his last card.

He tells the girl Carpenter loves that she must end the
terror by going to the man herself and killing him. Traps
here are useless. He will only meet her in the park, and
how can you trap the invisible in the open? Succeed or
fail, she bravely goes. The Invisible Man takes her to his
hide-out, he believes she loves him and he trusts her,
although in his rage against the public he is now preparing to loose invisible rats inoculated with bubonic plague
in the sewers of New York. She is prepared to go to bed
with him and kill him with a knife she has concealed under
the pillow. We prepare for this, then shift to a less
objectionable and more exciting windup.

———————————————————

You gentlemen will observe that I would scarecely
think itnecessary to discuss this thing in terms of
its dynamics in a memorandum if I entertained no doubts
as to the perfection of the text at the moment. It has
been jammed through in less than two weeks and it needs
more work, and that it can be put across.

THE INVISIBLE MAN - - THE PLOT

During 17 years of work on his invisibility formula,
Carpenter, a recluse, ugly and friendless, decides if he
can to make himself invisible, and enforce his view on social
and political regorm by punishing the guilty in high places
and creating a reign of terror.

When th epicture opens, in profound secrecy as to
his aims he is using as assistant Baxter, a young amateur
physicist. He needs some biological work, and so engages
by correspondence a qualified young woman from the Medical
Center who comes during an octopus experiment. She turns
out to be attractive, and, moreover, the first attractive
woman who has crossed his path since he shut himself up and
commenced his stupendous researches and experiments

Carpenter though attracted to her has too much will-
power and concentration of purpose to be thrown out of his
stride. When they first meet, we see the attraction, followed by his immediate reconcentration on the job. He con
tinues work as planned. The last experiment is to be on a
large monkey. If he can make that invisible, he will carry
out his secret scheme at once and operate on himself. But
from the atmosphere of mystery, Carpenter's obsessions, mental
queerness, and his actions that day, both boy and girl feel
that he is "up to something" more than merely scientific work.
This leads to a strain that culminates in the girl's refusal
to help with the monkey experiment.

Carpenter by this time has integrated his yen for
the girl into his strange mental phantasy. We mus make

clear in Swquence "B" and later the innocence and purity of
the man's soul, contrasted with his diabolical proceedings.
He is absolutely sincere in his desire to reform the world
and the abuses he will attack are those which our audiences
feel to be the real crying abuses of today. He believes that,
when he is no longer ugly but invisible, he can win the girl's
love by proving his greatness not merely as a scientist but
as a reformer and master of events through terror. But as
often happens with these terrorists, his love as it develops
later, is romantic and pure - he wants her to come to him
of herself - and he is conviced that all mankind, when at the end
she betrays him and seeks his death.
Returning to the plot, his anger when the girl refuses to stay in the room for the last experiment but one,
and Baxter quits with her, is both scientific and personal.
He cannot do either monkey or himself without assistance. Also,
he wants the girl to live through his triumph with him. So
when they both quit Carpenter becomes cunning, gets the boy
out with the monkey and then locks the steel door. He has
little time, he knows Baxter will get hlep, so he must at
once go through with the second part of his final experiment
on himself, and take the risk, without having experimented on
the monkey. This is plausible; he not only wants the girl
there, he must have her there, because he must have help and
Baxter, if there, would stop him by force from suicide or
worse. Thus we motivate without any melodramatic
mechanism the girl locked in the room with him while with
her help he makes himself invisible - she must help him once
he has started it, or he will die. During this terrible
scene he gives away to her his feeling for her and hints of

his intentions in New York and perhaps later the rest of the
world - his megalomania come out for the first time.

(This memo is dictated after Sequence "A" and "B" have
been written - it is now clear, after trying to work out
the picture as a whole, that they need a few deft touches of
characterization and motive to bring out Carpenter more clearly
on the lines expressed above, but otherwise I thik they are
all right.)

Carpenter has planned his operations in New York carefully. He has his hide-out ready, an abandoned stable containing clothers, disguises, tinned food, chemicals and even a few
rats in case he needs more experiments. But his punitive
murders, which he terms "executions" , must of course be done
when he is completely invisible, and hence stark naked and
carrying nothing, so each must be done with whatever weapon
he finds to hand beside his intended victims. Accordingly
when he kills the ganster in the Tombs it is with a table
knife as the victim is eating his sumptuous meal. When he
kills as the victim is eating his sumptuous meal. When he
kills the newspaper editor who refuses to print his proclamation
to the public, it is with the big spike for copy that always
stands on the editor's desk. But when he comes to attack the
great bear whose pools are smashing securities, he is on the
floor of the Stock Market, there is no weapon, and he is
forced to strangle the man with his bare hands.

To return to character and motivation - (the outline
of the picture in continuity is being worked out separately).

Carpenter's scene with the girl in her room alone in
New York in Sequence "C" reveals him to us fully for the first
time. As a lover he is pathetic and appealing - he trusts
the girl to come to him when he has proved himself to be the

master mind and agency for good - she is in no danger from
him, and we must believe this. But Baxter when he hears
about this interview does not believe it, the girl is carefully guarded against any attempt. Meanwhile, Carpenter has
hinted to the girl, so that the audience knows what is coming,
that he intends to reform abuses and execute the guilty. She
doesn't believe him. The murder of the gangster is at first
not connected with this strange yarn from Jersey about an
invisible man. At any rate not connected by the police or
public or press. Neither is the murder on the Stock Exchange.
But on the Big Bear's throat are the marks of Carpenter's
strangling fingers. And it is shortly after this second murder
that he kills the editor who refuses to print his message to
the world, that we see the typewriter writing by itself the
threat to the editor's assistant - - and that the truth comes
out - - that this man in invisible, that he is murdering people
and in an effort to put things to rights he is threatening to
murder other unnamed leaders of public life who have been
faithless to their trusts. Wild panic follows, fruitless
search for Carpenter.

Now we come back to the girl and her motivation. We
are anxious to get apparently - - though not really as appears
later - - completely away from the old physical "menace" to
the girl formula of so many mystery serials and films. We
have plenty of violent melodrama without that, if we can get
the right twist to put this whole thing on a more plausible
and better story plane, and this we think is the twist:

Carpenter's yen for the girl now is as much of an
obsession as his attempt to make himself an invisible dictator
through terrorism. He longs for her to come to him and is
astonished and disappointed that she doesn't. He is a love-sick

"menace". He can't understand! After all, has he not
offered her a throne beside him, are they not to be king
and queen of his invisible empire? By this time his megalomania
has made great strides and he is much more obvouly insane
than at first - - as of course he would be, considering what
he is and what he has done. We hear of a couple of other
murders. We don't want to go on showing these - -we've shown
enough of them - - what we show are significant details on
other lines - - his escape from a police dog in a crowd, etc - -
but we establish, with these new crimes and the threats made
against practically all leaders of public life, that no man
in high position considers himself safe - - guards are every-
where - - the panic is terrific - - other countries have declared
an embargo against all ships from America lest the man might
visit them - - things are in the worst mess possible.

Now we come back to the girl and approach the climax.
After the first blaze of publicity following his escape from
Jersey, she has dropped out of public attention. The invisible
man's yen for her is not known to the public. But Baxter
sees that she is most carefully guarded. One man appointed
by the President as head of the far flung organization which
is trying to catch Carpenter, now called "The Committe of
Public Safety," has learned about the girl's real situation
in this mess and he talks to her and points out that it is
only through her that this menace who is strangling society
can be extirpated. Not by any trap. Every possible trap
has been tried and failed. The creature is too cunning. Only
one thing will do it. If she herself goes to him, pretending
that she loves him and that she will share his invisible throne,
then she and nobody else will have the opportunity of killing
him. It's clear from his experiments tha he can stop a

bullet, a knife would finish him as it did the octopus.

Note that on these lines there is no trouble about bringing them together. Carpenter is keeping an eye on the girl, from a distance of course. He has told her that if she'll shake everybody off and walk in the park near the obelisk he will know that she is ready to come - - she is to leave the rest to him.

The girl has a terrific struggle with herself. She has th enormal yen of a high spirited courageous girl when told that she like Joan of Arc is the only person who can save the country. But it is much more than this. She reproaches herself for having gone through with the experiment with Carpenter, and helped him. She knows it's true as he told her in her hotel room in New York that she's responsible - - she could have let him die - - without her help he couldn't have done it - - he trusted her to pull him through at the crisis and she did not fail him - -and of course she now bitterly reproaches herself that she did not understand his meglomaniac hints in the lab and let him die, as she could so easily have done. From every point of view, it is her duty to use this man's passion for her and his trust in her to kill him. But she mustn't tell Baxter - - their love is avowed by now, and of course Baxter would stop her, take her away. What she does is therefore profoundly secret. She only has the cooperation of the head of the Committee of Public Safety. And this man's respect for Carpenter's cunning is so great that he is afraid to use her as a bait and set a trap - - if the trap failed the girl would be useless in the future and she is the last hope! She must do it alone. She is risking her life. He says it and she knows it.

She walks in the park by the obelisk. Carpenter, be- lieving in her, but taking precautions against her being

followed, turns up, invisible, using a baby carriage pushed
by a nursemaid as a shield. She tells him she has come to
him and she loves him and that she will hellp him bump off these
villains, etc. She claims the old horror of him has vanished,
she asks him to take her arm - -to show him that she won't
even shudder. He does, and now that she knows exactly where
his body is beside her she pulls out her gun or knife or
whatever you like - - we haven't worked this out - - and tries
to kill him. She fails, he gets the weapon. There is a taxi
or a car pulled up in the drive with a chauffeur. He holds
the gun or knife at the head of the baby in the pram and tells
her to get into the car. She knows the baby; must die if she
doesn't. She does. He gets in beside her and forces the
chauffeur to drive them off and gets her to his hide-out.

Returning to the characterisation again. Carpenter's
mental explosion when this creature whom he has idealized and
trusted tries to murder him changes completely his curious
love for humanity which he is trying to serve by bumping off
their oppressors. Given the character we have worked out,
this I think if plausible. Hate for the girl, hate for all
mankind, for the people who have been trying to track him
down like a wild beast when he was only trying to help them!
The man is now a violent maniac. His one idea is destruction
and revenge. He has the girl in his power. This leads us
into the wedding scene in the hide-out - - he puts powder and
rouge on himself making his face visable, dressed himself up
in wedding clothes, provides the girl with a wedding repast - -
he's going to rape her, we see how his crazed mind resents
her treachery and how he has changed from a perverted sort
of love for humanity as well as her, to terrible sadism.
The invisible rats, inoculated with bubonic plague, are now
to be released in the streets, they will breed in the sewers - -
New York will be stricken by pestilence - -and out of this

situation we work to a quick climax in which he is bitten by his own rats or suffocated by chlorine gas as in the first script, or some better twist at the end which we haven't thought out yet.

Note particularly that this memorandum deals not with continuity but with character - - with motive - -following out the dogma which I think will make this a successful picture and one different from others of its kind, and that dogma is this:

The audience will accept one completely impossible premise - - In this case invisibility - - they see it happen and they will believe it - - provided the invisible man himself, the girl and everyone else in the picture, sane or insane, act as they would act in real life in such a situation. There must be nothing impossible or even improbable in what happens after Carpenter becomes invisible. Stick to this formula throughout and the audience will go with us all the way.

MEMO

1.   Establish public acceptance of the facts and ensuing excitement.

2.   Show police with Baxter and Daryl in apartment. Establish guard over Daryl - - safer here than if taken out. Establish Baxter's anxiety to her.

3.   Broadcasting.

4.   The tired police - - completely fagged out - - and to values already existing in text add here commissioner's belief that the only hope is a cold spell to keep him indoors.

5.   The Capitol and White House scenes. Instead of appointing House as director Public Safety, let him have been appointed and taken over the situation in New York by Act of Congress.

6.   Daryl hears from Carpenter by post or phone - -he's waiting for her in the park - - why doesn't she come etc. If she lets him down he will visit his vengeance on New York - - they will die in heaps in the streets - - How can one man do all this? No one can guess - - but I can and will, etc. He might add that he'll kill another banker or two to show that he means business. If so, the banker thrown out of the window would come at this point. Anyway, this leads us to:

7.   The President tells Colonel House that he must play his last card - - the girl - - because the President, and this must be plausible, takes Carpenter's threats seriously.

8.   House goes to the girl and if Carpenter has threatened the public with massacre and she believes it, her motive for going to him is much stronger.

9.   Play the park scene as now and the first part of the scene in the hide-out. But meanwhile, Baxter has found her gone, suspected, gone to police, been fobbed off, tried to see House and failed, talked to his mother, got hold of the taxi driver and the nurse maid, and tracked Carpenter down to the immediate neighborhood of hide-out.

10.   Girl puts knife under pillow, is going through with it, then somehow - - and how and how - - there is a plausible interruption - - Baxter if possible - - again how? - - and he takes off his clothes in the rat room, tries to get out the window with the expected results which the audience will have seen coming five minutes back.

Dog. I agree that the present chase is out but dog idea is a good one. And Baxter, if he really is to break in at the end, could use a dog. His dog, from the apartment, to track Daryl from where the taxi set Daryl and Carpenter down. Let Baxter give the dog Daryl's show to smell. He can plausibly trace them to where the taxi discharged them but no further but the dog might do the rest. While I don't think this too hot, as Carpenter would have thought of everything of the sort, yet if we play for the immemorial ending, then this is as plausible or more so than most.

The dog angle would be much more effective as a whole, though perhaps not coming in just where we wanted it to and, if after those murders, the police used bloodhounds so that Carpenter could have a narrow escape. The invisible man would leave a trail for a dog. The police would have Carpenter's clothes from the lab and they could have every bloodhound in town all pepped up to do its duty if they got the smell.

- - - - - - -

Baxter (on sidewalk)   "Give yourself up to some scientific society."

- - - - - - -

Introduce telephone business into bedroom scene.

- - - - - - -

Baxter says: Carpenter let him live out of a cat and mouse complex.

- - - - - - -

Mrs. Baxter says: "It's indecent" when old that Carpenter wears no clothes.

- - - - - - -

Baxter in disguise?

- - - - - - -

Carpenter has business with photograph of himself in final scene.

This is the end of the Balderston material that was available. One can only speculate on how his full script would have been - Editor

FROM: John Huston

"INVISIBLE MAN"

Writer/Director John Huston

JUNE 29, 1932

CARPENTER: Head of the greatest endowed scientific institution
               in the world. An utterly mysterious man, saturnine,
electrically intelligent, given to sudden, infernal flights of
anger. Big frame, wasted, revoltingly ugly face of Albino-like
whiteness, save for a birthmark - a black discolored patch over
his temple and right eye.

MARIN: Experimenter in Carpenter's laboratory. Twenty-
               five, sharp, imaginative, gifted, prepossessing.

DARRYL: Marin's sweetheart. A Tansgra-type of beauty.
               Olive skin, black hair, coiled into heavy knots;
               full, carmine lips; dark, slanting eyes.

THE CITY

A skyline - clouds floating from the tips of spires of
skyscrapers - metal towers brilliant in the heavens - giant
sculptured figures poised loftily on gleaming pinnacles- - the
city of tomorrow, not the futuristic's dream of a metropolis,
but New York or Berlin fifteen years hence - -   A dirigible
cuts through one corner of the picture, mosquito-like helio-
copters buzzing around it.

                    ****

INTERIOR LABORATORY: Bletheim Foundation. Elaborately
equipped. Fifty or more white-garbed experimentors at work.

Now pausing to scan a report, now to look at a
culture, Carpenter makes the rounds of the laboratory - -
a crash of glass. The scientist in a rage, cursing a
paling worker for his stupidity, using his can like a
sword, overturning bottles, breaking test tubes. The
experimentors, trained to expect his sudden outbursts,

simply hold their breathing and wait for the storm to pass, and in due time, Carpenter proceeds, calmly enough, down the line of benches to a young man at a microscope whom he jabs lightly in the back with his stick.

"Marin."

Carpenter jerks his thumb, leads the way through a door into his private sanctuary.

"Your experiment - I congratulate you upon its success."

"Thank you, sir."

Carpenter makes inquiries about the background of the young man. What mathematics does he know? Ah, yes - the author of a paper on celestial mechanics. Carpenter himself is engaged in an experiment related to that field, a unique branch of optics. He needs an assistant. He's had Marin under observation, and approves of Marin. Would Marin care to join him - -

An invitation to become the conferee of the great Carpenter! The young man is dumbfounded. It was said of Carpenter that he was a greater mathematician than any other biologist and a great biologist than any other physicist. His contributions extended even to astronomy and medicine.

"Our work," Carpenter continues, "will be of a revolutionary nature, and the results of our experiments will be made secret. At first, even you shall be kept blind to the real significance of our research. You will work in my private laboratory. Begin by making a quantitative analysis of the refractions of the 'Y' ray."

Marin asks Carpenter no questions, simply does his bidding. He marvels at the man, his tirelessness, his searchlight intellect. At times he has even felt twinges simply hold their breathing and wait for the storm to pass, and in due time, Carpenter proceeds, calmly enough, down the line of benches to a young man at a microscope whom he jabs lightly in the back with his stick.

"Marin."

Carpenter jerks his thumb, leads the way through a door into his private sanctuary.

"Your experiment - I congratulate you upon its success."

"Thank you, sir."

Carpenter makes inquiries about the background of the young man. What mathematics does he know? Ah, yes - the author of a paper on celestial mechanics. Carpenter himself is engaged in an experiment related to that field, a unique branch of optics. He needs an assistant. He's had Marin under observation, and approves of Marin. Would Marin care to join him - -

An invitation to become the confrere of the great Carpenter! The young man is dumbfounded. It was said of Carpenter that he was a greater mathematician than any other biologist and a great biologist than any other physicist. His contributions extended even to astronomy and medicine.

"Our work," Carpenter continues, "will be of a revolutionary nature, and the results of our experiments will be made secret. At first, even you shall be kept blind to the real significance of our research. You will work in my private laboratory. Begin by making a quantitative analysis of the refractions of the 'Y' ray."

Marin asks Carpenter no questions, simply does his bidding. He marvels at the man, his tirelessness, his searchlight intellect. At times he has even felt twinges

of pity for Carpenter. What a frozen life he leads, his
hideous ugliness ruling out any chance for love, making the
very idea of Carpenter and a woman a repellent one. Day
by day, Marin becomes more puzzled over the nature of the
quest, but the measurement's he's made, the analyses, all of
which seemed so disconnected at the time they were performed
are beginning to fit into a structural scheme - a scheme of
what?   Marin feels as a savage, without the faintest
concept of steam, would feel were he put to assembling a
modern engine.

The revelation, when it comes, is blinding. A
piece of saturated white wool fabric is treated with ray
vibrations and placed on the glass disc of the ray machine.
Marin watches it, soft and white in the flicker of the
flashes, fade like a wreathe of smoke and vanish. Carpenter
puts his hand into the emptiness, then hands Marin the
invisible thing, unmistakably woolen, solid as ever. Marin
holds it for a moment, then throws it on the floor. Carpenter
laughs.

"You think it odd, eh? You know the rules of
visibility. Absorption and reflection of light. A Body
does one or both of these things. You can see an opaque red
box, for example, because the color absorbs some of the
light reflecting the red part back to you. Reflecting all
the light would make it shining white, like silver. A
glass box reflects only here and there, flashing gleams
and translucence - the skeleton of light. Put the glass
box in oil, it vanishes almost altogether. Smash the
glass box, grind it into a powder, and what in air would
be opaque white dust, is wholly invisible in oil. Paper-
would - is like the powdered glass. Oil white paper,
fill in the interstatices between the particles with oil
and it becomes transparent as glass. That's what's

happened to this slip of wool, only we've treated it with substances far more subtle than oil..

"I tell you, Marin, that living matter is subject to the same phenomena. Flesh, Marin - hair, Marin - Nails, Marin - bones and nerves - -"

Marin shivers.

"Me, Marin - I, John Carpenter, shall become invisible!"

******

Darryl, Marin's sweetheart, is frightened by his palor and heavy-circled eyes. He is driving himself like a slave. What does she care about scientific honors. Marin needs sleep. He will kill himself, working for Carpenter. If they could make this a holiday in the country. Marin laughs - - if Carpenter knew he had stolen so much as this hour. . . Now, he must hurry back or Carpenter will be furious.

Marin seldom leaves the laboratory now, snatching a half hour's sleep on a laboratory bench when best he can. If he is at the point of exhaustion, Carpenter is more appallingly energetic than ever. The scientist literally dances from test tube to microscope. His temper is re-markably even, almost gleeful his disposition.

What fantastic things have been happening! The episode of the cat still brings prickles to Marin's skin. The performance with the piece of wool had been duplicated, this time the subject being a live cat. Marin had watched it vanish into thin air - fangs and fur and claws - until all that was left of the cat was a pair of yellow eyes and a 'meow'. Turn off the lights and two flashing amber discs would appear in a cage in a corner of the laboratory. The cat was non the worse for its transformation (Had not Marin stroked its invisible back and heard it purr?

****

Darryl calls at the laboratory to see Marin.
Carpenter meets her. She does her best to hide the effect
his ugliness has on her, but Carpenter recognizes it and
it stabs him like a knife. Again Marin feels profound pity
for his master, whose ugliness makes him ashamed in the
presence of a woman.

******

The hour of the great experiment arrives. Scores
bottles are arranged alphabetically, the contents to be
administered in the order of the letters.

There was an interim during the experiment with
the cat when the poor animal suffered unbelievable anguish,
passing from rigid convulsions to periods of limp coma,
thence into a frenzy of action when it hurled itself around
the room, biting and scratching its two tormentors.

Carpenter, however, evinces no sign of weakness. On
the contrary, he is in the highest spirits, giving himself
to outbursts of merriment, all of which adds to the unreality
of the occasion for Marin.

The corporeal transformation of Carpenter from visibility
to invisibility occurs shortly before the dawn of a grey
winter day. Drugged by sleeplessness, the whole affair
has a nightmare-ish aspect for Marin. Carpenter goes
through the same horrible torments as did his predecessor
into invisibility, the cat; but he is in his full senses during
the last stages of the transformation when his naked body is
bathed in the rays and as his form loses its opaqueness and
human definition, he talks aloud, proving himself to be
wholly rational.

An invisible hand spins Marin around. whisper in
his ear. He gazes blankly ahead.

"Answer me - can you see me?"
Marin shakes his head.

"Here I am before you."

"I cannot see you."

The room rings with a joyous cry. A hand grips
Marin's wrist. His own hand is pulled out til it touches -
a naked chest.

"Do you want to join me? Shall I bring you over?"

"No." Marin gasps.

"Go away," says the voice. "Come back tomorrow. I
am all right. I want to be alone."

Marin stumbles down to the street. How strange the
outside world looks! In what a black abyss its people dwell!
If they but knew that upstairs in that building is a man,
bone and sinew and muscle - a man of flesh and blood, eve
as themselves, who is invisible!

******

Footprints in the snow across Hyde Park (or Central
Park). The invisible man is abroad and in a prankish mood.
An old dandy's cane is whirled away, his silk topper squashed
down over his nose, and coat tails fluttering, he flies headlong into an icy pond. A sauntering policeman is suddenly
minus his club,, his star and his cap, only to discover these
appurtenances adorning a felonious-looking bum - - but before
long Carpenter's teeth are chattering and his invisible
feet freezing.

The police are summoned to a customer's shop where the
shopkeeper testifies to a half hour of utterly unbelievable

occurrences when he witnessed wigs whisked away from their
headstands, watched empty books go clumping around the
floor, saw coats and breeches soaring through the air, and at
last, a number of these articles float out the door in a
bundle. The unlucky costumer is, of course, interned in
the psychiatric ward of the city hospital.

A man in black clothes, coat collar turned up, lower
portion of his face swathed in a muffler - the rest of his face
hidden, wearing black glasses and a hat hung low over his eyes,
takes a room in a house in the tenement district of the city.
His appearance the strangest conceivable, calls forth a good deal
of comment, and it is the opinion of the landlady with which
rented the room, that the poor soul in the fourth floor back,
has been the victim of an accident or an operation. However,
upon her sympathetic inquiries, the man rebuffs her and in
so surly a manner, that she changes her judgment and is of
the frank suspicion that he is a fugitive from justice, his
funny get-up being a disguise. His money is good though.
He paid in advance and almost double the rent asked. So
(even if the money is stolen) who is she to turn him in?
His luggage is nearly as mysterious as the man himself,
consisting mostly of bottles - bottles of all sizes, green bottles
blue bottles, red bottles, white bottles, hundreds of them.

******

The disappearance of Carpenter holds the front pages
for more than a week. Has he been kidnaped? - murdered?
Marin, the one who had seen him last, is grilled by the
police, but he guards Carpenter's secret zealously (had he
been minded to do otherwise, he would not have believed,
of course).

******

Night. Darryl tosses restlessly in her bed. She cannot
sleep. She is sure Marin knows more than he has told. A

stir in the darkness - a whisper: her name. She sits up, startled.

"Darryl - Darryl - don't be afraid."

"Who is it?"

"I - Carpenter - "

"Carpenter!" She stares around the room. "Where are you?

A low laugh. "Here, Darryl - beside you. You cannot see me, but you can feel me."

An invisible hand touches her throat, then covers her mouth as she starts to scream.

"Be still. I'll not hurt you. Don't be afraid. Hush, Darryl....Yes, I am invisible."

She stops struggling.

"I'm not ashamed to come to you now, Darryl." Briefly he tells her the story of his invisibility.

"What do you want?"

"You - Darryl - to be your lover. I, who could have any woman in the world, choose you. Kiss me, Darryl."

Invisible arms embrace her. She fights free.

"Forgive me. I shall not force you. You must learn to love me, Darryl.

******

Marin's blood freezes as he hears from Darryl about Carpenter's visit, then he tells her the whole weird story of the experiment. Darryl must be guarded - must never be alone, night or day.

****

Word at last from Carpenter, which says that on the following day he, Carpenter, will, as is his custom, lecture in the Bletheim ampitheatre - no more.

The packed auditorium stares in astonishment at the man in black and painted face on the speakers' platform. Is he Carpenter? If so, what has happened to him? Marin, icy shivers, running through him, looks on open-mouthed.

The babel on interrogations is hushed as Carpenter begin his lecture. His voice coming through the bandages is muffled.

First Carpenter renounces his position as head of the Beltheim laboratory. Only that much does the audience understand. What follows, they vaguely realize. It is a kind of challenge, a personal defiance to Carpenter's learned colleagues in science and to the world at large, succeeded which is the announcement of Carpenter's sovereignty and the declaration of himself - "Invisible Man, the first."

The crowd is on its feet. Is Carpenter insane? He should be seized. There is a movement toward him. Off comes his garments. Shouts - men tumble over one another. The clothes and bandages Carpenter wore are scattered over the platform.

The city is in an uproar.

"The Invisible Man. Invisible Man." The words are on everyone's lips.

******

Carpenter pays a second visit to Darryl. Marin and two others are guarding her, lying in wait. They attack Carpenter. A flash of metal in the darkness. Carpenter escapes. When the lights are turned up, one of Darryl's guards lies dead, a pair of scissors in his heart.

****

The invisible man is a murderer. An organized invisible man hunt. A reward is offered for his capture. Thousands join the search.

******

Carpenter declares war. One against the world. A scientific genius now is bent for destruction. A plague overtakes the city when he sets loose rats with the bubonic plague. The city reservoirs he turns into poison lakes. Explosions rock the skyscrapers.

*****

NOTE: The remainder of the story follows per Balderston's manuscript.

Darryl is importuned to be the bait in a trap for the invisible man. She is to go to him, teach him to trust her, and eventually, come it must, the opportunity for his capture.

In their last meeting, Carpenter had asked Darryl to come to him in the park (what chance is there to catch an invisible man in a park?) - that he will see her and talk to her.

The meeting takes place. Darryl goes with Carpenter to his hideaway. Marin follows the trail. A human chain is formed around the block. Doors and windows of the house are barricaded from the outside. Then begins the siege on the invisible man.

The invisible man, when he discovers he is in for certain destruction and is convinced that Darryl has not betrayed him, sends her out.

The battle lasts for hours - the cunning of Carpenter against the resources of society. Liquid flames are poured into the house. Men in suits like divers' costumes, enter and spray the rooms of the burning house with liquid fire. Carpenter is forced to the roof. At last he is cornered - and killed.

****

END

(Richard Schayer)

" THE INVISIBLE MAN "

```
      *
    *  *
   *    *
    *  *
      *
```

September 21, 1932
(Same as copy of
  August 1, 1932

"THE INVISIBLE MAN"

Adaptation by . . . . . Richard Schayer

NOTE:

This treatment presupposes a technique of camera movements,
silent action and weirdly impressive musical background.
There is to be very little dialogue and whenever possible
the camera will be on the faces of the listeners rather
than the speaker, which technique will make dubbing a sound
track in a foreign language a very simple proposition, this
opening up a world market for this picture. - R.S.

MUSIC
FADE IN. . CLOSE SHOT

Of a hideous octopus in a small glass
aquarium. As it waves its tentacles
and crawls about on the glass side of
the aquarium we he offscene the
clink of glasses, the rattle of steel
implements and then the sharp buzz of
an electric spark similar to that of
wireless telegraphy. We hold the
footage long enough for the audience
to get a good shudder or horror out
of the octopus and then slowly TRUCK
CAMERA along the shelf on which the
aquarium in standing.
It is a shelf-like workbench and it
runs the full length of the laboratory
wall. As CAMERA MOVES ALONG, a panor-
ama of weird looking bottles, retorts,
machines and other laboratory devices
passes the eye. The clink of glasses
become louder and finally we come to
a shot where a pair of man's hands in
rubber gloves are skillfully mixing a
series of chemicals in a glass beaker
of about one litre capacity. The
operator's arms are covered by the
sleeves of a stained laboratory apron.
The addition of a few drops of another
chemical to the mixture causes it to
seethe, bubble and turn color.

> A VOICE (triumphantly)
> The exact reaction - quick,
> Honan - the octopus.

CAMERA DRAWS SLOWLY back to disclose the figure of the experi-
mentor standing before the workbench staring triumphantly at the
glass beaker which he holds up to
the light streaming down upon him
from a great, shaded lamp hanging
from the ceiling. He is a young-
ish man, with a strong and highly
intelligent face. (Colin Clive)
His eyes gleam with the fanatical
flame of discovery and the haggard
lines and shadows of long days of
incessant toil seem to fade in the
light of imminent success

He moves toward the center of the
floor space where stands a strange
electrical ray machine constructed
to a great degree of long glass
vacuum tubes of the violet ray type.
There are several metal globes
arranged at various distances from
each other, and in the center, surrounded by the tubes is a platform
covered by a thick, soft rubber mat.
The experimenter swings part of the
device open so as to make an opening to the round, rubber matted platform.
CAMERA MOVES UP CLOSE to him. A
pair of ugly, hairy, hands come into
picture holding the glass aquarium in
which writhes the hideous little octopus. As these hands reach in to place
the aquarium on the platform the
CAMERA PANS UP to show the face leaning
over the tank. It is a horrible face. .
never better than merely repulsive, but
rendered completely terrific by a destruction of practically all of one side
of the countenance. Obviously some sort
of explosion had left this side of the
face a mere scar. Even the eye is gone
and the lid fastened down over the
empty socket. The one good eye glares
savagely down at the octopus in the
tank and a twisted smile of anticipation
curls the thin, cruel lips. The experimenter's hands empty the beaker of
chemicals into the tank.
The experimenter then orders his assist-
tant back with a gesture, then, as CAMERA
DRAWS BACK to give scope to the scene,
the two men proceed to lower over the
tank a great glass dome that hangs down
on chains. The edge of the dome press
down into the rubber matting.

                    EXPERIMENTER'S VOICE
                      Honan - the vacuum pump.

The tall, lean figure of the one-eyed
assistant turns to switch board and
throws two switches. A low humming
sound begins. The two men stand by,
watching the machine intently. A
sudden buzzing call sounds above the
hum of the motors. The experimenter
turns to a nearby table and clicks
the key of a dictograph.

                    EXPERIMENTER
                      Yes - who is it?

                  VOICE FROM DICTOGRAPH
                      It is I, Felix.. Dr. von Trenken.

                  EXPERIMENTER
                      Come in.. you're just in time!

He presses a button in a
panel.

We cut to a heavy metal door at
one end of the room. Automatic-
cally the three great metal bolts
barring the door slide to one
side and the door opens, disclos-
ing on the threshold a man of advanced middle age and scientific
aspect, somewhat carelessly dressed in summer clothing. As he
steps into the room the door
clangs shut behind him and the
bolts reseat themselves in their
sockets. The doctor pauses and
sniffs the air.

> VON TRENKEN
>> Colloids! - - you've been mixing
>> colloids, Felix.

> FELIX - (OFFSCENE)
>> Don't stand there sniffing the
>> air... come quickly!

CAMERA TRUCKS with the doctor
to the machine where Felix is
now closely attending certain
dials and switches. The doctor looks the scene over with
immense scientific interest.

> VON TRENKEN
>> So this is the great experiment!
>>> (peering into machine)
>> An octopus... and alive!

CAMERA PANS to show the aquarium inside the glass dome.

> FELIX'S VOICE (IN A NOTE OF EXALTATION)
>> So you see him, my dear doctor.
>> Pretty little devil, isn't he?
>> Watch closely, my good friend..
>> for if I am not mistaken you
>> won't see him for long.

CUT TO:

CLOSE SHOT...FELIX

He pulls a couple of switches
and a great sparking is set
up within the machine.

> FELIX
>> Honan! - - the lights out!

The tall assistant throws a
switch at another panel
leaving the room in compara-
tive darkness. His hideous
face turns toward the snapping
and buzzing machine and a weird
flickering light plays upon it.
We PAN BACK to the machine
showing all its tubes glowing
and great sparks of electricity
jumping back and forth across
the metal globes surrounding
the glass dome. Felix and the
doctor stand staring into the
dome at the aquarium.

CLOSE SHOT..AQUARIUM

Bathed in a weird light, the octopus
beings a terrific commotion within
the aquarium. It writhes as though
in great agonized convulsions. Slowly it turns white (which can be done
by LAP DISSOLVING to a pie of negative).

                    FELIX'S VOICE - (IN RISING TRIUMPH)
                         Primary reaction.. Watch now..
                         Doctor.. watch closely.

The octopus begins to FADE
SLOWLY into a transparency.
                    VON TRENKEN'S VOICE
                         Gott in Himmel! ... It is unholy!

                    FELIX'S VOICE (with rising crescendo
                              of excitement)
                         Merely the transmutation of
                         visible living cells to cells
                         that no longer react light...
                         and hence, my dear doctor, are
                         invisible!

With these last words the
octopus fades from view.
                    VON TRENKIN'S VOICE
                         Miraculous!

CAMERA SWINGS AROUND to
sow the doctor gazing in
horrified amazement into
the glowing machine. Then
in PANS to Felix's exultant
face, then to the hideous
face of Honan, the assistant
who is gazing out of his one
eye with malevolent satisfaction, at the result of his
master's experiment.
                    FELIX'S VOICE
                         Honan.. the lights!

Honan pulls a switch and the
bright lights come on.
A LONGER SHOT as Felix throws
off the switches of the machine
and starts the contrivance that
raises the huge glass dome from
over the aquarium. He then
swings open the machine and Honan picks up the aquarium and
carries it to a table under a
bright dome light. Felix and the
doctor move to table and study
the aquarium.

CLOSE SHOT

The two faces as seen through the
glass side of aquarium..which dis-
torts their features somewhat horribly.
In the aquarium a column of bubbles
rises to the water's surface. The doctor starts to put his hand in the water..

                              FELIX (grabbing his hand)
                                    Careful! He can give you a
                                    nasty bite!
                              VON TRENKEN
                                    You think then, it survived
                                    such an ordeal?
                              FELIX
                                    Certainly! If it were dead it
                                    would no longer be invisible..
                                    my formula affects only living
                                    tissues.. Watch!

CAMERA IS PANNED to one
side as Felix thrusts a
glass rod into the aquar-
ium. Instantly there is
a terrific stirring around
in the tank, as though the
water were being threshed
about by the invisible
octopus.

                              FELIX'S VOICE
                                    You see! Well, what do you say
                                    now.. my good friend?

Dr. von Trenken draws back
in loathing.

                              VON TRENKEN
                                    Horrible! --
                              FELIX (disappointedly)
                                    Is that all you have to say?
                                    I show you - one of the world's
                                    leading scientists -- something
                                    that no man has done or seen
                                    before and you don't even con-
                                    gratulate me!

The doctor puts his hand on
Felix's shoulder.

                              VON TRENKEN
                                    I can't congratulate my boy,
                                    until I know what is in your
                                    mind...how far you intend to
                                    carry this experiment.

                              FELIX
                                    As far as possible--

CUT TO:

CLOSE SHOT..HONAN
He is wiping the tanks of the
ray machine with a cloth and
pauses to listen to his master.
As he listens he glances up at
the glass dome over his head
and it is apparent that he is
getting some sort of terrific
idea.

                              FELIX'S VOICE
                                    Who knows... if I can render
                                    this octopus..bony beak and all,
                                    invisible, I can operate success-
                                    fully upon vertebrate creatures.
                                    I mean to try it on some lesser
                                    mammals first..perhaps.. even
                                    man.

Honan throws a sharp glance
toward his master and stands
in profound thought.

CLOSE SHOT..FELIX AND DOCTOR

We SHOOT OVER the doctor's
shoulder into Felix's face
as the doctor speaks, so as
to avoid the movement of the
doctor's lips. Felix is re-
moving his rubber gloves and
laboratory apron.

                    VON TRENKEN
                         So! That is why I withheld my
                         congratulations... I was afraid
                         that your mind had leaped to
                         that monstrous idea- - -

                    FELIX   (half turned away)
                         Monstrous?

                    VON TRENKIN
                         Hideously monstrous.. my boy..
                         There are mysteries into which
                         even science has no right to
                         search. There are laws we have
                         no right to alter or defy...

                    FELIX   (tauntingly)
                         Religion!

                    VON TRENKEN
                         No! Nature!! The laws of nature
                         are omnipotent... defy them and
                         we sicken.. go mad.. or die....
                         You are tampering with one of
                         nature's most closely guarded
                         secrets.. I warn you, my boy..
                         be content with what you have
                         done.. don't pursue this ghastly
                         investigation.. don't let loose
                         upon this already tormented earth
                         knowledge as filled with poten-
                         tial evil as your formula for
                         invisibility.

Before Felix can answer
there is the sharp sound
of the dictograph call.
He opens the circuit.

                    FELIX
                         Who is it?

                    GIRL'S VOICE
                         Hello! - - Felix!
                    FELIX
                         Dorothea! Your father didn't
                         tell me you came with him.
                         Come right in.

He pushes the button and
we hear the door unbolt
itself, then as we PAN
WITH Felix as he moves toward the door...

                    DOROTHEA'S VOICE
                         Ugh! What a smelly place..
                         Hello Darling.. so this is
                         where you've been hiding for
                         two weeks

By this time the two have
met and embraced. WE SHOOT
into Dorothea's pretty face
over Felix's shoulder.

                          FELIX
                    Has it really been that long?

                     DOROTHEA   (Laughing)
                    Your surprise isn't very flatter-
                    ing.. you're supposed to say,
                    'it seems ages to me, too!'

                          VON TRENKEN
                    You'll never make a parlor
                    knight out of Felix, my dear.

                          FELIX
                    I'm sorry, sweetheart.. but I've
                    been working night and day.. on..

                          VON TRENKEN
                    A great experiment.. and he needs
                    your consolation, my child.

CUT TO:

SHOT OF HUNAN

putting the bottles away
and watching the girl out
of his one eye. There is
undoubted desire in his
gaze.

                          DOROTHEA
                    Oh! - - Was it a failure?- - I'm
                    so sorry...

                          FELIX
                    On the contrary.

BACK TO GROUP.

                          VON TRENKEN
                    Not a failure..exactly.. but he
                    has decided that further exper-
                    iments along the same line are
                    useless and intends to give up
                    the investigation.

Felix watches the Doctor
curiously during this
speech.

                          DOROTHEA
                    Splendid..then we'll see some-
                    thing of him again
                          (looking him over)
                    Of all the untidy spectacles..
                    Now you go and make yourself
                    presentable and we'll take you
                    home to dinner.

                          FELIX
                    But darling.. really!

                          DOROTHEA
                    I won't listen..run along..
                    I'll wait for you here.
                          VON TRENKEN
                    Come along my boy... I want to
                    talk to you while you dress.

FELIX (Kissing Dorothea's hand)
I won't be long.. There are
some jars of synthetic crystal
forms that you might find interesting.

He and the doctor exit,
through a door in the rear
of the laboratory. The
CAMERA MOVES ALONG with
Dorothea as she walks along
a shelf of jars containing
various crystal form in
different shades and colorings.

A CLOSE SHOT OF HONAN

As he watches her.. His
single eye burns with desire
and his lips twitch. He
moves toward her.

CLOSE SHOT..DOROTHEA

As she looks closely at a
particular jar of crystals.

                    HONAN'S VOICE
                Good evening, Miss von Trenken.

Dorothea starts at the
sound of the voice and
turns around.

CLOSE SHOT..HONAN

As he turns to her and
stares at her with his
one eye.

                    DOROTHEA'S VOICE
                Oh! Honan! - - you frightened me.

CLOSE SHOT..BOTH

SHOOTING so as to watch
the movement of Honan's
lips.

                HONAN
                I frighten many people, Miss...
                I'm very sorry...

                DOROTHEA   (moving away
                It's all right, Honan.

WE TRUCK WITH her until
she pauses by the aquarium,
containing the invisible
octopus.

                HONAN'S VOICE
                Has Mr. Landers told you the
                nature of our - - his experiment
                Miss?

                DOROTHEA (her face away from camera
                        as she looks at the aquarium)
                No- -

                        HONAN'S VOICE
                            Would you like to know?

                        DOROTHEA
                            Not unless he wants me to
                            thank you, Honan.

She is looking at the
bubbles in the tank..
wondering what they are
coming from. She pokes
a finger in the water.

                        HONAN
                            Beg pardon, Miss.

CLOSE SHOT.. HONAN

He makes a gesture as though
about to warn the girl..then..
with a drafty and luring smile
appears to decide to let her
go ahead with her investigation
of the aquarium mystery.

CLOSE SHOT..DOROTHEA

She pokes her hand further into
the tank as though to feel the
bubbles rising from its bottom.
Suddenly there is a swirl in
the water and her hand plunges
deeper in as though dragged into
the tank by an unseen force.

                        DOROTHEA (a startled scream — then
                                    a series of screams

As she struggles to draw her
hand out of the tank Honan
rushes into her.. takes her
arm in his and plunges a long
knife into the tank again and
again..as he get her freed
she faints and he holds her
close to him in his arms..
looking down gloatingly into
her face just as Felix and von
Trenken come rushing in with
ad lib exclamations of alarm.
Felix takes Dorothea from Honan
and the girl opens her eyes and
clings to Felix.

                        HONAN
                            The octopus, Mr.. Landers.. she
                            put her hand in the tank.. it
                            seized her.. I had to cut it to
                            ribbons to free her arm.

All look toward the tank..
the dead octopus is slowly
coming to view.

                        FELIX
                            You see, Doctor.. with death..
                            visibility.

von trenken

                            I see..

112

FELIX   (bending over Dorothea)
>   Sweetheart.. I'm so sorry.. I
>   should have warned you.. are
>   you hurt?

DOROTHEA
>   My arm stings a little.. it's
>   all right.. Take me home, Father..

FELIX
>   We'd better forget about dinner..
>   Rest awhile and I'll come over
>   this evening..
>>   (Moving with them toward the
>>   door)

DOROTHEA
>   You promise!

FELIX
>   I promise.

VON TRENKEN
>   And your other promise made to
>   me just now.. I have your word
>   that all this.. this nonsense..
>   is ended.. no more octopi.. or
>   worse.

CUT TO:

CLOSEUP OF HONAN

Listening intently to the
Doctor and Felix. His
eye gleams wickedly.

FELIX
>   You have my word.. I'm through
>   with the business.. The thought
>   of possible danger to Dorothea
>   would stop me when nothing else
>   would.

Honan licks his lips.

CUT BACK TO GROUP

DOROTHEA
>   What is all this mystery?

VON TRENKEN
>   Never mind, my dear.. Let it re-
>   main.. a mystery.. We'll see you
>   later, Felix

FELIX
>   Yes.. tonight.. goodbye, darling

He and Dorothea embrace,
affectionately, and separ-
ate at the door. Felix closes
the door which bolts automatic-
cally.

CLOSE SHOT..HONAN

He stares at Felix bale-
fully out of his one eye.

>   FELIX'S VOICE
>   Dismantle all that apparatus
>   and pack it away.. we're
>   through with this horrible
>   business.

CUT TO: Felix at a desk
gathering up a sheaf of
paper memoranda as though
preparing to put them out
of sight forever. Felix
turns sharply at this tone
of voice from his assistant.

>   HONAN'S VOICE (a sudden firmness
>   of tone
>   So you haven't the courage of
>   your convictions, Mr. Landers?
>   An old man trembles.. a pretty
>   girl screams.. and you abandon
>   an investigation that will
>   make you the greatest scientist
>   of all time.

CUT TO: Honan as he finishes
his speech and throws a
smiling sneer in Felix's
direction.

>   FELIX'S VOICE
>   How dare you!

MEDIUM SHOT OF BOTH

The CAMERA MOVES UP as the
two men face each other.
WE SHOOT AN ANGLE that keeps
Honan's face partly averted
so that we don't see his lips
moving. Felix is amazed at
this transformation of his
silent laboratory slave into
a dominating personality.

>   HONAN
>   I dare because I have given the
>   best of my life in your service..
>   I too, have paid the penalty of
>   devotion to scientific investiga-
>   tion.. Have you forgotten that it
>   was in your service that I became
>   disfigured? Who has more right
>   than I to demand that you continue
>   these experiments..even to their
>   ultimate conclusion.. the end you
>   so bravely acclaimed to Dr. von
>   Trenken.. and then so weakly
>   abandoned.. the creation of..
>   Invisible Man.

          FELIX
               Invisible Man? You mean...
               you would subject yourself to
               this experiment.

          HONAN
               Is my visible presence so pre-
               possing that I should cling
               to it to an even more hideous
               old age? For years I've seen
               the look of loathing on the
               faces of all who pass me by on
               the street.. Dogs bark at me...
               children fly from me.. women
               shrink back in horror.. No pretty
               blonde girls invite me to dinner..
               or kiss me tenderly in goodbye.
               But, have you thought what a man
               might do - - if invisible?

          FELIX
               Thought? ... I have dreamed of
               nothing else for months.. it was
               that spur that drove me on to
               complete the experiment... but....

          HONAN
               But now.. you are afraid to enter
               this invisible kingdom yourself.
               You shrink from it in horror...
               and why not? You have youth..
               money.. good looks.. even love
               while I have nothing.

CLOSE SHOT..FELIX

While Honan bends over
him and pleads his final
temptation.

          HONAN (humbly)
               Give me this new life.. master..
               I will be your invisible slave..
               Your genii of the fairy tales..
               You will be an Aladdin.. with me
               to do your bidding you will be-
               come master of the earth. What
               secret of man or nation will be
               safe from your eyes? Make me
               your invisible slave, master.
               I will spy for you.. steal for
               you..even kill for you.

          FELIX   (tempted beyond endurance)
               You will suffer agony during
               the process of transition...
               you may even die!

          HONAN
               Better that, than remain as I am.

          FELIX
               There is a strong possibility of
               failure.
          HONAN
               I'll risk it...Come! Make ready!

FELIX
Now? ....tonight?

HONAN   (almost a hiss)
Yes! ... Now!!

Felix slowly rises to
his feet. He stares
hesitantly at Honan who
is watching him as a snake
watches a bird. Honan
drops on one knee and bows
his head humbly before
Felix. Honan's face turns
up slightly to let the
CAMERA catch the sardonic
gleam in his eye - the
smile that belies his words.

HONAN
Master.. your slave beseeches
you!!

FELIX   (with sudden determination)
Right! Let us get to work!!!

DISSOLVE TO:

INTERIOR VON TRENKEN'S HOME

A prettily furnished European
sitting room. The music
changes in the dissolve to
the music of a piano playing
an old-time love theme.
Dorothea is at the piano and
Dr. von Trenken is reading by
a lamp. The CAMERA moves up
to a CLOSE SHOT of Dorothea;
as she comes to the end of
the melody she is playing she
looks down at her right wrist
- thinks of the experience
she had with the octopus -
grasps her wrist with the
other hand and gives a shudder
of reminiscent horror. Then
she turns her head away from
the CAMERA to speak to the
doctor.

DOROTHEA
Father.. do you suppose some-
thing could have happened to
Felix?

DOCTOR   (offscene)
Happened? Of course not!

CLOSE SHOT..DOCTOR

He is looking at Dorothea
over the tops of his
glasses as though having
just spoken.

                DOROTHEA   (offscene)
                But it's after ten.. and you
                heard him promise to be here
                this evening.

Dorothea appears in the
scene and seats herself
on the arm of the doctor's
chair. The angle is such
that we do not read the
words on her lips.

                Father.. while I was playing
                the piano, I felt that horribly
                slimy, invisible thing grip my
                wrist again! There is something
                terrible going on! And you know
                what it is.. You must tell me!

              DOCTOR   (putting his arms about her)
              Nonsense. my dear.. your nerves
              are overwrought. What you need
              is rest. Run along to bed, and
              I'll bring you a bromide.

              DOROTHEA
              Then you won't tell me?

              DOCTOR
              There is nothing to tell...
              Felix is all right. I'm sure
              of it. He is worn out..
              probably lay down for a nap
              and fell asleep. Run along
              now. We'll see him tomorrow.

              DOROTHEA
              All right, dear. Goodnight.

The two embrace and
Dorothea exits from
the scene. The Doctor
watches her until we
hear a door close, then
frowningly he removes
his spectacles, wipes
them on his handkerchief,
his face reflecting a
deep anxiety. Suddenly
he makes up his mind to
act, and rises. THE
CAMERA PANS WITH HIM A
LITTLE WAY TOWARD THE DOOR,
THEN IN A WIPE DISSOLVE
we pick up the Doctor in
a hallway getting his hat
and stick. As he starts
out the front door, another
WIPE DISSOLVE brings us to:

INTERIOR ..LABORATORY

A CLOSE SHOT of Felix
working at the controls
of the ray machine. The
humming and sparking
noise is in full chorus.
As Felix manipulates the
levers he watches intent-
ly over his shoulder and
the CAMERA PANS WITH HIS
GAZE to disclose within
the glass dome and bathed
in the weird glow of the
rays and sparks the nude
form of Honan. He is
seated on a metal stool
his hands gripping a cross
bar brace within the dome.
His face is contorted with
agony and his body writhes
and strains. Slowly his
form assumes a chalky whiteness.
Felix is nearly beside himself with excitement as he
watches the coming of this
first reaction. He manipulates rapidly more controls.
The whiteness of Honan's
body begins to fade and the
skeleton outline begins to
show as though seen through
an X-ray. In a moment there
is nothing visible but this
seated skeleton, which writhes
gruesomely within the glass
dome.
Felix throws another switch
and the humming noise rises
to a higher whining note.
Hunan's skeleton begins slowly to fade from view. The
skull turns and gazes for a
 moment toward Felix and its
ghastly grin is accentuated
by a nodding motion as though
Honan were aware of the transformation taking place and
were nodding encouragement to
Felix to continue.
Felix throws in the last switch
and pulls open some others..
the hum dies down and a hissing
sound arises as though air were
being admitted to the glass dome.
The skeleton form of Honan fades
entirely from view. Felix throws
off all the rays, then floods
the room with the overhead light
and jumps to the switch that controls the motor which raise the
glass dome on its chains. The
dome chains rattle as the glass
rises slowly toward the ceiling.

Felix throws open the
section of tubing that
comprises the gate to
the central platform
of the machine. He
stares at the empty
metal stool as though
he hardly believes that
the experiment has suc-
ceeded. He starts to
put out his hand as
though to touch the in-
visible Honan...but
does not dare.

      FLEIX   (breathlessly)
        Honan!

      HONAN'S VOICE (weakly)
        Water! Water!

Felix turns quickly to
a bottle of distilled
water and ours a beaker
full. He brings it back
to the metal stool and
holds it out as though
to the invisible man.
The beaker is apparently
taken out of his hand,
tipped upward as though
to an unseen mouth. The
water appears to be ab-
sorbed in thin air as it
disappears from the glass
container.

      FELIX   (after a pause)
        How do you feel now?

      HONAN
        Better.. stand aside.. I'm
        coming out.

Felix draws back and
gazes fascinatedly at
nothing as though try-
ing to see if he can
detect the movement of
Honan as the invisible
man comes from the ray
machine.

        See anything?

      FELIX
        No! -- light rays pass through
        and around you as though you
        were not existent.

      HONAN
        I cast no shadow?

      FELIX
        None!

                        HONAN
                        But I might leave footprints?

                        FELIX
                        Yes.. you must be careful of
                        that!

                        HONAN
                        So! It is a success, my master..
                        a complete success..
                                (his voice rises to a
                                pitch of high excitement)
                        Invisible! .. Ha! Monarch of
                        an invisible empire! Look my
                        master... look!

THE CAMERA PANS ABOUT   (his exclamations are
the room as various ob-   punctuated by the crash
jects are hurled into the   of glasses and thud of
air by an unseen hand.   books as he hurls things
                                     about.

Books fall at Felix's feet   (mockingly)
                        Your servant awaits your orders,
                        master.. Is it books you want..
                        here! "Honan! Bring me that
                        test-tube rack" .. Here master!

A test-tube rack crashes
at Felix's feet.   Where am I, master.. Where am I
                        now?.. For all you know I may
                        be creeping upon you to throttle
                        you as easily as one wrings the
                        neck of a chicken.. like this!

Felix is apparently seized
at the throat by the un-
seen hand of Honan.. He
draws back in horror.   FELIX   (gasping)
                        Honan! Take your hand off me!
                        Stand away! Do you hear?

He is suddenly released
and fingers his throat
in mingled terror and
relief.   HONAN   (ironically)
                        Your pardon, master...
                        For a moment I forgot myself..
                        Your servant most humbly
                        craves your pardon.

The sharp buzz of the
dictograph breaks in
on the scene. Felix
turns to the instrument
quickly and opens the
circuit.

                        FELIX
                        Yes!

                        VON TRENKEN'S VOICE
                        Dr. von Trenken, Felix -
                        May I come in?

FELIX
> Oh! - - Certainly Doctor- -
> just a moment.

He snaps the circuit
shut.

> Honan! He must not find out- -
> gather up these books - quickly
> - and in the name of Heaven
> don't betray our secret.

HONAN   (maliciously whispering)
> Of course not - Master!

Felix hastens to the
door while behind him
we hear the sound of some
of the books being re-
placed on the desk - we
follow him to the door
which he throws open by
hand, admitting the doctor/

VON TRENKEN
> Felix. How wild you look -
> what has happened?

CAMERA FOLLOWS THEM INTO
THE ROOM.

FELIX
> Nothing Doctor - I must have
> fallen asleep - is it late?

VON TRENKEN
> Nearly eleven - Dorothea was
> greatly upset by your absence
> - it worried me, too.

FELIX
> I am very sorry.

VON TRENKEN
> It's quite all right if every-
> thing is all right with you.
> You are sure nothing has happened?
>   (he glances about)
> You have kept your promise -
> about these dangerous experiments?

FELIX   (uneasily)
> Of course, Doctor.

DOCTOR
> Where is Honan?

FELIX
> I - I have sent him away -
> told him I was going to take
> a long rest - and would need
> him no longer.

CUT TO: a swivel-chair
by the desk - the chair
turns part way round
then tilts back with a
slight creak as though
Honan was sitting in it.

> DOCTOR
> Good! I hope you will never
> reengage him. There is some-
> thing evil about that man -
> something potentially horrible
> - deadly.

> FELIX   (changing the subject)
> Oh! Honan's all right
> He's harmless enough.

> DOCTOR
> Maybe - but I'd rather not be
> around him. Well, my boy,
> excuse this intrusion, but I
> was worried. I'll be going
> home - get a good night's rest
> and come over tomorrow - I
> have some interesting new germ
> cultures I want to show you.

The swivel chair
straightens up as
though relieved of
the invisible weight
in it.

> FELIX   (at the door)
> I'll be over - goodnight -
> and give Dorothea my humblest
> apologies.

Felix opens the door.

> DOCTOR
> Certainly - goodnight - huh!

The doctor gives a
little start and looks
quickly over his
shoulder, sideways.

> FELIX
> What's the matter?

> DOCTOR
> I could have sworn something
> brushed by me as you opened
> the door
>   (he laughs)
> You see what your octopus
> has done to my imagination!

> FELIX   (laughing somewhat hollowly)
> Yes! - and mine too. We must
> forget it - goodnight.

> DOCTOR
> Goodnight my boy.

Felix closes the door,
then turns quickly
into the room.

               FELIX   (excitedly, in hoarse
                        whisper)

                 Honan! - Honan! Where are
                 you? Speak to me!
                 Honan!   - - Ah!

He swings again to the
door. He realizes that
Honan has gone out with
the doctor. He is
filled with consternation.

DISSOLVE TO:

NOTE: Music, of course
      through all this
      sequence.

EXTERIOR STREET..NIGHT

This can be the street
we used in Frankenstein
- a foreign appearing
street, but one not
definitely associated
with any particular
country. It is rather
 poorly illuminated and
except for the sturdy
figure of Doctor von
Trenken plodding his
way homeward, it appears
quite deserted. Some-
where in the distance a
dog howls - the only
sound we hear except for
the steady clicking of
the good doctor's heels.
The CAMERA TRUCKS along
behind the doctor, grad-
ually drawing up behind
him as he passes across
a portion of pavement
over which water has re-
cently been spilled. The
CAMERA - still moving forward, now TILTS to point
downward at the pavement
and one by one wet foot-
prints - prints of a man's
barefeet - appear behind
and a little to one side
of those made by the
doctor. With a shudder
of horror we realize that
the invisible Honan is
following the doctor,
closely. The doctor
passes through a dark
arch and we wonder if
anything is going to happen
to him in the gloom of
that structure. As he
emerges into the light of
a street lamp on the other
side of the arch, he suddenly stops and looks sharply
around and the CAMERA
closes up to him. The
doctor looks about him
with a puzzled air, as
though he had a sense of
someone following him and

can see nothing to cause
such a sensation. After
a moment, the doctor with
a shrug of contempt for
his imagined fears moves
on again, but he grips
his heavy walking stick
in a defensive manner and
watches the shadows from
right to left as he walks
on.

A WIPE DISSOLVE
Takes the doctor to the
front doorway of his house
- a modest European dwelling. As he unlocks and
opens the front door a large
German shepherd dog appears
on the threshold, wagging
his tail solemnly.

                    DOCTOR
          Yes, Lupo - it is I - my
          good fellow.

As the doctor starts to
enter, the dog, disregard-
his master, appears to
scent something mysterious
and gazes past the doctor
toward the street, baring
it's teeth with a snarll-
ling growl.

                    DOCTOR
          Come - come - Lupo - no cat
          chasing tonight - inside
          with you.. Do you hear me?
          Come! You'll awaken your
          mistress.

INTERIOR..FRONT HALL

The doctor takes hold of
the dog's collar and
closes the front door.
The dog reluctantly per-
mits the restraint, then
when released, goes quickly to the front door and
sniffs at the bottom of
it suspiciously.

                    DOCTOR
          Come Lup - to bed with you!
          No more nonsense! What a
          houseful of nerves this is
          tonight - eh! Boy? Come on,
          off with you!

At it's master's repeated
commands the dog moves
away from the door, but
glances back over it's
shoulder as though still
interested in some mysterious thing beyond the door.
DISSOLVE TO:

INTERIOR..DOROTHEA'S BED-
ROOM..MOONLIGHT EFFECT

A close shot of the girl
asleep and most attract-
ive in her filmy night
dress - her blonde hair
tousled on the pillow and
the sheet, because of the
warmth of the night,
partially kicked aside so
as to exposse the swelling
curves of her shoulder and
breast. THE CAMERA DRAWS
SLOWLY AWAY from her then
PANS to make a circuit of
two sides of the room.
Along one side are French
windows, open to the night
air, except for lacy cur-
tains that hang closed and
away slightly to the breeze.
THE CAMERA PASSES these curtains then PANS to the end
of the room, and centers on
the door to the hall. The
door slowly swings open and
the audience will gasp - as
they expect the Invisible
Man to enter. Instead, we
see the kindly face of
Doctor von Trenken, peering
in to see if all is well
with Dorothea. Satisfied
with his inspection he retires, gently closing the
door after him.
THE CAMERA SWINGS again to
the window curtains. Slowly
one of the lace curtains
draws aside as though held
by an invisible hand. One
can almost imagine the evil
face of Honan peering into
the room at the sleeping
girl.
A CLOSE SHOT of Dorothea
as she stirs a little in
her sleep and smiles as
though in a happy dream.
ANOTHER SHOT at the window
curtain - it drops back into
position. A chair near the
window is moved slightly to
one side.
A CLOSE SHOT at Dorothea.
She stirs again and the
movement further loosens
the nightgown at her shoulder
-exposing a little more of
her rounded breast. Her lips
part and she whispers in her
sleep.

DOROTHEA (whispering
        Felix! --Darling

HONAN'S VOICE   (in a throaty whisper)
        Yes -- my love!

DOROTHEA
        I forgive you, dear, -- kiss me!

THE CAMERA SLANTS DOWN
toward Dorothea as though
it were Honan himself
bending close to her.
Dorothea's arm comes up
and makes an encircling
movement as though it
actually were closed
about a man's neck. Her
lips part as though for
a kiss. Her eyelids flutter
and her breath comes more
quickly. Suddenly her eyes
open and stare upward into
the CAMERA lens. Instantly
a look of dazed horror
comes over her face.

                (half-awake)
        Felix! Let me go! -- what are
        you doing here? Felix! --
        Ah! -
                (she utters a sudden
                piercing scream)

CUT TO: Lupo, the dog. He
is leaping up a flight of
stairs.

CUT TO:

INTERIOR..BEDROOM..
MEDIUM SHOT

From behind Dorothea. She
is sitting bolt upright
in bed - uttering scream
after scream while beyond
her the window curtain is
flung aside by an unseen
hand as though Honan had
made his escape that way.
Then above her screams
comes the furious barking
of Lupo at the door.
THE CAMERA ANGLE changes
to include the hall door,
which bursts open to admit
the excited dog and the
figure of Doctor von Trenken, partially undressed
and carrying a pistol.
The dog rushes toward the
window and stands by the
curtains barking furiously.

                              DOCTOR
                         Dorothea!.. My child - - what
                         on earth! Lupo! Lupo - stop
                         that noise! - -

The dog draws back from
the window and goes sniffing
about the floor, while the
doctor hastens over to the
bedside.

                              DOROTHEA (excitedly)
                         Father! Someone was here - -
                         I could feel his arms about
                         me - he kissed me - I was
                         dreaming it was Felix - when
                         I awakened fully - I could
                         see no one.

CLOSE SHOT von Trenken.
He looks alarmed. A
sudden suspicion..
then he tries to hide his
feelings.

                              DOCTOR
                         There! There - my dear -
                         It was nothing but a night-
                         mare! We are all greatly
                         upset tonight - even Lupo!
                         Calm yourself, my child!

                              DOROTHEA (brokenly)
                         I could feel him. I tell you -
                         even when I opened my eyes -
                         his arms were still holding me.
                         He didn't let me go until I
                         screamed. It couldn't have
                         been a dream - - it was to real - -
                         too horribly real.

                              DOCTOR
                         Sometimes we dream that we have
                         awakened and we are still sleep-[]
                         ing. It must have been such a
                         dream. Compose yourself, my
                         darling. Lupo will sleep here
                         by your bed.. nothing can harm
                         you, here in our own house.

A SHOT OF LUPO standing
gazing at the window
curtains and baring his
teeth in a low growl.

                         (SOUND; OFFSCENE)
                         (A telephone bell tinkles)

Dr. von Trenken turns to
a French phone on a table
by the bed.
                              DOCTOR
                         Yes? - - Oh! Felix....

CUT TO:

FELIX

He is at the phone in his
laboratory. His face in-
dicates great relief at
the sound of the doctor's
voice. He tries to appear
casual and natural.

                    FELIX
                        Oh! Doctor - I just wanted
                        to apologize for not walking
                        home with you. It didn't
                        occur to me until you had
                        been gone sometime.
                        Everything all right, I hope?

CUT TO:

DOCTOR AT PHONE

He keeps his face averted
from Dorothea to hide the
suspicion that clouds his
expression.

                    DOCTOR
                        Of course - what made you
                        worry about us? Yes -
                        naturally all our nerves
                        are a little upset tonight.
                        No, Dorothea is quite all
                        right. Yes - - we'll see
                        you tomorrow. Goodnight,
                        my boy.

He frowns at the instru-
ment as he hangs it up.
Then he assumes a calm
manner as he turns back
to Dorothea. The CAMERA
PANNING to include her in
the shot.

                    DOCTOR
                        No need to alarm Fleix.

                    DOROTHEA (more calmly)
                        Of course not - - it must
                        have been a dream - as you
                        said.

The doctor pats her head
and Lupo comes and puts
his head on the bed bedside
her.

                    DOCTOR
                        of course, my dear - -a dream
                        - - just a bad dream.

But there is something
in the doctor's express-
ion that belies his words.
He suspects it was not a
dream - at all.

DISSOLVE TO:

DISSOLVE IN:

EXTERIOR STREET..NIGHT

We are in front of a
house that sets back
a little from the side-
walk. One small tree
grows in front of the
house. An extremely
intoxicated man in silk
hat and evening dress
and carrying a walking
stick comes zig-zagging
along the pavement and
starts to turn in at the
house guarded by the one
little tree. He clings
to this tree a minute to
steady himself, then
makes a valiant effort to
reach the front door, but
swerves in an eccentric
circle and curves back to
the tree and clings there
again to steady himself.
He does this twice more -
then assumes a doleful,
helpless expression -
swaying as he holds on to
the lone little tree.
(Of course, music of an
appropriate comic nature
plays through this se-
quence).

                    DRUNKEN GENTLEMAN
                Losht! - losht, in the woods!

The drunken wayfarer
now prepares to spend the
night in what he consid-
ers a dense forest. He
removes his hat, jabs his
cane upright into the
ground and hangs the silk
hat on it. He then - with
comic difficulty O gets
out of his coat and rolls
it up for a pillow, placing it
against the tree trunk. As
he starts to remove his sus-
penders from his shoulders
as though about to take off
his trousers, he stops suddenly and stares at his cane
and hat.
the hat revolves a
couple times on the cane.
The drunk blinks comically,
then makes another move toward
taking off his trousers -

again his hat spins around
on the cane. The drunk
considers this miracle with
comic gravity for a moment
then resolutely turns his
back toward the hat and cane
and starts once more to remove his trousers. He can't
resist peeking over his
shoulder and as he does so
the hat spins violently
around the cane. This is
too much for the drunk -
he stealthily picks up his
coat and starts tip-toeing
away from the tree as
though bent on escape from
this haunted spot. He looks
back once more and the hat
rises off the cane and remains suspended in the air
at about the height of a
man's head.

TRUCKING SHOT:
The drunks moves on faster - -
now partially sobered. The
hat and stick start to
follow him up the street -
the stick clicking on the
pavement as though carried
by an invisible pedestrian.
The drunk breaks into a
wobbly run and at the corner runs into the arms of
a gendarme.

                    GENDARME
          What's this? What's this?

The drunk is almost too
frightened to speak -
but points back around
the corner - then manages
to mutter:

                    DRUNK
          My hat and cane - they are
          chasing me up the street.

The gendarme looks sus-
picious and drunk makes
signs to him to listen
and look - then both
peek cautiously around
the corner. The hat and
stick are lying motion-
less on the sidewalk -
the gendarme laughs -
goes and picks up the hat
and stick - brings them
back to the drunk - sticks
the hat on the drunk's head
and puts the cane in his
hand.

GENDARME
Off to bed with you - - and
sober up.

The gendarme turns his
back on the drunk who
stands trying to figure
out what had happened to
him. Suddenly the gen-
darme makes a violent
motion forward as though
he had received a terrific
kick in the behind - -
with a roar of rage, he
turns and seizes the un-
fortunate drunk and starts
taking him off to jail.

SOUND: (a low chuckling
laugh - as though
honan were enjoy-
ing the result of
the prank he had
just played)

WIPE DISSOLVE TO:

EXTERIOR..ANOTHER HOUSE

A young man stands be-
fore the house looking
up at a lighted window
by a balcony. He whistles
a soft little call - which
works in with the musical
accompaniment. An attractive woman of voluptuous
figure - clad only in night-
dress - appears on the balcony. She makes a gesture
of warning, then beckons
to the young man to come up.
The girl disappears within
the balcony door. The Young
man starts to climb the
trellis work to the balcony.
Suddenly he appears to receive a heavy blow from an
invisible hand and falls into
a sitting posture at the
bottom of the trellis in an
unconscious state. The
trellis and vines shake as
though an invisible form
were clinging to them. The
CAMERA ASCENDS to the balcony, then moves to the dim-
ly lighted window and peeks
into the room. The woman is
apparently waiting inside.

Her attitude is that of
an expectant lover. A
guttural man's voice is
heard from another room.

                    HONAN'S VOICE   (in whisper)
                         The light - put out the light.

The woman makes a warn-
ing gesture of finger to
lips - nods her head -
points warningly in the
direction from which
comes the snoring - then
turns out the light.
There is a pause - then

                    WOMAN'S WHISPER   (in darkness)
                         My darling.

DISSOLVE TO:

CLOSE SHOT..TRELLIS AND
VINES

They shake again and the
CAMERA DESCENDS from the
balcony to the ground.
The young man is regain-
ing consciousness. He
gets to his feet - looks
around dazed - then gives
his low whistling call.
The woman again appears
oh the balcony - she leans
over. The man makes signs
that he is coming up. The
woman shakes her head.

                    WOMAN'S VOICE
                         What - again! Go home, you
                         greedy boy!

The woman retires. The
young man rubs his head
in great bewilderment -
then moves off - shaking
his head as though he
couldn't figure out what
she could have meant by
'again'.

DISSOLVE OUT:

DISSOLVE TO:

INTERIOR.. MANSION

A canopy extends from
a handsome front en-
trance to the curb
where a swell limousine
with two uniformed flunkeys
is standing. A very dig-
nified and stately woman
in evening dress is just
leaving the house to get
in her car. One of the
flunkeys holds the door
open for her. She moves
in a very pompous manner.
As she bends over to get
in the car she does a
leap forward into the car
as though she had been
well goosed by an invisible
hand. She turns on her
seat and glares at the bewildered flunkey who closes
the door and gives her a
struggling gesture as though
meaning he had done nothing.
Then as he starts to climb
up beside the chauffeur he
too, gets the goose from
the invisible hand and
leaps into the seat and
strikes out wildly at the
chauffeur - uttering a loud
exclamation as he does so.

(VOICES: OFFSCENE)
Goodnight, your highness - -
Goodnight, Duchess!!

             FOOTMAN
              Ha! !

FADE OUT

FADE IN:

INTERIOR FELIX'S BEDROOM
MORNING

Felix is in a uneasy sleep.
The tumbled condition of his
bed clothes indicates that he
has tossed restlessly through
the night.

The Camera pans to include
the door, which opens slowly
with a slight creak.

Felix awakens with a start
and looks off toward the door,
which is shown in this angle
from behind the man in bed.
There is nothing visible in
the doorway

          FELIX   (his back to camera)
            Who's there?

         HORAN'S VOICE
           Good morning, Master.

Felix gives a startled
laugh, then swings out
of bed and starts putting
on a lounging robe as the
following dialogue is heard.

          FELIX   (exultantly)
           Horan! - -Then it was not
           just a dream - I have
           succeeded - you are here -
           and invisible - Ha! - Pass
           in front of that sunbeam
           by the window - Marvelous!
           Not the faintest outline
               (suddenly stern)
           But why did you go out last
           night - without my permission?

         HORAN'S VOICE
           Adventure! - Romance! -
           Master, last night - for the
           first time in many years -
           I held a warm, soft young
           woman in my arms - her lips
           to mine - in ecstacy. I
           patrolled the street - play-
           ed childish pranks - peered
           into bedrooms - kicked a
           policeman - followed amorous
           lovers - my naked body bathed
           in the balmy air of summer
           night - What a night, my
           master - and now - I am
           hungry.

FELIX
>I'll order breakfast

Felix rings a bell.

HORAN
>Order enough -

FELIX
>Be careful when Otto enters -
>He must never suspect.

HORAN
>Of course.

The door opens and
Otto, Felix's man ser-
vant enters - a fat and
stupidly humorous type
like Bert Roach - He
looks around.

OTTO
>Good morning, Mr. Felix. I
>thought I heard you talking
>to someone, sir.

FELIX
>I was reciting - Otto - a hymn
>of praise to the morning sun -
>I am happy, Otto - my work has
>been a success - and now I
>shall play - Breakfast, my boy,
>and plenty of it. I have been
>starving myself for weeks.

OTTO
>Yes, sir.

FELIX
>Fruit - bacon - eggs - toast -
>coffee - enough for two.

Otto peers around as
though still expecting
to see signs of another
occupant of the room.

FELIX
>Hurry! Idiot.

OTTO   (smirking)
>Yes, sir, for two, sir.

As Otto reaches the door
he suddenly leaps over the
threshold as though goosed
from behind.

(NOTE: This in case we don't
use the Duchess gag in the
street.)

DISSOLVE TO:

CLOSE SHOT FELIX

finishing his breakfast.
He is now nearly dressed.

> HORAN'S VOICE
> Master, I am starving.

> FELIX
> I forgot - sit down and eat -
> We'll always have to take
> turns eating - as there is

He pushes back his
chair. The Camera
follows him as he
moves toward the
telephone. From the
direction of the table
offscene, comes the sound
of a man using table-ware
for a meal.

> HORAN'S VOICE
> Not always - I have thought
> of a plan -

> FELIX   (picking up phone)
> Yes? - what plan -

> HORAN'S   (off-scene)
> A little surprise for you -
> wait and see.

> FELIX   (into phone)
> Six - seven - three! -
> please.
>   (to Horan)
> I don't like surprises.

> HORAN
> This one will amuse you.

> FELIX   (into phone)
> Dorothea? - Good morning,
> darling...Yes, quite all
> right - I'm terribly sorry
> about last night - overwork,
> I guess. Forgive me? -
> That's a dear. I'll be over
> right away - what do you say
> to a drive through the park -
> Splendid! - I'll be right
> over - Goodbye dear.

Felix turns and starts to
get into his jacket and
straighten his tie and hair.

> HORAN'S VOICE
> Charming girl! - Lovely!

> FELIX   (at mirror)
> None lovelier!

> HORAN'S VOICE   (mingled with clatter
>   of knife and fork)
> Looks particularly adorable in bed.

Felix turns about abruptly,
his hand arrested in the act
of straightening some portion of his attire.

                    FELIX   (amazed)
                        What?

                    HORAN'S VOICE   (tantalizingly re-
                                    miniscent)
                        All flushed in slumber - her
                        golden hair strewn on the pillow -

Felix takes a stride or two
toward the table, the camera
panning to include the table
as he nears it. The knife and
fork drop on the plate and
the chair moves back and
partly turns.

                    FLEIX
                        You devil! - You dared?
                    HORAN'S VOICE   (ironically)
                        No harm, my master. I escorted
                        the good doctor safely home -
                        and then - I could not resist
                        a little visit to the fair
                        Dorothea's bedroom. She was
                        sleeping soundly - and dream-
                        ing, master - dreaming of you.
                        She whispered your name -
                        I pressed a chaste kiss on her
                        lips - for you - my dear master.

                    FELIX
                        You hound!

Felix leaps forward and
clutches at the empty
air over the chair as
though reaching for Horan's
throat. There is nothing
there. Then Horan's mocking laugh rings out from
another part of the room,

                    HORAN'S VOICE (tauntingly)
                        Here I am - master -

                    FELIX   (in fury)
                        Listen - you fiend - if ever
                        you dare approach Miss Von
                        Trenken again- - if you so
                        much as lay your loathsome
                        hand on her - I'll hunt you
                        down and kill you like a rat -

                    HORAN
                        Easily said - but not so easily
                        done -

                    FELIX
                        I'll find a method! - - Keep
                        away from her - do you hear
                        me - keep away from her!

                    HORAN   (sarcastically)
                        I am my master's humble slave
                        to hear is to obey.

                    FELIX
                        Oh! - -

In fury and disgust he
rushes from the room,
Horan's mocking laugh
ringing after him as
the door slams shut.

DISSOLVE TO:

EXT. WOODLAND DRIVE
MED. SHOT FELIX & DOROTHEA

They are in the rear seat

of an open touring car of
foreign appearance. Otto
is driving.

CLOSE SHOT FELIX & DOROTHEA

They are leaning back on
the cushions, their heads
close together, their hands
entwined. Dorothea is just
finishing an account of what
happened to her the night
before. Felix's face is
thoughtful and worried.

>   FELIX
>   And that was all that
>   happened?
>
>   DOROTHEA
>   Yes - it was just a hideous
>   nightmare - but horribly vivid
>   and real.
>
>   FELIX
>   It must have been.
>
>   DOROTHEA
>   But how did you know anything
>   unusual had happened to us?
>   Father didn't want you to
>   know.
>
>   FELIX
>   I can't tell you - yet.
>   Darling - promise me you'll
>   say nothing to your father -
>
>   DOROTHEA
>   Of course, dear.
>
>   FELIX
>   And you'll keep the dog with
>   you - always - at night.
>
>   DOROTHEA
>   Yes, dear - if you want.

                         FELIX
                              I don't mean to frighten you,
                              dear - There is nothing to be
                              afraid of - and soon, I hope
                              I'll be able to explain ever-
                              thing.

                         DOROTHEA
                              I hope so, too - I can't stand
                              mysteries...

                         FELIX   (teasingly)
                              Isn't love - a mystery?

                         DOROTHEA   (snuggling her face to his)
                              Not to a woman - silly!

Their lips meet.

CLOSEUP OTTO

He gets a reflection in the
rear sight mirror of his master and sweetheart in an embrace, and heaves a comic
sentimental sigh.

DISSOLVE TO:

INT. HALLWAY ROOMING HOUSE

It is a rather shabby dwelling
and the landlady is standing
facing the camera and talking
to a tall man in simple dark
clothes who carries a battered
suitcase in his gloved hand.
He is back to camera and keeps
his hat on.
                                   LANDLADY
                              It is a nice room, sir - with
                              a private bath.

                         MAN'S VOICE
                              Show it to me.

The landlady looks a
little in awe of this
tall stranger. She starts
up a flight of stairs and
the man follows.

DISSOLVE TO:

INT. BEDROOM

A plainly furnished room -
European in type, with an
old-fashioned bathroom ad-
joining.   LANDLADY
                              The bath is there, sir - hot
                              and cold running water - and
                              towels free. You can have
                              breakfast sent to your room -
                              but no cooking is allowed.

(continued)

As she bustles about
opening windows and
drawing curtains...the
man's face is kept away
from camera.

LANDLADY (continuing)
That's the only rule I stick
to - You can have all the company you want - (simpering)
and if you're a stranger in
town I know some nice, pretty
girls - -

MAN'S VOICE (sharply)
Thank you - all I shall want
is complete privacy - -

LANDLADY (a little startled at
                    his tone)
Y-yes - of course, sir - -
        (at the door-brave again)
But no cooking!

She crosses to door.

MAN'S VOICE (sharply)
I understand!

The landlady gives a
sniff and exits.

CLOSE SHOT MAN'S BAG

His gloved hands come into
scene and open the bag.
He takes out some articles
of clothing and then a jar
of cold cream and some sticks
of grease-paint, which we show
in CLOSEUP.

MEDIUM SHOT

A tall figure moves into
the bathroom, still without
revealing his face. The
Camera follows him and watches
him place some of the toilet
articles and grease-paint box
on a shelf. There is a horrible
furtiveness about his movements.
Of course we will feel that this
must be Horan, miraculously visible
again, but we won't let the audience
know positively - -until later.
They will be tortured with curiosity to see the face of this tall
man in black and we will keep them
curious a little longer.

The Camera shooting close - - follows
the figure over to the washstand and
one of the gloved hands starts the
water running into the bowl. One
hand then begins drawing off a glove
from the other and we DISSOLVE TO....

THE DISSOLVE shows a bowl
full of greasy-looking water
running out through the drain
with its customary sucking
noise - - the Camera PANS to
show a pair of dark glasses
on a shelf- a wig - and then
a black suit of clothes on a
chair.

The Camera trucks along into the
bedroom and as it nears the hall
door the door opens and camera
goes through it as though following the invisible man down the
hall to the stars.

The Camera starts down the stairs,
at the foot of which the landlady
is talking with another woman, a
flashy-looking brunette of the
street-walker type.

The Camera pauses about two steps
up from the hall as though Horan
himself had paused to listen to
the conversation.

> LANDLADY (imitating Horan)
> "All I want is privacy", he
> says, in a voice that would
> freeze your heart, dearie.

> GIRL
> Grouchy, eh? - - I like 'em
> that way - they make good
> spenders once you warm them
> up.

> LANDLADY
> If you can do yourself any
> good with this one you're a
> wonder, dearie - -

> GIRL (starting upstairs)
> You never can tell till you
> try.

> LANDLADY
> Good luck.

Just when we think the girl
is going to bump into the
invisible man on the stairs
the Camera starts backing
upstairs in front of the girl,
focussing especially on her
firm, full breasts as they
shake seductively to the girl's
step. At the head of the stairs
the Camera draws back to allow
the girl room to move up the
hall, then follows right behind
her to her room door. The Camera
appears to center on the right-
ness of her skirt where it
clings to the curves of her
tempting behind.

The Camera follows the girl
into her bedroom and then
watches her as she prepares
to make herself comfortable.
She removes her street things-
turns on a lively radio or
phonograph record - moves
about humming snatches of
the jazz tune that is being
played, while she kicks off
her slippers and drops her
dress about her feet. She
gets disrobed to underwear
and stockings, then sits on
the edge of the bed and pulls
off one stocking.

Suddenly she is apparently
thrown backward on the bed by
invisible forces - she utters
a short half-stifled scream
then struggles violently against
unseen power. Her hands act as
though she were trying to loosen
an invisible grip on her throat...

DISSOLVE TO:

INT. HOSPITAL WARD
CLOSE SHOT AT GIRL

We fins the dame girl lying in
a small iron cot with a nurse
bending over her. The patient's
throat is bandaged and she looks
haggard and weak.

The Camera draws back to disclose
several men standing about the cot.
One is obviously the hospital doctor, in white jacket - another is
a police officer and the third is
De. von Trenken.

                    HOSPITAL DOCTOR

                         Then you still maintain
                         that your assailant was
                         invisible?

CLOSEUP..GIRL

The girl nods her head -
weakly - her eyes dilating
in horror.

CLOSE SHOT GROUP OF MEN

The hospital doctor turns to
the others and shrugs his
shoulders.

                        HOSPITAL DOCTOR

                        You see - - emotional
                        hysteria - - that's all.

                     DR. VON TRENKEN

                        And the finger marks on
                        her throat?

                     HOSPITAL DOCTOR
                        Undoubtedly self-inflicted -
                        some sort of nightmare with
                        violent subconscious muscular
                        reaction.

                     DR. VON TRENKEN (thoughtfully)

                        You are probably right,
                        Doctor.

                     POLICE OFFICER (disdainfully)

                        Invisible Man - -

                            (he laughs
                            scornfully)

                     DR. VON TRENKEN (smiling)

                        Absurd - isn't it - Well
                        she'll be all right in a
                        few days - - Goodbye, gen
                        tlemen.

                     others

                     Goodbye, doctor

As he turns to leave
the group ....

DISSOLVE TO:

EXT. VON TRENKEN'S GARDEN

A pretty little formal
European garden adjoining
a small terrace or loggia.
The garden is walled about,
and the wall is entirely over-
grown with vines. Felix and
Dorothea are at the far end
of the garden engaged in tender and animated conversation,
which we do not hear because
of the distance from the Camera.
The big police dog, Lupo, is
lying at their feet.

(Into the musical love theme
comes an undertone of the theme
used whenever the Invisible Man
is about to enter a scene.)

CLOSE SHOT OF VINE-COVERED WALL

The vines at the top of the wall
rustic and shake a little as tho
something invisible were stirring
them.

MED. LONG SHOT GROUP

The police dog suddenly stands up
and looks off toward the wall. It
bares its teeth and growls - Felix
and Dorothea stop talking and look   DOROTHEA
at the dog. The Camera comes closer   What is it Lupo?
to the group. The dog bristles at
it, stares off toward the wall.   FELIX
Felix is paring an apple with small   What's the matter with
but sharp kitchen knife.   him?

                                                      DOROTHEA
                                                          You'd think he saw a
                                                          ghost - Down, Lupo!
                                                          there is nothing there-
                                                          down, sir!

Felix reacts to this as though the
idea strikes him that Horan might
be around. The dog reluctantly lies
down by Dorothea but keeps his attention forward on the wall.

We CUT to Von Trenken coming out
into the garden from the house.
His face wears a serious and thoughtful expression as he observes Felix
and Dorothea in the garden.   DOROTHEA'S VOICE
                                                          Hello dear.

                                                      VON TRENKEN (assuring a
                                                                   natural manner)
                                                          So there you are - -

He advances toward them.

MEDIUM SHOT. . .GROUP

Felix and Dorothea rise to
greet the doctor, who comes
into the scene and embraces
Dorothea affectionately.

                    DOCTOR
               well - you're looking yourself
               again.

                    DOROTHEA
               We had a glorious drive through
               the park -

               FELIX   (shaking hands)
               How are you, sir?

                    DOCTOR
               Quite well - I want to chat with
               you, young man, if Dorothea will
               excuse us.

                    DOROTHEA
               Of course. I want to get ready
               for tea, anyway - Come on, Lupo.

               FELIX
               Goodbye, dear.

She moves off with the
police dog and both men
watch her go. Von Trenken's
face settles into very serious lines. Felix tosses the
fruit knife on the table.
The Camera closes up on the
two of them.

                    Well, Doctor?

                    DOCTOR
               So you broke your promise to
               me - Felix.

               FELIX   (taken aback by this direct
                              accusation)
               What do you mean, sir?

                    DOCTOR
               Your promise not to continue
               those devilish experiments.

               FELIX
               Why do you say that?

                    DOCTOR
               Has Dorothea told you of her
               experience last night?

               FELIX   (dissembling)
               She said something about a
               dream- a nightmare.

DOCTOR
It was no dream!

FELIX
Explain, please.

DOCTOR
Several strange occurrences
have been reported to the
police today. Only one of
them was of a serious nature -
I have just come from the
hospital where there is a
young woman who claims to
have been attacked in her
room by - an invisible man!

FELIX
And you believe - -

DOCTOR   (angrily)
Don't dissemble with me, Felix -
I can read the truth in your
face -

FELIX   (voice rising)
Nonsense

DOCTOR   (his voice rising)
You are lying to me, young man -
Where is your assistant - Horan?
Where is he?

felix
How should I know?

DOCTOR
You know only too well - you
used him as your subject - you
have turned loose upon the world
a potential monster who has already started upon a program of
violence - Heaven knows how far
it may lead!

FELIX
This is ridiculous!

DOCTOR
If you persist in your attitude
young man, I shall be forced to
forbid you the hospitality of
my house - and the friendship
of my daughter -

FELIX
You insult me, sir -

Dorothea in her room is
changing her dress. From
off-scene the doctor's and Felix's
voices raised in angry tone,
but the words are not dis-
tinguisable. She listens
with a startled expression
then starts to rush into
some sort of presentable
garment.

CUT TO:

The two men in the garden.
The quarrel has reached its
climax.

                    FELIX
                        Very well, Doctor - you may
                        do as you please, but if you
                        think you can keep Dorothea
                        and me apart, you're mad!
                        As for your threats about
                        the police - go as far as
                        you like - you will only
                        make yourself ridiculous
                        in the eyes of the world.

                    DOCTOR
                        Ridiculous or not - I mean
                        to carry this investigation
                        to the end - and if this
                        invisible monster of yours
                        becomes the dreadful menace
                        I fear he is inclined to-
                        you shall share full re-
                        ponsibility for his crimes -
                        Good day, sir.

                    FELIX
                        Good day!

He turns and strides
angrily toward the
house. As he dis-
appears, the doctor
takes one step to
follow him, then
suddenly groans,
throws out his arms,
stumbles and falls
face downward in the
garden path.

A CLOSEUP OF THE DOCTOR
shows the fruit knife in
his back, buried to the handle.

INT⬚ VON TRENKEN HOUSE
MED. SHOT

As Felix passes through
the living room and goes
to the front door, Dorothea
comes downstairs, in a
negligee. She is dread-
fully perturbed.

                DOROTHEA
            Felix! - Felix!

The answer is the front
door slamming shut. Suddenly Lupo begins to bark furiously off-scene and Dorothea
rushes for the garden windows -
An old servant, perhaps, rushes
into the scene also.

A shot of the doctor lying
dead in the garden and Lupo
barking furiously. Dorothea
rushes toward her father,
screaming.

DISSOLVE TO:

Felix is pacing restlessly
about, deeply agitated over
his interview with Dr. Von
Trenken. The buzzer of his
doctograph sounds sharply
He hastily opens the circuit.

              FELIX
            Yes?

            HORAN'S VOICE (in mock subservience)
            Good evening, Master

            FELIX (savagely)
            Come in!

He presses the button that
operates the automatic door.

SHOT AT THE DOOR

The door bolts slide open
and the door swings inward -
But instead of the expected
invisible entrance of Horan -
there stands in the doorway
the tall, black-clad figure
of Horan himself - - only partially disguised by black glasses.
He wears gloves and as he removes
his hat we see that he now wears
a wig, instead of his former
bald head.

CLOSE SHOT FELIX

He stares in amazement at Horan.

>   FELIX
>   Horan!
>
>   HORAN'S VOICE (as door clangs shut)
>   At your service, Master.
>
>   FELIX'S VOICE
>   But it isn't possible -

CLOSE SHOT HORAN

He moves further into the
room.

>   HORAN
>   It is very simple - Remove these
>   clothes and my body would be
>   invisible as before. As for my
>   face - merely an opaque appli-
>   cation of grease paint - a touch
>   of the theatre - These
>   glasses screen my invisible
>   eyes - this wig -a touch of
>   pardonable vanity - and behold
>   the old Horan - perhaps, I
>   hope, a little more presentable
>   than before - not quite so
>   hideous.
>
>   FELIX   (aghast)
>   More hideous than ever - there
>   is something unearthly about
>   you - uncanny like a living
>   corpse.
>
>   HORAN
>   A moment at a wash basin and
>   I can disappear from view a-
>   gain - if I displease you.

He moves as though to
go to the wash room.

                              FELIX
                                   No - wait! - I must talk
                                   to you - now -

                         HORAN
                                   Yes, Master

                         FELIX
                                   Enough of that mockery - -
                                   You are no servant of mine -
                                   and never intended to be one -
                                   I was a fool to listen to you -
                                   Scarcely a day has passed and
                                   you have already brought about
                                   my head the danger of complicity
                                   in your offenses ...Dr. Von
                                   Trenken has forbidden me the
                                   house - he knows our secret and
                                   threatens to reveal it to the
                                   police.

                         HORAN
                                   Dr. Von Trenken no longer
                                   stands in our way.

                         FELIX   (alarmed)
                                   What do you mean by that?

The buzzer rings
sharply. Felix opens
the circuit of the
dictograph.

                                   Yes - -

                         OFFICER'S VOICE
                                   Open in the name of the law.

                         FELIX
                                   The law?

He presses the button for
the door and turns in that
direction in mingled sur-
prise and alarm.

The door opens and two or three
policemen, accompanied by a man
in civilian clothes enter.

Horan moves quietly toward an
open door leading to a washroom

Felix meets the officers half
way. The man in civilian clothes
makes a gesture and two policemen
place their hands on Felix.

                         FELIX
                            What is the meaning of this?

                         PREFECT
                            Felix Landers, you are under
                            arrest for the murder of
                            Dr. Hugo Von Trenken!

                         FELIX   (aghast)
                            Murder? - Dr. Von Trenken!

                         PREFECT
                            You may save your breath for
                            the examining magistrate - -
                            Take him along.

Felix puts up a struggle.

                         FELIX
                            But this is ridiculous - Dr.
                            von Trenken is my friend. I
                            am engaged to his daughter. I
                            know nothing about this murder.

                         PREFECT
                            Miss von Trenken has testified
                            against you - Come - you are
                            inviting us to use force.

The terrible thought that
Horan had killed Von Trenken
comes suddenly to Felix. He
glances about the room, but
Horan is out of sight.

                         FELIX
                            Just one minute - please! -
                            I beg of you! - When and how was
                            the Doctor killed?

                         PREFECT
                            I am not supposed to answer
                            questions - but since you per-
                            sist in your innocent attitude - -
                            he was found dead in his gar-
                            den, an hour or so ago - a
                            fruit knife in his back. Take
                            him away!

                         FELIX   (horrified)
                            Wait! - the man who killed
                            Dr. von Trenken is in that
                            wash room. Get him quickly, or
                            he will disappear - believe me!
                            - do as I say - for the love
                            of Heaven - -

The prefect motions to
one of the officers, who
steps to the washroom door.

We look into the washroom
with the officer - a suit
of dark clothes hangs on a
nail - also a hat - nothing
else is visible.

                         OFFICER
                    There is no one there, sir.

Back to the group. Felix
exclaims in despair. The
Prefect is angry.

                    PREFECT
                    You heard - there is no one there.

               FELIX   (half to himself as tho he
                            realizes the futility of
                            trying to make these men
                            believe him)
                    He has made himself invisible
                    again! -

               PREFECT (scornfully)
                    The Invisible Man! — More of
                    that nonsense - Take him away.

They drag Felix off.
As they go his voice
continues trying to impress
them with the truth.

                    FELIX
                    He is still in this room, I
                    tell you. Let me go! - I'll help
                    find him for you - Won't you
                    believe me? Oh God! Why did
                    I do this thing!

                    PREFECT
                    You see - he confesses!

As they exit, dragging
Felix through the door,
which clangs about after
them.

                    SOUND: Horan's croaking laugh
                            rings out after the door
                            is shut.

As Horan's laugh is heard
invisible hands shatter a row
of bottles and then begin
shattering the structure of
the ray machine by hurling
stools and other equipment
against the glass dome and
the violet ray tubes.

DISSOLVE TO:

INT. MAGISTRATE'S COURT

A small courtroom of European
type - - more like an office than
a courtroom - -with the examining
magistrate behind a raised desk
and a few clerks and uniformed
bailiffs or police. Dorothea
is just terminating her
testimony. She is deeply
 distressed at having to give
evidence so damning to the man
she loves and at the moment
we pick up the examination
she is on the point of breaking down in tears.

Felix is seated facing
the magistrate ... a guard
on each side of him -

>

                    MAGISTRATE
                         Just one more question,
                         Miss von Trenken .. You are
                         positive that the voice of the
                         man you heard quarreling with
                         you father was the voice of
                         Mr. Landers?

                    DOROTHEA (lowering her head)
                         Yes!

                    MAGISTRATE
                         The witness is excused - -

Dorothea sinks back in
the witness chair- -
staring at Felix - -as tho
she hardly could believe this
is the man she once loved.

                    MAGISTRATE
                         The prisoner understands that he
                         is not yet on trial - - that this
                         is merely a preliminary examination
                         and any evidence he brings to light
                         may be used against him later.

                    FELIX
                         I understand, your honor- -

                    MAGISTRATE
                         Proceed with the examination

(CONTINUED)

Felix turns to Dorothea
and studies her tenderly
and imploringly...a moment,
The girl tries to pull herself
together to meet the ordeal
of her lover's questions.

                    FELIX   (imploringly)
                    Dorothea - - before you put
                    your hand in that glass
                    aquarium in my laboratory you
                    looked at it closely.

                    DOROTHEA
                    Yes.

                    FELIX
                    And you saw nothing?

                    DOROTHEA
                    Nothing but air bubbles.

                    FELIX
                    But your hand was gripped by
                    something alive .. yet invisible!

                    DOROTHEA
                    It appeared - invisible

                    FELIX
                    Why do you say - - "appeared"?

                    DOROTHEA (brokenly)
                    I asked Father about it...and he
                    told me it was a chemical trick...
                    an optical illlusion...which made the
                    water appear transparent...
                    when it was not....

There is a stir in
the courtroom and a
chorus of "ah's"

                    MAGISTRATE
                    Silence in the court.

The murmur dies down.

                    FELIX
                    Then you do not believe me when I tell
                    you that the octopus in that tank was
                    alive...but invisible..until its death?

                    DOROTHEA (heart brokenly)
                    I - - believe my Father....
                    FELIX
                    And you really believe that I - I
                    killed him?

                    DOROTHEA (brokenly)
                    Please...I can't stand any more...
                    FELIX   (sadly)
                    That is all.

Dorothea comes from
the witness box and sinks
down sobbingly beside her
middle-aged housekeeper... who tries   (CONTINUED)

155

to comfort her. Felix faces
the court - - grimly - -sadly- -
hopelessly...

                         FELIX
                    Your honor...if I cannot convince the
                    woman I love of my innocents it is
                    useless for me at attempt further argu-
                    ment in the court. Hold me for trial
                    condemn me to death ... for in a measure
                    I am guilty .. I have unwittingly
                    turned loose upon humanity an invisible
                    force whose potentialities for evil are
                    unlimited .. I warn the court that unless
                    this invisible murderer is tracked down
                    and destroyed there will be further and
                    even more terrible crimes .. This creature
                    has already tasted blood - - from this to
                    homicidal mania is but a step - - he
                    may conceive himself as an avenging angel
                    of destruction and reduce who cities - -
                    entire nations - - to ruin ....

There is another titter of laughter
through the courtroom and the magistrate thumps on his desk for order.

                         MAGISTRATE
                    Silence! Silence!

The court attendant advances
and whispers something to
the magistrate, who appears
to receive the information
with great interest. The
magistrate then thumps again
for order and turns toward
Felix.

                         MAGISTRATE
                    Prisoner - - you have stated in the court
                    that the man who murdered Doctor von
                    Trenken was your former laboratory
                    assistant, Alfred Horan .. whom you have
                    rendered invisible.

                         FLEIX
                    Yes!

                         MAGISTRATE
                    You still persist in this extraordinary
                    statement?

                         FELIX
                    Yes!

                         MAGISTRATE   (to one of the bailiffs)
                    Bring in...Alfred Horan!

There is great ex-
citement in the courtroom
and all present crane their
necks toward the little door
through which witnesses are
brought into court.

Felix looks amazed ... then
braces himself with a sudden
show of satisfaction..this
may play into his hands.

Dorothea stares toward Felix ..
reproachfully...The door opens
and Honan appears, flanked by
two policemen of bailiffs...He
appears in an ugly humor and glances
right and left like a caged animal.
They lead him down before the judge.

     MAGISTRATE
      Are you Alfred Honan?

    HONAN (gruffly)
      I am!

    MAGISTRATE (to bailiffs)
      Is there any doubt about the identity
      of the witness?

    BAILIFF
      None, you honor..He is well known
      throughout the city. Lately he has
      taken to wearing those dark glasses - -
      a wig - - and paint to disguise the
      scarred aide of his face.

    MAGISTRATE (to Felix)
      Prisoner - - do you admit this
      witness to be Alfred Honan?

    FELIX
      Yes .. your honor.

    MAGISTRATE (ironically
      The Invisible Man!

The courtroom titters
again and the Magistrate
pounds for order
    FELIX
      Yes!

    MAGISTRATE (to Honan ..apologetically)
      The prisoner claims to have rendered
      you invisible and accuses you of the
      murder of Doctor von Trenken.

    HONAN (getting calmer and
        resourceful)
      I see, your honor .. I was afraid of
      this .. Mr. Landers was pursuing an
      experiment in the invisibility of matter
      and it became such an obsession with
      him that I was forced to leave his
      laboratory. Obviously his man is
      deranged.. It is a pity.
    MAGISTRATE
      Have you any knowledge that might indicate
      a motive for the quarrel between the
      prisoner & Doctor von Trenken?

                                    HONAN
                                        Only that I heard the Doctor warn
                                        Mr. Landers if he did not drop his
                                        mad experiments he would forbid him
                                        his house...and his daughter's hand.

                                    MAGISTRATE
                                        I see!
                                            (turns to Felix)
                                        Prisoner..have you anything further
                                        to say?

Felix is now coldly
calm, though his eyes are
blazing...He is determined
to play his trump cards.

                                    FELIX
                                        Your honor..this court is being
                                        deceived by outward appearances.
                                        Beneath those garments and that
                                        paint the still solid body of
                                        Alfred Honan is invisible to the
                                        human eye. Through chemical
                                        changes wrought in my laboratory
                                        the cells of his flesh and bone
                                        permit the passage of light as though
                                        nothing were there.

Honan shakes his head
pityingly and the
courtroom spectators
laugh. The judge pounds
again for order.

                                    FELIX
                                        He could not paint the surface of
                                        his eyeballs ...Ask the witness
                                        to remove those black glasses!

                                    MAGISTRATE   (to Honan)
                                        Do you care to humor the prisoner
                                        to this extent?

                                    HONAN
                                        It is impossible, Your Honor ...
                                        I am on the verge of blindness ...
                                        to remove these glasses for even
                                        a moment may make me sightless
                                        forever.

Fleix is beginning to
realize that he is
trapped.

                                    FELIX
                                        He lies .. behind those glasses
                                        are no visible eyes at all ...
                                        nothing but dark holes - vacancy.

Honan gives a pitying
shrug. The magistrate
shakes his head, too
as though in pity for
Felix's mental state.

                                        (CONTINUED)

MAGISTRATE
Enough of this! You may
go, Mr. Honan.

FELIX
No! - No! Make him remove
his gloves - you will see
his hands there - Don't let
him go! You will regret
to the last day of your life!

MAGISTRATE
Silence! Felix Landers
I hold you for trial charged
with the murder of Doctor von Trenken!
-Take him away! And guard him well -
there is no knowing what turn his madness
may take.

The bailiffs seize
Felix.

FLEIX
I'm not mad! I'm not mad. I tell
The bailiffs are   you!- Dorothea! - Dorothea! There leading Felix away,
leading Felix   stands your midnight visitor -
away struggling.   Your father's murderer!

Honan turns to Dorothea
and bends over her
sympathetically. She
stares up into his face
is fascinated horror. She
is getting the big idea.

HONAN
Permit me to add my condolences to
those of your other friends.

Dorothea suddenly reaches
up and snatches the black
glasses from Honan's eyes.
Two black holes appear where
the eyeballs should be
(THIS IS A SIMPLE MAKEUP
TRICK but should prove
very horrible.)

Dorothea emits a piercing
scream. Honan snatches
for his glasses, but she throws
them aside.

DOROTHEA
His eyes - - look - - Felix is
right - there are no eyes. Look!
Look!

Honan lunges to get
his glasses from the
floor. Two bailiffs
seize and hold him. His
eyes are black holes, but his face
is contorted with rage and murderous
mania.

(CONTINUED)

The spectators stir with
excitement and exlaim -

                                 CRIES OF
                                         Look at his eyes - - Black holes!
                                         Heaven above! Landers was right!

The Magistrate pound
for order. The bailiffs
who have been holding
Felix release him and
Felix rushes to Dorothea's
side.

                                 MAGISTRATE
                                         Order! - order in court!

Honan throws off the
two bailiffs and takes
a stand with his back
to the wall - brandishing
his heavy cane. He is on
the platform by the judge's
desk. The wall back of him
should be of the correct
tint and decorative scheme
to enable the CAMERA to
perform the TRIPLE EXPOSURE
STUFF that now follows,

                                 HONAN
                                         Stand back you people! - -
                                         Stand back! So it's
                                         magic you want! - Mysteries!
                                         Tricks! - I'll show you one
                                         never before seen by mortal eyes!

He takes a large hand-
kerchief from his pocket
and gets it in the water
pitcher on the judge's desk.
He throws his wig aside
and spreads the wet hand-
kerchief over his face as
he appears to rub his features
vigorously.

A CUT OF THE GROUPS staring
in amazement. Then they react
in sudden horror at what they
see.

CUTTING BACK to Honan we see
his apparently headless body
standing there, as he tosses
the wet handkerchief aside.

                                 HONAN
                                         You scream! - You tremble! - -
                                         Wait! - - and watch!

(CONTINUED)

He throws his gloves
off and his hands vanish
from the full's down.

Felix suddenly realizes   FELIX
that in another moment   Stop him - he'll escape!
Honan will vanish!

Honan's black suit suddenly falls to the floor as
though it were controll-
ed by strings. His shoes
clatter to one side.
                                 BAILIFFS
                                          Look out! - Guard the doors!

                                 FELIX
                                          The window - the window!

A bailiff rushes toward
the open window - he is
apparently struck forcibly
by and unseen hand.

                                 HONAN'S VOICE
                                          Out of my way! - - I'll
                                          kill anyone who stands in
                                          my way - just as I killed
                                          von Trenken!

The window is thrown
wide open - then as the
CAMERA FOLLOWS a rush of
police to the window, we
see the branches of a
tree outside suddenly
bend down as though by
a weight, then fly upward
as though released. And
from the courtyard outside
comes Honan's mocking
laugh.

Felix holds Dorothea in
his arms, soothingly, as
the girl clings hysterically
to him.

The magistrate is still pound-
ing his desk. He is purple
with amazement and shattered
dignity.

                       MAGISTRATE   (vainly)
                                 Order in court! - -
                                 Order in the court.

                              FADE OUT

And that, dear reader, is the end of Richard Schayer's treatment - Many other writers tried their hand at
a script but non were acceptable to Carl Laemmle Jr.'s standards. And Whales's either. To make up for the
unfinished endings on the treatments - I have next put in the first shooting script by R.C. Sherriff, to whom
James Whale assigned the project at this point.

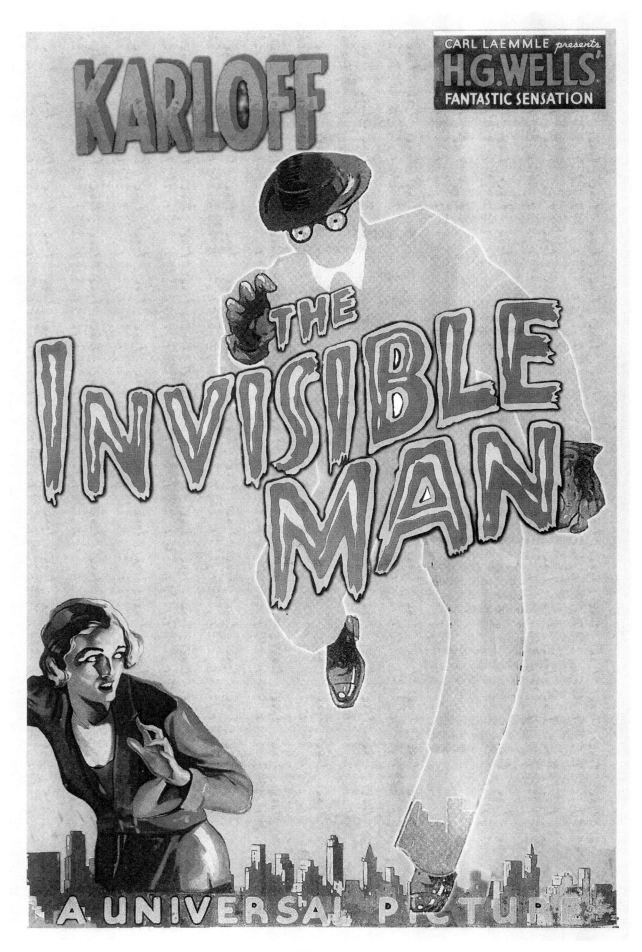

"T H E   I N V I S I B L E   M A N "

From the Novel by

H. G. WELLS

Screenplay by

R.C.SHERRIFF

*
***
*

*
***
*

FILE COPY
FOR CENTRAL FILES

PICTURE NO: 623

DIRECTED BY: JAMES WHALE

JUNE 12, 1933

UNIVERSAL PICTURES
C O R P O R A T I O N
Universal City, Calif.

"THE INVISIBLE MAN"

IMPORTANT NOTICE

This script is the property of Universal
Pictures Corporation and is merely loaned
to you for use in connection with the
picture for which it is issued.

You have accepted this script upon the
distinct understanding that if same is not
returned to the Stenographic Department
immediately after the completion of your
work in connection with this picture, you
will pay to Universal Pictures Corporation
the sum of Twenty-five dollars for its
retention.

CARL LAEMMLE JR.
General Manager

SCRIPT NO: 22

SEQUENCES	SCENES	PAGES
A	42	11 - 2 - 25 - 34 - 38 - 4
B	72	11 - 19 - 21 - 24 - 25 - 2 53 - 58 - 6
C	12	5
D	79	21 17 - 34 - 37 - 42 - 44 - 62 - 71 -
E	123	33 2 - 15 - 16 - 34 - 43 - 44 - 5 3 - 77 - 78 - 79 - 82 - 86 - 88 - 96 - 98 - 99 - 101 - 104 - 106 -
F	83	20 2 - 12 - 18 - 19 - 21 - 30 - 32 - 68 - 81
G	57	12 - 1 - 30 - 23 - 26 - 34 - 38 - 45 - 48 - 49 - 50 - 55 -
H	11	4 - 3 - 4 - 7
TOTAL: 8	479	117

113 - 114 - 117

*
***
*

*
***
*

A-6   EXT. ROAD..MEDIUM LONG SHOT
WITH MAN IN FOREGROUND

     The man has just turned from
reading the sign and starts
towards CAMERA which DRAWS
BACK as we see below us, in a
velly, a little group of houses-
dark walled, white roofed - grey
smoke zigzagging to the gust of
wind. The man moves forward dark-
ening the picture which...

     DISSOLVES TO:

A-7   INT. VILLAGE INN (NIGHT.) LONG
SHOT.

     High CAMERA shooting down on the
people in the Inn. A striking con-
trast to the bitter loneliness of
the world outside. An automatic
piano is playing joyfully in a corner, and the saloon is crowded with
men, possibly one giggly woman.
Tobacco smoke, talk and laughter
fill the air. We hold on this long
enough to get a general impression
of the atmosphere of the Inn.
CUT TO:

A-8   INT. VILLAGE INN...AT BAR

     A cheery party lounging against
the bar; rough, sturdy country types-
each with his glass of beer.

                 FIRST CUSTOMER
                 Did you hear about Mrs.
                 Mason's little Willy. Sent
                 him to school and found him
                 ten foot deep in a snow
                 drift!

                 SECOND CUSTOMER
                 How'd they get 'im out?

                 FIRST CUSTOMER
                 Brought the fire engine
                 along. Put the hose pipe in-
                 pumped it backwards - and
                 sucked 'im out!

     A gust of laughter greets this
sally as the CAMERA MOVES across
the saloon to a beery looking
individual who is pretending to
play the automatic piano -- he
runs his fingers over the keys,
swaying his head dreamily to and
fro. The music stops - he lowers
his hands to his knees, swings
around and bows and smiles.
CUT TO:

CG   A-9   INT. VILLAGE INN. CLOSE SHOT

Man, with a large mustache, who
has been standing beside the
piano, drops in another penny.
CUT BACK TO:

A-10   INT. VILLAGE INN...TWO SHOT

The music starts again and the
beery looking man hastily swings
round to pretend once more that
he is playing -- just too late to
carry out the illusion to the
audience.
CUT TO:

A-11   INT. VILLAGE INN...DOLLEY SHOT.
MEDIUM

CAMERA leaves the two men at the
piano and MOVES AROUND the saloon
getting in the different types-
to a party of earnest villagers
playing at darts in a corner by
the door.
CUT TO:

A-12   INT. VILLAGE INN. CLOSE SHOT

We see the set profile of a
competitor as he raises a dart
and throws it. CAMERA SWINGS TO
MEDIUM SHOT taking in the darts
board and the door beside it. We
see a dart fly, to bury itself,
quivering, amongst other darts on
the board, as there comes a per-
emptory rap on the door. A moment's
pause, then the door abruptly opens
to reveal the wierd stranger, standing on the threshold.
CUT TO:

A-13   INT. VILLAGE IN...MED. CLOSE ON
STRANGER...LOWY CAMERA

WE can see him clearly now for the
first time; the light of the room
on him; the darkness of the night
beyond. The borad brimmed hat is
pulled low over his eyes -- covering
his ears and forehead. The two
eerie goggles slowly glare around
the room. Beneath it is the long,
peaked nose-- and beneath that only
the high buttoned collar of his
coat. The bandaged cheeks are
practically hidden.

CUT TO:

A-14 INT. VILLAGE INN..MED. LONG
SHOT ON DOLLEY

   AS the stranger advances. There
   is a power and authority in his
   slow stride; the surprised dart
   players instinctively fall back.
   CAMERA moves into TWO SHOT --
   as stranger without pause goes
   to the bar and stands looking over
   it st Mr. Hall, the plump little
   keeper of the Inn. There is a
   moment of silence before the
   stranger speaks.
   CUT TO:

A-15 INT. VILLAGE INN..CLOSEUP
STRANGER

   SHOOTING over Mr. Hall's shoulder
   on the stranger as he speaks - his
   voice is strong and even.

        THE STRANGER
          I want a room -- and a
          fire.
   CUT TO:

A-16 INT. VILLAGE INN..MEDIUM SHOT

   Mr. Hall standing behind the bar.
   The stranger facing him. Mr. Hall
   with difficulty tears his gaping
   face away from the strange apparition,
   and calls into the passage beyond.

        MR. HALL
          Janny!

        MRS. HALL (offstage)
          'Ullo!

   A short, exceedingly fat lady
   pops a round fat face round the
   corner of the door.
   CUT TO:

A-17 INT. VILLAGE INN. CLOSEUP OF MRS.
HALL.

   AS Mrs. Hall looks off in the
   direction of the bar.

        MR. HALL (offscene)
          Here's a gent wants a room
          and a fire.

   CAMERA DRAWS BACK to a THREE
   SHOT as Mrs. Hall comes forward
   surprised and flushed.
        MRS. HALL
          What? A room!

   (CONTINUED)

A-17   (CONTINUED)

                                        THE STRANGER (in a patient,
                                                level voice)
                                        I said a room.

                                        MRS. HALL (eyeing the stranger
                                                curiously)
                                        We ain't got none ready --
                                        not this time o' year. We
                                        don't usually get folks
                                        stopping except in the
                                        summer.

                CUT TO:

A-18   INT. VILLAGE INN..CLOSE PROFILE
        SHOT ON THE STRANGER
        _____

        AS he looks at Mrs. Hall, there
        is a quiet authority in his voice.

                                        THE STRANGER
                                        You can get one ready.

                CUT TO:

A-19   INT. VILLAGE INN. CLOSE SHOT
        ON MRS. HALL
        _____

        SHe looks at the stranger.

                                        MRS. HALL
                                        Certainly, sir!

        As she turns and calls thru the
        door from which she has just
        emerged, we
        CUT TO:

A-20   INT. VILLAGE INN..MEDIUM SHOT
        ON THE THREE
        _____

        All standing at the bar - Mrs.
        Hall looking off to door.

                                        MRS. HALL
                                        Milly!

                                        THE STRANGER
                                        I Want a private sitting
                                        room, too.

                                        MRS. HALL (sensing good
                                                business)
                                        Certainly, sir! -- Will you
                                        come thru, sir - this way!

        Mrs. Hall throws open the door
        in the bar and the stranger walks
        thru. The villagers, now silent,
        follow him curiously with their
        eyes.
        CUT TO:

cg   A-21   INT. HALL...FOLLOW SHOT

As the stranger followed by Mrs.
Hall comes out into the hall doorway, she closes the door, picks up
a lamp, and the stranger follows her
as she preceeds the way up a short
stairway to the door of the sitting
room. CUT TO:

A-22   INT. HALL..INTO SITTING ROOM CAMERA
        ON DOLLEY

Mrs. Hall opens the door and they
go into the sitting room. CAMERA
ENTERS WITH THEM. The usual type.
A small fireplace with ornaments
on the mantelplace - an old arm-
chair, a round table in the centre
of the room - various pieces of
furniture round the walls. The
stranger crosses to the window -
standing rigidly with his back to
the room. He still wears his hat,
and overcoat with the snow clinging
to them. Mrs. Hall goes to the fireplace, gets down on her knees, busy
laying the fire.
CUT TO:

A-23   INT. SITTING ROOM...TWO SHOT

                        MRS. HALL   (sociably)
                        It's the coldest winter
                        we've had down 'ere for
                        years. They've had all the
                        sheep and cows in for a
                        fortnight now, poor things
                        can't get a blad of green
                        grass.

She glances up, but the stranger
neither moves nor replies. Wonder-
ingly, she returns to the fire -
lights it, and rises.

CAMERA MOVES IN CLOSERS ON THE TWO

                        MRS. HALL
                        Can I take your hat and
                        coat, sir -- and give 'em
                        a good dry in the kitchen?

                        THE STRANGER (without moving)
                        No.

Mrs. Hall is so surprised that
she is not sure if she heard
aright.

CUT TO:

A-24   INT. SITTING ROOM..CLOSEUP
              STRANGER'S HEAD ..LOW CAMERA

          There is a pause, then the
          stranger slightly turns his
          head.
                                        THE STRANGER
                                            I prefer to keep them on.

          He turns back to the window.
          CUT TO:

      A-25   INT. SITTING ROOM...MEDIUM SHOT
              OF THE TWO

                                    MRS. HALL
                                        Very good, sir. The
                                        room'll be warm soon.

                                    THE STRANGER (his back to Mrs.
                                                    Hall)
                                        I've got some luggage at
                                        the station. How can I
                                        have it sent?

                                    MRS. HALL
                                        I'll get it brought over
                                        tomorrow, sir. Are you
                                        going to stay a bit?

                                    THE STRANGER
                                        Yes
                                            (pause)
                                        Is there no way of getting
                                        it tonight?

                                    MRS. HALL
                                        Not tonight, sir!

                                    THE STRANGER
                                        Very well.
                                            (another pause)
                                        You'll bring me some food?

                                    MRS. HALL
                                        Right away, sir!

          CAMERA PANS to the door with
          her as she furtively exits,
          then swings back holding the
          silent, unmoving stranger. He
          slowly puts out his gloved
          hand, and draws down the
          blind until it meets the
          curtains on the lower half
          of the curtain.
          CUT TO:

      A-26   INT. SALOON...MEDIUM SHOT

          CAMERA BEHIND BAR shooting into
          FULL SHOT of saloon. The Darts
          competition has begun again, but
          the men round the bar are discus-
          sing the stranger. They are round-
          eyed and confidential.   (CONTINUED)

                              170

A-26   (CONTINUED)

                    FIRST CUSTOMER
                         If you ask me, he's a
                         criminal - flying from
                         justice --

                    SECOND CUSTOMER (disgustedly)
                         Gar! He's snowblind --
                         that's what he is. Has to
                         wear goggles to save his
                         eyes.

                    FIRST CUSTOMER (leaning over the
                                    bar and speak-
                                    ing to Mr.Hall)
                         Anyway, you be careful -
                         and lock your money up!

A-27   INT. SALOON..MEDIUM CLOSE SHOT

         Mrs. Hall passes along behind
         the bar with a tray of supper.
         THE CAMERA FOLLOWS her to the
         door of the sitting room, which
         she nervously knocks at and opens.
         We follow her into the room.
         CUT TO:

A-28   INT. SITTING ROOM. MED. CLOSE
         AT DOOR

         She pauses by the door in surprise
         to see the stranger standing ex-
         actly as she left him; rigidly;
         his back to the room -- his eyes
         to the window.
                    MRS. HALL
                         Your supper, sir.

         CAMERA PANS with her to the
         table and takes in the stranger
         at the window. He makes no sign
         that he has heard.
                    THE STRANGER
                         Is there a key to that
                         door?

                    MRS. HALL (surprised)
                         A key, sir? I haven't
                         ever seen one. I don't
                         think there was one when
                         we came here.

                    THE STRANGER
                         I want to be left alone,
                         and undisturbed.

                    MRS. HALL
                         I'll see nobody disturbs
                         you, sir.

         CAMERA PANS with her as she
         leaves the room and closes
         the door -- then SWINGS BACK
         to the stranger.
         CUT TO:

CG   A-29   INT. SITTING ROOM..CLOSE SHOT
ON STRANGER
_____

Slowly he turns into CAMERA -
raises his gloved hand and begins to unbutton his coat, as we
CUT TO:

A-30   INT. KITCHEN...FULL SHOT
_____

Milly, an untidy servant girl,
is vigorously stirring a pot
of mustard. Mrs. Hall comes in.
Milly hastily turns and holds
out the pot.
CUT TO:

A-31   INT. KITCHEN..CLOSE SHOT MILLY
_____

                MILLY   (innocently)
        Here's the mustard, mam!

CUT TO:

A-32   INT. KITCHEN...FULL SHOT
_____

Mrs. Hall gives an exclamation
of disgust and snatches the pot.

              MRS. HALL
        You'll be the death of me,
        with your slowness! Here
        you let me take the gentle-
        man's supper in - and for-
        get the mustard! and him
        wanting to be left alone!

She turns indignantly on her
heel and bounces out of the
room.

A-33   INT. HALL...MEDIUM SHOT
_____

As Mrs. Hall carrying the
mustard enters and goes to
the sitting room door and
knocks,
CUT TO:

A-34   INT. SITTING ROOM...MED.CLOSE
AT DOOR
_____

Mrs. Hall on the threshold-stops
with an exclamation of surprise
and horror. The stranger is sitting at his supper, and the sight
of him is enough to make anyone
start back in fear.
CUT TO:

A-35   INT. SITTING ROOM..MED. CLOSE ON
STRANGER
_____

He is sitting quite still staring
at Mrs. Hall (off) thru his great
blue goggles.

CUT TO:

172

OF STRANGER

> Not a scrap of his face is visible
> save the long thin nose. His fore-
> head, cheeks and ears are swathed
> in white bandages. A mop of untidy
> brown hair escapes here and there
> from the bandages that cross the
> top of his head, and projects like
> tails and horns in all directions,
> giving him the wierdest and most
> horrifying qppearance. As we
> first see him he raises his gloved
> hand with a lightning movement and
> holds a handkerchief over his mouth
> and chin.
> CUT TO:

A-37   INT. SITTING ROOM..CLOSEUP OF MRS.
HALL

> She is transfixed with astonishment
> and fear.
> CUT TO:

A-38   INT. SITTING ROOM..MEDIUM CLOSE
SHOT OF STRANGER

> At last the stranger speaks - in
> an ominous, muffled voice.

                    THE STRANGER
               I told you not to disturb
               me.

> CUT TO:

A-39   INT. SITTING ROOM...TWO SHOT

> Mrs. Hall comes up to the table
> with the mustard.

                    MRS. HALL
               It's - it's only the
               mustard, sir. I forgot it.
               I'm sorry.

               CUT TO:

A-40   INT. SITTING ROOM..CLOSEUP ON
STRANGER

> He looks up at Mrs. Hall.

                    THE STRANGER
               Thank you.

> CUT TO:

A-41   INT. SITTING ROOM..MEDIUM
SHOT.

                    MRS. HALL
               You been motoring on them
               slippery roads, sir?

(CONTINUED)

                              THE STRANGER (without answering
                                             her question)
                                   You can take my overcoat,
                                   and dry it.

                                 MRS. HALL
                                   Very good, sir.

                              THE STRANGER
                                   Leave the hat.

                                 MRS. HALL
                                   Yes, sir.

          Mrs. Hall reaches forward and
          puts down the mustard as if she
          expects him to bite her - she
          backs away from the table, turns
          and leaves the room with alacrity.
          THE CAMERA FOLLOWS her out, then
          slowly returns to the stranger.
          He is sitting quite rigidly, glanc-
          ing over towards the door. CAMERA
          MOVES UP to CLOSE SHOT. His gloved
          hands rest on the table - the
          handkerchief no longer covers his
          mouth and chin. The bandages be-
          low his nose have been pulled down
          to enable him to eat. And where
          his mouth and chin should be there
          is nothing - just an empty space.
          The whole of his bandaged head
          seems to be supported by the tiny
          place where his hair comes down at
          the back to meet his collar.
          CUT TO:

A-42   INT. SALOON..FULL SHOT

          Mrs. Hall, breathless, comes running
          into car - and is quickly surrounded
          by the loungers at the bar - her hus-
          band stands by with his mouth open,
          she speaks tremulously and confidentially.

                                 MRS. HALL
                                   Bandages! - right up to
                                   the top of his head! All
                                   round his ears!

                              FIRST CUSTOMER (in a hoarse
                                               whisper)
                                   Any blood?

                                 MRS. HALL
                                   No - no blood. Looks like
                                   some kind of horrible ac-
                                   cident!

                              SECOND CUSTOMER (dryly)
                                   Bumped his head on the
                                   prison wall, getting over.

          He nods knowingly and spits
          as we .....
                                 FADE OUT

                                    174

SEQUENCE "B"

B-1   FADE IN:
CRANLEY'S HOME.. LIBRARY
LONG SHOT.. (DAY)

    A long comfortable furnished
library.. at one end.. in large
bow windows, there is fitted a
small scientific laboratory, a
bench with instruments and shelves
lined with bottles. DR. CRANLEY,
a distinguished looking man of
middle age, is at work by the
windows. He holds a test tube to
the light.. shakes it, and holds
it up again. He is too absorbed in
his work to hear the door open
at the library end of the room.

    CUT TO:

B-2   INT. LIBRARY.. MED. SHOT
AT DOOR

    A girl has entered. She stands
for a moment, watching the white-
coated doctor busy at his work.
FLORA CRANLEY is a beautiful girl..
dressed in outdoor costume.
She is quiet, but there is a
burning anxiety beneath her outward
control.

               FLORA
                 Father!

    CUT TO:

B-3   INT. LIBRARY.. MED.
CLOSE SHOT

    Dr. Cranley looks over his
shoulder with a frown. He speaks
with a mixture of kindness and
severity.

               DR. CRANBY
                 I wish you would leave me
                 alone, Flora, when I'm work-
                 ing.

               FLORA   (Coming into shot)
                 I can't bear it. We've got
                 to do something.

               DOCTOR   (Vaguely)
                 Do somethin.. what about?

               FLORA
                  About Jack.

    Dr. Cranley patiently
returns to his experiment.

               DOCTOR
                 He'll come back.. don't you
                 worry.

    (CONTINUED)

Flora can scarcely
control herself.

                              FLORA
                              Father! --Put that horrid
                              thing down, and listen!

Dr. Cranley lowers the test
tube in surprise and comes
over to his daughter. She
is trembling.

CAMERA MOVES IN CLOSER.

                         FLORA   (continues)
                              It's nearly a month now..
                              without a word.

                         DOCTOR   (kindly)
                              But the note he left was
                              quite clear! He said we
                              might not hear for a while.
                              It's a good thing sometimes
                              to go right away by yourself
                              when you're finishing a
                              difficult experiment.

                              FLORA
                              What kind of experiment is
                              it, Father?

                         DOCTOR   (with a shrug)
                              Something of his own.

                              FLORA
                              I had a terrible feeling
                              last night. I felt he was
                              in desperate trouble.--

Flora starts in fear..
her nerves are on edge.

CUT TO:

B-4   INT. LIBRARY..
       AT FRENCH WINDOWS

They have opened abruptly,
and a tall young man, in
the white coat of a scientist,
is standing on the threshold.
He comes in. He is good looking,
but there is an unpleasant harshness
about him. He stands looking off in
the direction of the Doctor and Flora.

                              FLO
                         DOCTOR   (offstage)
                              Hello, Kemp.
                                   (pause)
                              Flora's worried about Grif-
                              fin.

CAMERA PANS WITH KEMP
as he comes and joins the
other two.

                         KEMP   (dryly)
                              I don't wonder. I should
                              have thought at least he
                              could drop a line.

                         DOCTOR
(CONTINUED)   It's a queer thing.

B-4   (CONTINUED)

                                        KEMP   (lighting a cigarette)
                                            It certainly is. Considering
                                            he was in your employ.

                                        DOCTOR
                                            He had my permission to
                                            carry out his own experiment
                                            in his spare time.

                                        KEMP
                                            And to clear off when he
                                            liked.. for as long as he
                                            liked?

                                        FLORA   (bursting in)
                                            What does it matter!-- if
                                            he's in trouble?

    Flora turns quickly and
    leaves the room; she is on the
    verge of tears. The old Doctor
    looks after her.. perplexed and
    unhappy.

    Kemp's eyes are following Flora..
    some where in the room beyond
    the library. He turns and goes after
    her. CAMERA FOLLOWS HIM.. Flora
    is seen a little ahead of him..
    they go into the lounge.
    A tastefully furnished, comfortable
    room with big windows, that look
    out over the country. Flora cannot
    rest; she wanders over to a window
    and gazes out.

    Kemp comes over to her and stands
    by her side.
    CUT TO:

B-5   INT. LOUNGE.. MED. CLOSE ON TWO

                                        KEMP
                                            I've got the car outside,
                                            Flora. It'll be a rest to
                                            come for a run.

    Flora does not reply to his
    invitation. It seems as if
    she has not heard.

                                        FLORA
                                            Do you think there are any
                                            papers in his room to help us?
                                            He must have arranged where
                                            he was going? There may be
                                            letters.

                                        KEMP
                                            He left a heap of burnt
                                            papers in the fireplace..
                                            that's all.

        CUT TO:

                        177

B-6   (CONTINUED)

                              KEMP   (continued)
                              .. give me a chance, darl-
                              ing.. to tell you what I
CUT TO: feel! I can't work, or
                              sleep till I know...

B-7   INT. LOUNGE.. CLOSE
        SHOT.. FLORA

        As she sinks down into a
        chair. She buries her face
        in her hands and cries.

                              FLORA
                              For God's sake leave me
                              alone! -- How can you dare
                              when...

        Her words are lost in
        convulsive sobbing. CAMERA
        PANS UP TO KEMP who stands
        looking down at her.. there is
        no sympathy in his face..
        only unpleasant, rather
        sinister anger.

        DISSOLVE TO:

B-8   THE SITTING ROOM AT THE
        VILLAGE INN. FULL SHOT

        A remarkable change has taken
        place. The ornaments on the
        sideboard have given place to
        rows of bottles.. line upon line.
        Upon the table are other bottles,
        some scientific instruments of
        strange design and two large,
        open books.

        On a small table, in a corner
        beneath the lights, stands a
        delicate scientific balance of
        weights and scales and other
        instruments. Beside the table
        stands the stranger.. with his
        eerie, bandaged head and gloved
        hands. He is not wearing his
        greatcoat or hat, and the bandages
        can be seen to come right
        down, round his neck, till they
        disappear beneath his collar.
        He is very carefully stirring a
        mixture in a small glass container;
        observing its colour, and
        occasionally turning to note down
        his observations in one of the large
        books on the table behind him.
        CAMERA PANS WITH HIM as he goes
        to the window and back to the table.
        All the time he is muttering feverishly
        and incoherently to himself... only
        once are the words a little
        louder and understandable.

                                      (CONTINUED)

B-8   (CONTINUED)

                                    STRANGER
                                There's a way back, you
                                fool! -- there must be a
                                way back!

        There comes a knock at
        the door.

        CUT TO:

B-9   INT. SITTING ROOM
       MED. CLOSE SHOT STRANGER

        He starts up with an oath.

                                THE STRANGER
                                    What is it?

                            MRS. HALL (outside)
                                Your luncheon.

                                THE STRANGER (shouting)
                                    Take it away.

        CUT TO:

B-10   OUTSIDE SITTING ROOM DOOR
       MEDIUM SHOT

        Mrs. Hall with a tray in her
        hand stands listening.
                                MRS. HALL
                                    You don't want it cold, do
                                    you?

        There is a marked difference
        in Mrs. Hall's attitude. Her
        politeness and fear of the
        stranger have gone. She is
        truculent and angry.

                                MRS. HALL
                                    D'you suppose I'm going to
                                    carry trays backwards and
                                    forwards all day! Luncheon's
                                    at one.. and it's one now!

        She impatiently pushes
        the door with the tray.. but
        it opens reluctantly. A large
        chair has been placed against
        it inside the room. The stranger
        comes forward in fury.

        CUT TO:

B-11   OUTSIDE DOOR.. CLOSE TWO SHOT

                                THS STRANGER
                                    Get out I tell you!
        He viciously thrusts the
        door back with his fist.
        The tray crashes to the
        floor outside. Mrs. Hall screams
        and runs down the passage.

        CUT TO:

B-12 INT. SITTING ROOM
MEDIUM SHOT

    CAMERA PANS WITH STRANGER
     back to the table. He is
     quivering with fury.

                                    THE STRANGER
                                    My God! Why can't they
                                    leave me alone!

    He holds up the glass con-
    tainer he has been stirring;
    the mixture has gone cloudy.
    He holds it above him.
                                    ... and a day's work ruined by
                                    a damnable, ignorant woman!

    He crashes the container
    into a corner of the room
    and sinks into a chair with
    his hands clutching his head.

    CAMERA MOVES SWIFTLY UP TO A
    CLOSE UP
                                    ...there's a way back..
                                    God knows there's a way
                                    back.. if only they'd leave
                                    me alone!

    CUT TO:

B-13 INT. SALOON BAR
FULL SHOT

    SHOOTING TOWARD THE BAR.
    Mrs. Hall, crimson with
    indignation, is pouring out her
    anger to a sympathetic circle
    of customers around her. Her
    husband stands by with his
    mouth open.
                                MRS. HALL
                                He's not goin' to stay
                                under this roof another
                                hour! Crashed the tray out
                                of me hand and swore at me..
                                turns my best sitting room
                                into a chemist's shop..
                                spills it on the carpets..
                                and a week behind with his
                                money!
                                    (she swings around on
                                    her husband)
                                Go and tell him now. Tell
                                'im if he isn't packed up
                                and gone in half an hour
                                we'll have the law in to
                                turn him out.. and take 'is
                                bill, too.. three pounds
                                ten.. and see you get it
                                before you come out!

    She thrusts the bill into
    Mr. Hall's nervous hands
    and gives him a shove to-
    wards the stranger's room.
    Mr. Hall proceeds anxiously
    for a few steps and suddenly
    turns with an appealing face.

    CUT TO:

                                180

B-14   INT. SALOON CLOSE
       TWO SHOT

    On Mr. and Mrs. Hall.

                    MR. HALL
                    Let's leave him a bit,
                    Janny... till he cools off.

                    MRS. HALL
                    Go on.. do it now! Him and
                    his goggles and his chemist
                    shop! If you don't kick
                    him out.. I'm clearing out
                    meself.. and that's the
                    truth!

    Mr. Hall reluctantly goes on.
    CAMERA FOLLOWS HIM THROUGH
    DOOR AND UP THE STAIRS.
    He pauses at the door and
    timidly knocks. There is no
    reply. Mr. Hall looks surprised,
    then slowly pushes the door and goes
    in.

    CUT TO:

B-15   INT. SITTING ROOM
       MEDIUM SHOT

    The stranger is sitting as we
    left him.. his head in his hands..
    a pathetic picture of despair.
    Mr. Hall comes up to the table;
    fidgets, clears his throat and
    speaks..

                    MR. HALL
                    Look 'ere, Mister. We can't
                    'ave this no more. You've
                    broke the wife's best china
                    and you're a week behind in
                    the rent. You got to pack
    CUT TO: up and go.

B-16   INT. SITTING ROOM.
       CLOSE UP

    The Stranger raises his head.
    He is eyeing Mr. Hall queerly
    and rigidly thru his great
    blue goggles. There is something
    pitiful, and broken about him...
    his masterful manner has gone.

                    THE STRANGER
                    I'm expecting some money,
                    Mr. Hall. I'll pay you di-
                    rectly it comes.

                    MR. HALL   (offstage)
                    You said that last week..
                    and it hasn't come.

    (CONTINUED)

B-16   CONTINUED

                                          THE STRANGER
                                              I came here for quiet -
                                              and secrecy. I'm carrying
                                              out a difficult experi-
                                              ment. I must be left
                                              alone. It's vital - it's
                                              life and death that I
                                              should be left alone. You
                                              don't understand!

B-17   INT SITTING ROOM. MED CLOSE
        TWO SHOT

        The quiet, pleading manner
        of the stranger makes Mr. Hall
        bolder.

                                          MR. HALL
                                              I understand all right!
                                              You don't pay and what's
                                              more, you're driving folks
                                              away from our house!

                                          THE STRANGER
                                              I've had a serious accident.
                                              It's disfigured me - affect-
                                              ed my eyes.

                                          MR. HALL
                                              I don't mean that. I mean
                                              the way you carry on -
                                              throwing stuff on the car-
                                              pets and swearing. It's no
                                              good, mister, you gotter
                                              go.

B-18   INT SITTING ROOM.
        CLOSEUP STRANGER

        Looking up at Mr. Hall
        pleadingly.

                                          THE STRANGER
                                              I implore you to let me
                                              stay! I beg of you! --

B-19   INT SITTING ROOM. CLOSE
        SHOT MR. HALL

                                          MR. HALL
                                              The wife says if you don't
                                              go she is, so it's gotter
                                              be you.

        CAMERA DRAWS BACK to a
        MED SHOT as he comes forward
        to collect the books and in-
        struments on the table.

                                              Come on. I'll help you
                                              get the stuff packed up.

        The stranger leaps from
        his chair in sudden fury.

                                          THE STRANGER
                                              Leave that alone!

        (CONTINUED)

B-19   CONTINUED

          Mr. Hall starts back,
          astonished.

                                        THE STRANGER (Cont'd)
                                          -- and get out of here!

                                        MR. HALL   (blustering)
                                          Look 'ere - is this my
                                          house or yours?
          Mr. Hall proceeds to
          pick up the books; a mania-
          cal fury sweeps over the
          stranger. He rushes forward
          and strikes Mr. Hall a terrific
          blow that sends him reeling onto
          the floor in a corner.

B-20   INT SITTING ROOM. MED LONG SHOT

          HIGH CAMERA SHOOTING DOWN. He
          is over him in a second; he seizes
          the little struggling, shouting
          man by the waist and flings him
          brutally into the passage. He
          crashes the door to, and stands
          sobbing and groaning with his whole
          weight against it. Mr. Hall is heard
          shrieking outside.

B-21   INT PASSAGE. MED SHOT

          SHOOTING DOWN FROM STAIRS.
          Mr.Hall lies prostrate on the floor.
          Mrs. Hall is wailing and crying on
          her knees beside him. A crowd of
          gaping villagers is peering at the
          astonishing sight.

                                        A VILLAGER
                                          Gawd! He's a raving
                                          lunatic!
          A tall, gaunt countryman
          has knelt down beside Mr.
          Hall.

B-22   INT PASSAGE. CLOSEUP MAN

          He raises his head to the
          crowd.

                                        MAN
                                          Go and get the policeman.

B-23   EXT INN. FULL SHOT

          A crowd of curious sight-
          seers has collected, attracted
          by Mrs. Hall's screams. A man
          comes out of the Inn and glances
          around.

                                                    (CONTINUED)

B-23   CONTINUED

> THE MAN
> Here! Go and find Jaffers,
> and tell him to bring his
> handcuffs. There's a mad-
> man inside.

> A VOICE
> What! The bloke with
> goggles?

> ANOTHER VOICE
> I said he was off his nut!

> ANOTHER VOICE
> Here's Jaffers coming now.

B-24   EXT INN. MED CLOSE SHOT

A stout, solid policeman
pompously advancing down the
village street. He hears a
voice call - "Here, Jaffers!
Come along here!" Jaffers
advances and joins the crowd
outside the inn.

> JAFFERS   (officially)
> What's all this?

The gaunt man comes out
of the inn.

> GAUNT MAN
> That stranger with the
> goggles. He's gone mad.
> Assaulted Mrs. Hall and
> damn near killed her hus-
> band.

Jaffers looks perturbed.

> JAFFERS
> Where is he?

> GAUNT MAN
> In the sitting room.

Jaffers solidly enters
the inn - the crowd surge
in after him.

B-25   INT SALOON. FULL SHOT

Mr. Hall has been raised to
a chair; he is dazed, but con-
scious. There is a bad cut over
his eye which his wife is dab-
bing with a handkerchief. Jaffers
comes in, pauses apprehensively.
Mrs. Hall turns excitedly and
points to the sitting room door.

> MRS. HALL
> He's in there -- in the
> sitting room! He's homi-
> cidal!

(CONTINUED)

B-25   (CONTINUED

  Jaffers looks still more
  worried. He does not relish
  the job at all. CAMERA PANS
  ACROSS taking Jaffers thru
  the door towards the hall, as
  he slowly goes, followed by a
  little group of villagers.

B-26   INT PASSAGE. MED SHOT

  shooting over the backs of the
  people on Jaffers, as he goes
  up the stairs to the door of
  the sitting room.

B-27   INT PASSAGE. MED CLOSE SHOT

  on Jaffers as he takes the handle,
  slowly turns it, and goes in.

B-28   INT SITTING ROOM. MED CLOSE
   SHOT STRANGER

  The stranger is standing by
  the table. He is calm now, quiet
  and ominous.

B-29   INT SITTING ROOM. MED SHOT

  There is something so uncanny
  in the stranger's appearance
  that Jaffers pauses, irresolute.
  Numerous heads are peering into
  the room behind him.

        JAFFERS
         Here. What's all this?

       THE STRANGER (commandingly)
         Keep back there!

        JAFFERS
         Keep back! Who d'you
         think you're talking to!

       THE STRANGER
         I give you a last chance -
         to leave me alone!

B-30   INT SITTING ROOM. MED CLOSE

  on Jaffers and group at door.

        JAFFERS
         Give me a chance, eh!
         You've committed assault--
         that's what you've done! --
         And you can just come
         along with me to the
         station.

        (CONTINUED)

B-30   CONTINUED

As the stranger does
not move, Jaffers takes
a step forward.

                                JAFFERS
                      Come on! Better come
                      quietly - unless you want
                      the handcuffs on.

B-31   INT SITTING ROOM
        MED SHOT LOW CAMERA

The stranger rises to his
full height - there is tremendous, ominous power in
him.

                                THE STRANGER
                      Stop where you are! --
                      You don't know what you're
                      doing!

CUT TO:

IH   B-32   INT. SITTING ROOM
            MED. LONG SHOT ON GROUP

            Jaffers despite himself is
            awed. He shuffles.

                                        JAFFERS
                                        I know what I'm doing
                                        all right -- come on.

                                        VOICES FROM CROWD
                                        Get hold of him!
                                        Put him in gaol!

            They surge forward.

            CUT TO:

     B-33   INT. SITTING ROOM
            MED. CLOSE ON STRANGER

                                        THE STRANGER
                                        All right, you fools!
                                        You've brought it on
                                        yourselves! Everything
                                        would have come right
                                        if you'd left me alone.
                                        You've driven me near
                                        madness with your
                                        peering thru keyholes
                                        and gaping thru the
                                        curtains! And now
                                        you'll suffer for it.

            He pauses.
            CUT TO:

     B-34   INT. SITTING ROOM
            MEDIUM SHOT (CLOSE)

            Jaffers, with the little group
            behind him, is rooted to the
            ground by the outburst. The
            stranger gives a fierce, de-
            risive laugh.

            CUT TO:

     B-35   MEDIUM SHOT STRANGER

                                        THE STRANGER
                                        You're crazy to know
                                        who I am -- aren't you?
                                        All right then! I'll
                                        show you!

            CAMERA MOVES SWIFTLY IN and
            FOCUSES on his gloved hand as he
            raises it up to his nose -- CAMERA
            PANS UP TO HIS FACE - he lowers
            his hand with the nose between
            his fingers, and throws it at the
            foot of the policeman.

                                        -- there's a souvenir
                                        for you!

            CUT TO:

                              187

B-36   MEDIUM SHOT ON GROUP

There is a gasp of horror
from the group. They stand
gazing in amazement at the
nose on the ground before and
slowly raise their heads to the
stranger.

CUT TO:

B-37   CLOSEUP ON STRANGER

He removes his glasses and
throws them in front of the man
beside the policeman.

                         THE STRANGER
                              -- and one for you.

No eyes look out from be-
neath; a hideous cavity.

CUT TO:

B-38   INT. SITTING ROOM
         CLOSEUP .... MAN

There are gasps of horror;
someone whispers.

                    MAN
                         Gawd! -- he's all eaten
                         away!

CUT TO:

B-39   MED. SHOT ON ... STRANGER

The stranger's hands go to
his head and begin to unwind
the bandages - his voice sweeps
over the shivering group that
shrinks towards the door.

                         THE STRANGER
                              I'll show you who I am --
                              and what I am.

He tears off his matted wig,
then roll after roll of the
bandages fall away - revealing
emptiness beneath. At last
there is nothing but a headless
man beside the table - and a
loud diabolical laugh.

CUT TO:

B-40   INT. SITTING ROOM...MED. SHOT
         GROUP

There are shrieks from the crowd,
then panic and a mad rush to get
from the room

CUT TO:

B-41   FRONT DOOR OF THE INN
        MED. LONG SHOT

        of people rushing out - shouting
        and crying.

        CUT TO:

B-42   INT. SITTING ROOM...MED. CLOSE
        STRANGER

        of the headless stranger shaking
        with mad laughter by the table.

        CUT TO:

B-43   INT. SALOON...MED. SHOT

        on Jaffers, the policeman who,
        with two or three more courageous
        villagers, stand in the saloon.

                              JAFFERS
                        He's invisible! That's
                        what's the matter with 'im.
                        If he gets them other
                        clothes off we'll never
                        catch him in a thousand
                        years! Come on!

        The men rush towards the
        sitting room.

        CUT TO:

B-44   INT. SITTING ROOM...MED. SHOT
        ON STRANGER

        SHOW here, as far as can be
        devised, the stranger undressing
        himself. His coat should slip
        to the ground - revealing a head-
        less figure in shirt and trousers...

        CUT TO:

B-45   CLOSE SHOT

        ...the trousers slip down onto
        the floor revealing nothing re-
        maining in the air, but a shirt.

        (NOTE: I suggest that trick photo-
        graphy be employed here as far as
        possible with the aid of invisible
        wire frames minipulated by the
        marionette method. Exact details
        depend upon the extent to which
        these methods - or other methods -
        oan be employed.)

        CUT TO:

B-46   INT. SITTING ROOM
MED. SHOT ON... (CLOSE)

The policeman, with his two
companions, burst into the room
and stand transfixed at...

CUT TO:

B-47   CLOSE SHOT ON...

the sight of a shirt bobbing
about behind the table, cutting
fantastic capers.

CUT BACK TO:

B-48   INT. SITTING ROOM
MED. SHOT ON...:.(CLOSE)

the three men.

                         A VILLAGER
                              Put the handcuffs on!

                         JAFFERS (indignantly)
                              How can I handcuff a blooming
                              shirt?

                         VILLAGER
                              Quick! - Get hold of it!

CAMERA DRAWS BACK as he
darts forward. There is a
hoarse laugh from the emptiness
as the shirt moves away. The
man grasps hold of the tail of
the shirt; it writhes and falls
to the floor as the Invisible
Man slips out of it. The room
is empty, save for the scattered
clothing of the Invisible Man - the
gasping policeman; the villagers
standing round as if in a dream,
and the men helplessly grasping
the shirt tail. A calm, strong
voice comes from the corner.

                         THE VOICE
                              Are you satisfied now, you
                              fools?

There is a moment of silence.
The policeman and villagers do
not move. The voice comes again
as the CAMERA MOVES searching
for the stranger - CAMERA   ---It's easy, really - if
FOCUSES on corner as if finding   you're clever. A few
him. A curtain moves as if   chemicals mixed to-
brushed by someone; also a   gether - that's all.
plant of flowers moves as   And flesh and blood
stranger apparently passes by.   and bone just fade
                                     away.

CUT TO:

B-49   INT. SITTING ROOM
         MED. CLOSE SHOT ON....

         A drawer opens and a bottle
         rises from it - as it would
         if a man were holding it.

                                    THE VOICE
                              A little of this injected
                              under the skin of the arm -
                              every day for a month. Only
                              one man in the world was
                              clever enough to find it;
                              no one else ever knew.

         The bottle falls and the
         CAMERA PANS to the floor.

         CUT TO:

B-50   SITTING ROOM...MED. SHOT ON

         We see a chair move as if the
         stranger is moving about.

                                    THE VOICE
                              An Invisible Man can rule
                              the world; nobody will see
                              him come - and nobody will
                              see him go! He can hear
                              every secret - he can rob,
                              and wreck and kill -

         CUT TO:

B-51   INT. SITTING ROOM
         MED. CLOSE ON...

         the group of men; huddled
         together - terrified.

                                    JAFFERS
                              Not if he gets no further
                              than this room he won't!

         He swings round to one of
         the villagers.

                              Here! Shut that door!
                                 (turns round and speaks
                                  to the emptiness)
                              Now then, you come along
                              quietly!

         There is no answer but a
         derisive laugh. There is
         silence - then suddenly...

         CUT TO:

B-52   SITTING ROOM
         CLOSE SHOT ON....

         the window shoots up. The
         policeman dashes across.

                                    JAFFERS
                              Look out! Mind that window!

         (CONTINUED)

B-52   (CONTINUED)

          He swings round as a laugh
        - comes from another corner
          of the room.

                                    THE INVISIBLE MAN
                                         You think I'd escape like
                                         a common criminal!

          The voice comes nearer -
          slowly and thoughtfully.

                                         You need a lesson. I think
                                         I'll throttle you.

          CUT TO:

B-53   SITTING ROOM..CLOSEUP ON...

          There is a moment of silence.
          The policeman stands bewildered
          by the window. Suddenly he
          raises his hands to his throat
          and screams. The voice of the
          Invisible Man comes close to the
          policeman's face.

                                    INVISIBLE MAN
                                         You must be made to under-
                                         stand what I can do.
          QUICK CUT TO:

B-54   MED. SHOT ON....

          one of the villagers at first
          too terrified to move - then he
          dashes forward and doubles up
          with a groan as he receives a
          kick in the stomach. The police-
          man's knees sag - he drops to the
          ground.

          QUICK CUT TO:

B-55   MED. SHOT ON....

          a villager by the door suddenly
          crashes back against it with a
          cry of terror and falls sideways,
          bringing down a table. The door
          flies open.

          QUICK CUT TO:

B-56   PASSAGE OUTSIDE OF SITTING ROOM

          Mrs. Hall and a shaky Mr. Hall
          are standing by - waiting for news.
          They see the door open, and then
          the coat rack crashes over as the
          Invisible Man rushes by. Mrs. Hall
          screams.

          CUT TO:

B-57   INT. SALOON...MED. SHOT

    of the bar as people are thrown
    back and glasses are swept from
    the bar with a crash.

    QUICK CUT TO:

B-58   EXT. INN...MED. LONG SHOT

    A crowd of gaping sightseers,
    standing by. The door of the
    Inn flies open. No one moves
    for a moment - then the whole
    crowd collapses outwards as the
    Invisible Man strikes a passage,
    between them. There are cries
    of terror.

    QUICK CUT TO:

B-59   EXT. STREET

    A woman with a pram. The pram
    suddenly flies sideways and
    collapses in the road.

    QUICK CUT TO:

B-60   EXT. ROAD

    An ancient villager; whose hat
    suddenly shoots off his head
    into a pond.

    QUICK CUT TO:

B-61   SHOT OF....

    A stone rising from the ground -
    and a window crashing.

    (NOTE: The following shots are
    taken with great rapidity to show
    vividly the spreading of a panic.)

    QUICK CUT TO:

B-62   EXT. STREET...LONG SHOT ON..

    a crowd of villagers racing panic-
    stricken down the street - shouting
    incoherently.
                    VOICES
                    Look out!
                    Get indoors!

    QUICK CUT TO:

B-63   SHOT OF....

    a woman snatching up a child
    and running into her house,
    slamming the door.

    QUICK CUT TO:

B-64   SHOT OF...

    a man, in a small jeweller shop,
    feverishly shovelling his goods -
    (watches, rings, etc.) from their
    show case into a safe. His wife
    is helping him.

    QUICK CUT TO:

B-65   SHOT OF....

    a man standing against the
    pavement with a bicycle.
    Suddenly the bicycle is snatched
    by invisible hands and peddles
    off by itself down the road.

    QUICK CUT TO:

B-66   EXT. STREET
    MED. SHOT ON.....

    People staring in open-mouthed
    wonderment as the bicycle goes
    by. Someone shouts:

                   VOICE
                   It's him....the Invisible
                   Man!

    There are shouts - some of
    anger, some of terror. Some
    people rush away - others more
    courageous dash after the reced-
    ing bicycle.

    QUICK CUT TO:

B-67   STEEP HILL OUTSIDE VILLAGE

    The bicycle comes in sight - runs
    at the hill, then wobbles and
    slows down. The men behind gain
    upon it, shouting:

                   MEN
                   Come on! We've got him
                   now!
    CUT TO:

B-68   EXT. HILL...MED. SHOT..

    Suddenly the bicycle rises
    from the ground and is flung
    back into the midst of the pur-
    suers. Some are thrown to the
    ground, injured. The others
    break and run, panic-stricken.

    CUT TO:

B-69   INT. VILLAGE INN.
CLOSE SHOT ON....

Jaffe s, exhausted, but still
game - telephoning from the Inn.

JAFFERS
On the Gospel it's the
truth! -- Tried to strangle
me, sir!

CUT TO:

B-70   INT. POLICE STATION CLOSE
SHOT ON....

Police Inspector Bird, a thick
set mustached, stupid bully,
sitting in the station, reply-
ing to the telephone call.

INSPECTOR BIRD
Where are you speaking from,
Jaffers? From the Lion's
Head Inn? Did you say an
'Invisible Man?' -- Well,
look here - you put more
water in it next time!

CUT BACK TO:

B-71   INT. VILLAGE INN..CLOSE SHOT ON

Jaffers, handing the telephone
to Mr. Hall, the Innkeeper, in
despair.

JAFFERS
He won't believe me -- you
tell him!

CUT TO:

B-72   A CITY STREET

A newsboy - running - calling
out:

NEWSBOY
All about the Invisible Man-
Special! Invisible Maniac-
Special!

People buy papers - and
stand still - reading.

FADE OUT

SEQUENCE 'C'

FADE IN:

C-1   INT. LABORATORY
      LONG SHOT...LATE AFTERNOON

HIGH CAMERA. A small laboratory which belongs to Dr.
Cranley and was used by Jack
Griffin before his disappearance. It stands in the grounds
of Dr. Cranley's house.

Dr. Cranley and Dr. Kemp are
searching through papers and
books that lie scattered on a
long table. Behind them down
the center of the room runs a
bench, fitted with the usual
instruments of a scientist's
work. CAMERA FOLLOWS THEM DOWN
the long table as they search.

> DR. CRANLEY
> Not the slightest clue.

As they reach the fire-
place, we...
CUT TO:

C-2   INT. LABORATORY
      MED. SHOT...SIDE ANGLE

Dr. Cranley standing by the
stove. - Kemp comes into shot
- pokes the fireplace with his
stick. It is filled with burnt
papers.

> KEMP   (dryly)
> Didn't expect there would
> be. That's where the
> clues are - he wasn't
> leaving anything to chance.

> DR. CRANLEY
> Griffin was never a man
> for secrets. He came to
> me with everything.

C-3   INT. LABORATORY
      MED. CLOSE SHOT ON...

Kemp and including a large
empty cupboard, which Kemp
turns and points at...

> KEMP
> He kept a lot of stuff
> locked in there. I came
> in one evening - when
> he didn't expect me...

(CONTINUED)

C-3   (CONTINUED)

                                        KEMP   (continued)
                                           ...he was standing by this
                                           cupboard - it was full of
                                           instruments. When he saw
                                           me he slammed the door and
                                           turned the key.

          CUT TO:

C-4   INT. LABORATORY
        MED. SHOT ON...

        Dr. Cranley who has wandered
        away. He shakes his head; is
        restlessly searching amongst
        the instruments on the table.

                                        DR. CRANLEY
                                           You say he brought a pack-
                                           ing case up here in his
                                           car?

                                        KEMP   (coming into shot)
                                           The night before he dis-
                                           appeared. I heard him
                                           hammering - packing every-
                                           thing up.

        Dr. Cranley does not reply.
        CUT TO:

C-5   INT. LABORATORY
        MED. CLOSE ON...

        Dr. Cranley - he has
        come upon a fragment of
        papers beneath an earthen-
        ware jar on the laboratory
        bench, or high shelf.
                                        DR. CRANLEY
                                                (eagerly fumbling
                                                 for his glasses)
                                           Here's something, Kemp!
                                                (he flicks some dust
                                                 off with his fin-
                                                 gers)

          CUT TO:

C-6   INT. LABORATORY
        CLOSE UP ON...

        Dr. Cranley, his glasses are
        on; he peers at the paper;
        slowly, as he reads, the eager-
        ness on his face changes to
        consternation and fear. He low-
        ers his hand to his side and
        looks up at Kemp in silence.
        CUT TO:

C-7   INT. LABORATORY
          CLOSE SHOT ON...

g
h
r

          Kemp and Dr. Cranley -
          as Cranley looks up at
          Kemp...

                              KEMP
                                What is it?

          Dr. Cranley does not
          reply.

                                ...Bad news?

                            DR. CRANLEY
                                (slowly)
                            It's only a rough note. A
                            list of chemicals. The
                            last on the list is -
                            Monocane.

                            KEMP
                            Monocane? What _is_ mono-
                            cane?

                          DR. CRANLEY
                            Monocane's - a terrible
                            drug.

                          KEMP
                            I've never heard of it.
                              (his vanity as a
                              scientist is hurt
                              by his ignorance)

          CUT TO:

C-8   INT. LABORATORY
          MED. CLOSE ON...

          Kemp and Dr. Cranley.
          Dr. Cranley leans against
          bench, wearily.

                          DR. CRANLEY
                            You wouldn't, Kemp. It's
                            never used now. I didn't
                            know it was even made.
                            It's a drug that comes
                            from a flower that grows
                            in India. It draws color
                            from everything it touch-
                            es. Years ago it was tried
                            for bleaching cloth. They
                            gave it up because it de-
                            stroyed the material.

                          KEMP
                            That doesn't sound very
                            terrible.

          CUT TO:

C-9   INT. LABORATORY
          CLOSE UP ON...

          Dr. Cranley -

                          DR. CRANLEY
                            I know. But it does some-
                            thing else, Kemp. It was
                            tried on some poor animal
                            - a dog, I believe. It

          (CONTINUED)

C-9   (CONTINUED)

                                        DR. CRANLEY
                                            (continued)
                                        was injected under the
                                        skin; it turned the dog
                                        dead white, like a marble
                                        statue.

                                    KEMP   (offscene)
                                        Is that so?

                                    DR. CRANLEY
                                        Yes. It also sent it
                                        raving mad.

              CUT TO:

C-10   INT. LABORATORY
        MED. SHOT

        There is a long silence.
        The two men stand facing
        one another. Kemp's jaunty
        manner has left him when
        he speaks again...
                                    KEMP
                                        - You sure don't think? -
        Dr. Cranley breaking in;
        his voice is level and
        controlled...
                                    DR. CRANLEY
                                        I only pray to God that
                                        Griffin hasn't been med-
                                        dling with this ghastly
                                        stuff.

                                    KEMP
                                        He'd never touch a thing
                                        with madness in it.

        CAMERA PANS
        as Dr. Cranley walks
        over to the cupboard.
                                    DR. CRANLEY
                                        He might not know. I found
                                        that experiment in an old
                                        German book just by chance.
                                        The English books only
                                        describe the bleaching
                                        power; they were printed
                                        before the German exper-
                                        iment.

        Dr. Cranley is staring at
        the empty cupboard as if
        trying to read its secret.
        At last he turns abruptly as
        Kemp comes into the shot.

        (NOTE: Possibly bring them
        out here and have the follow-
        ing dialogue walking across
        the lawn.)
                                    KEMP
                                        What are we going to do,
                                        Doctor?

        (CONTINUED)

C-10   (CONTINUED)

                                    DR. CRANLEY
                                  I think we must tell the
                                  police - that Griffin's
                                  disappeared - only that
                                  he's disappeared. I put
                                  you on your honour, Kemp,
                                  - not to breathe a word
                                  of this - to anyone.

        They go to the door.
        CUT TO:

C-11   INT. LABORATORY
       CLOSE SHOT ON...

        Dr. Cranley and Kemp stand-
        ing at the door. The old
        Doctor holds out the little
        fragment; then silently he
        drops it into his pocketbook.
        CAMERA PANS DOWN to pocket-
        book as he does so.
        CUT TO:

C-12   INT. LABORATORY
       MED. SHOT ON...

        Dr. Cranley and Kemp at
        door.

                                    KEMP
                                  Shall I come down to the
                                  station with you?

                                    DR. CRANLEY
                                  It's all right, Kemp.
                                  I'll go tonight - when
                                  Inspector Lane's on duty.

                                    KEMP
                                  I'll get along back home
                                  then. Goodnight.

                                    DR. CRANLEY
                                  Goodnight.

        Kemp goes out.
        Dr. Cranley stands
        thoughtfully gazing
        after him.

                        FADE OUT.

"THE INVISIBLE MAN"

SEQUENCE "D"

FADE IN:

D-1   INT. SITTING ROOM IN DR. KAMP'S HOUSE..
       LONG SHOT..NIGHT

       A tastefully furnished old-
       fashioned room with large French
       windows opening on to a dark lawn.

       Kemp is sitting smoking by the fire,
       reading a book by the light of a lamp
       beside him. He has a whiskey and soda
       by his side. The wireless is playing
       soft, but cheerful music in the opposite
       corner.

                                    SOUND: MUSIC

       CUT TO:

D-2   INT. SITTING ROOM..AT WINDOWS

       Very slowly the French windows
       are seen to open - scarcely more
       than a foot. They remain open for
       a moment, then softly close again.

       CUT TO:

D-3   INT. SITTING ROOM..MED. SHOT ON..

       Kemp seated with his back to the
       windows - (unsuspecting) and does
       not see the strange phenomenon,
       but the draught slightly sways the
       silk draping of the mantle-piece.
       He looks up, puzzled - turns to the
       windows that have closed again, and
       after a moment settles down to his
       book once more. The wireless music
       has stopped. There is a short silence,
       then the voice of the announces comes:

                       ANNOUNCER
                 This is the National Station
                 broadcasting this evening's news.
                 Remarkable story from country
                 Village. The police amd doctors
                 are investigating an atonishing
                 story told this afternoon by the
                 people of the Village of Iping. It
                 appears that a mysterious disease
                 has broken out infecting a large
CAMERA MOVES UP   number of the inhabitants.   It
UNTIL WE HOLD A   takes the form of a delusion that
CLOSE UP on KEMP   an Invisible Man is living among
during the an-   them. Several people have been se-
nouncing.   riously injured, probably through
                 fighting among themselves in their
                 belief that their opponent is an
                 Invisible Man. The whole village
                 is in a state of panic and every-
                 one --

       CUT TO:

D-4   INT. SITTING ROOM...CLOSE UP
       ON WIRELESS

     The wireless set showing the
     dial, which is seen to turn
     softly over - and there is
     silence.
     CUT TO:

D-5   INT. SITTING ROOM...MED SHOT ON..

     Dr. Kemp looks across in surprise.
     He is about to rise when he is
     startled by a low, unpleasant laugh.
     Then a voice, the voice of the In-
     visible Man, takes up the story cut
     short by the silent radio.

                 INVISIBLE MAN
                 - and everyone deserves the
                 fate that's coming to
                 them. Panic - death -
                 things worse than death -

     CAMERA MOVES IN TO CLOSE
     SHOT as if the Invisible Man
     gets nearer. There is a low
     horrible chuckle. Then silence.
     Kemp sits rooted to his chair
     in astonishment. Then the
     voice comes again, softly:
                 - don't be afraid, Kemp.
                 It's me, Griffin, Jack
                 Griffin. How are you, my
                 friend.

     He thumps Kemp on shoulder or
     ruffles his hair. Kemp passes
     his hand across his forehead as
     if to clear a ghastly dream.
     Then the Invisible Man speaks
     again:
                 I'm frozen with cold - dead
                 tired. Thank God for a
                 fire.

     Kemp sits petrified as...we
     CUT TO:

D-6   INT. SITTING ROOM...MED CLOSE ON..

     ...the rocking armchair opposite
     trundles up to the fire. Then
     a dent appears in the soft back
     of the chair as the Invisible Man
     sits down.
     CUT TO:

D-7   INT. STUDY...MED CLOSE ON...KEMP

     A wave of horror sweeps over Kemp
     as the realization comes. With a
     hoarse cry he springs up and retreats
     to the opposite wall. He is panting
     for breath - speechless with fear.
     The voice rings out, harshly and
     impatiently.
                 INVISIBLE MAN
                 Sit down, you fool! - and
     CUT TO: let's have a decent fire.

D-13   CONTINUED

                  comes forth - all as if the
                  Invisible Man were smoking.
                  Then the voice comes again:

                              INVISIBLE MAN
                        You always were a dirty
                        little coward, Kemp.
                        You're frightened out of
                        your wits, aren't you.
                        It's no good talking like
                        this.

                CUT TO:

D-14   INT. STUDY...TWO SHOT ON...

                  Kemp and the rocking chair -
                  Kemp makes no reply. The
                  chair leans forward.

                              INVISIBLE MAN
                        Have you got a good long
                        surgical bandage?

                  Kemp nods in a dazed
                  way.
                        - Good. And the dark
                        glasses you wear for X-Ray
                        work?

                  Kemp nods again.
                        All right. Go and get
                        them at once, and let me
                        have a dressing gown and
                        pajamas - and a pair of
                        gloves. You'll feel
                        better if you can see me -
                              (pause)
                        - won't you?

                  The chair opposite Kemp
                  is thrust back - CAMERA
                  PANS to the door, which opens,
                  and the voice barks out
                  again.
                        - Come on! We've no time
                        to waste!

                CUT TO:

D-15   INT. STUDY...MED SHOT

                  SHOOTING THRU DOOR FROM
                  OUT SIDE...
                  Kemp tries to pull himself
                  together. He rises unsteadily
                  and creeps to the door. He
                  goes out, and the door closes
                  behind him.
                  WIPE OFF TO:

nn   D-8   INT. STUDY...MED SHOT ON..

> The rocking chair rocks as
> if a man had risen from it,
> then a log rises from the box by
> the fireplace, hovers in midair,
> then settles with a splutter on
> the fire. The voice barks out
> again - viciously.

> > INVISIBLE MAN
> > D'you hear me! - sit down!
> > Unless you want me to
> > knock your brains out.

QUICK CUT TO:

D-9   INT. STUDY...CLOSE UP ON...

> Quick flash of Kemp too terror
> stricken to move. There is
> silence, then off-stage we
> hear:

> > Sit down! - or by God,
> > I'll --

QUICK CUT TO:

D-10   CLOSE SHOT

> The heavy poker rises men-
> acingly from the hearth.
> CUT TO:

D-11   INT. STUDY...MED SHOT ON...
          KEMP

> He creeps back in terror to
> his chair. The Invisible Man
> speaks again - calmly, but
> ominously.

> > INVISIBLE MAN   (off-scene)
> > I want you to listen care-
> > fully, Kemp. I've been
> > through hell today. I
> > want food - and sleep.
> > But before we sleep there's
> > work to do.

> The voice dies away. Kemp
> is huddled in his chair.
> CUT TO:

D-12   INT. STUDY...CLOSE UP ON...
          KEMP

> He is far too panic stricken
> to do anything but stare with
> protruding eyes at the empty
> chair opposite him. We feel
> that Invisible eyes are upon
> him, considering him - weighing
> him up.
> CUT TO:

D-13   INT. STUDY...MED CLOSE ON...

> The rocking chair as Kemp sees.
> A cigarette lifts out of box -
> match is extended in mid-air,
> cigarette is lighted and smoke

> CONTINUED

                      comes forth - all as if the
                      Invisible Man were smoking.
                      Then the voice comes again:

                                                    INVISIBLE MAN
                                               You always were a dirty
                                               little coward, Kemp.
                                               You're frightened out of
                                               your wits, aren't you.
                                               It's no good talking like
                                               this.

                      CUT TO:

D-14   INT. STUDY...TWO SHOT ON...

                      Kemp and the rocking chair -
                      Kemp makes no reply. The
                      chair leans forward.

                                                    INVISIBLE MAN
                                               Have you got a good long
                                               surgical bandage?

                      Kemp nods in a dazed
                      way.
                                               - Good. And the dark
                                               glasses you wear for X-Ray
                                               work?

                      Kemp nods again.
                                               All right. Go and get
                                               them at once, and let me
                                               have a dressing gown and
                                               pajamas - and a pair of
                                               gloves. You'll feel
                                               better if you can see me -
                                                    (pause)
                                               - won't you?

                      The chair opposite Kemp
                      is thrust back - CAMERA
                      PANS to the door, which opens,
                      and the voice barks out
                      again.
                                               - Come on! We've no time
                                               to waste!

                      CUT TO:

D-15   INT. STUDY...MED SHOT

                      SHOOTING THRU DOOR FROM
                      OUT SIDE...
                      Kemp tries to pull himself
                      together. He rises unsteadily
                      and creeps to the door. He
                      goes out, and the door closes
                      behind him.
                      WIPE OFF TO:

nn   D-16   INT. PASSAGE

A small room or cupboard in a
dark passage in Kemp's house
used for medical stores. Kemp
still dazed and trembling,
takes a large roll of surgical
bandages from a cupboard, and a
pair of rubber gloves. Then he
takes up a pair of dark glasses
and leaves the room. We follow
him down a short passage to the
bedroom.
CUT TO:

D-17   INT. BEDROOM...LONG SHOT

CAMERA ENTERS with Kemp as he
nervously opens the door and
goes in. CAMERA PANS as he goes
up to the bed to include the
Invisible Man. He is sitting
rigidly on the bed. He is clad
in pajamas, slippers and dressing
gown - emptiness where his head
and hands should be.
CUT TO:

D-18   INT. BEDROOM...MED CLOSE ON...

The Invisible Man as he raises
handless arm and points.

                        INVISIBLE MAN
                    Put them on the table.
CUT TO:

D-19   INT. BEDROOM...MED. ON KEMP

He comes forward and puts
the gloves and glasses on the
dressing table.

                        INVISIBLE MAN (off-scene)
                    Now go down and draw the
                    blinds in your sitting
                    room.

As Kemp obediently turns
to go we ....

CUT TO:

206

CG   D-20   INT. BEDROOM...TWO SHOT

             Kemp and the Invisible man.

                                    INVISIBLE MAN
                                        Are we alone in the house?

                                    KEMP
                                        Yes.

                                    INVISIBLE MAN
                                        Good
                                            (pause)
                                        All right. Go now. If you
                                        raise a finger against me
                                        you're a dead man. I'm
                                        strong, and I'll strangle
                                        you. You understand? Wait
                                        for me downstairs.

             Kemp goes out and the door
             closes.
             CUT TOP

       D-21   INT. HALL..LONG SHOT.

             Kemp, slowly and unsteadily
             descending the stairs. At the
             bottom he halts, hesitates and
             takes a step towards the front
             door. But even as he moves a
             voice comes from above.
             CUT TO:

       D-22   INT. HALL..SHOOTING UP THE STAIRS

             On the half open door and the
             Invisible Man empty clothes.

                                    INVISIBLE MAN
                                        The sitting room, I said,
                                        Kemp.

             CUT BACK TO:

       D-23   INT. HALL..MED SHOT ON...KEMP

             He hastily turns, and makes his
             way to the sitting room. The
             voice follows him as he goes.

                                    INVISIBLE MAN
                                        -- and if you try and es-
                                        cape by the window I shall
                                        follow you - and no one in
                                        the world can save you!

             Kemp goes into the sitting
             room as we...
             CUT TO:

       D-24   INT. SITTING ROOM

             Kemp goes to the blinds, and
             draws them, mechanically, as if
             he is walking in his sleep. He
             pauses by the telephone.
             CUT TO:

CG

D-25   INT.SITTING ROOM.MED.CLOSE SHOT

On Kemp by the telephone, looks
at it longingly, then glances in
fear towards the door. He dares
not use the telephone. He stands
there miserably waiting.
DISSOLVE TO:

D-26   EXT. VILLAGE STREET..LONG SHOT

The main street of the village
of Iping. A police car comes
swiftly down the road and pulls
up at the Inn. The villagers
gaping.
CUT TO:

D-27   INT. VILLAGE INN...FULL SHOT

A number of villagers are sitting
around waiting. There is an atmosphere of suspense. Mr. Hall,
with a bandage around his head,
still looks fuddled and shaken.
A police sergeant is waiting
anxiously b the windows, watching out. Now he starts to attention and makes for the door,
CAMERA PANS WITH HIM - speaking
over his shoulder to the waiting
people as he goes:
                    SERGEANT
            Here's the Inspector!
CUT TO:

D-28   EXT. VILLAGE STREET. MED. SHOT

The street outside. An important
looking Police Inspector gets out
of the car, followed by a smart
assistant. They go up the steps
into the Inn. The Inspector is
Bird.
CUT TO:

D-29   INT. VILLAGE INN..MEDIUM SHOT

The villagers have risen. The
Inspector enters. The Sergeant
salutes. The Inspector glares
around, obviously annoyed.

                    INSPECTOR BIRD
            Nice fool, you've made of
            me! I've got reports from
            ten miles round. Not a
            sign of anything.
                (he pauses)
            I'll tell you what I think
            of your Invisible Man.
            It's a hoax..

CUT TO:

CG   D-30   INT. VILLAGE INN..MEDIUM CLOSE
               SHOT

On Inspector Bird and his assistant as Bird continues.

> INSPECTOR BIRD
> I'll have an enquiry right now!

He turns to his assistant:

> Bring in everybody who says they saw or heard anything. I'll get to the bottom of this before the night's out.

CUT TO:

D-31   INT. VILLAGE INN...MED. LONG
               SHOT

The Sergeant salutes and goes to the door. The Inspector pulls a chair up to the saloon table, produces a large notebook and looks fiercely round at the uneasy people standing by the walls, Mrs. Hall among them.

DISSOLVE TO:

D-32   INT. KEMP'S HALL (NIGHT) PAN
               SHOT...ON

The door of the bedroom of Kemp's house. It opens, and the Invisible Man steps out. He closes the door and walks stiffly and erect downstairs. His head is completely covered by the bandages; he weaves the dark glasses and the gloves. He looks almost as he did when we first saw him at the Inn -- except that he wears no wig, and bandages takes the place of the false nose.
CUT TO:

D-33   INT. STAIRS...DOLLEY SHOT

The Invisible man coming down the stairs. We follow him as he reaches the bottom of the stairs and turns along the passage to the sitting room. He goes in.

CUT TO:

CG   D-34   <u>INT. SITTING ROOM...LONG SHOT</u>

>HIGH CAMERA. The Invisible Man
>closes the door. Kemp stands
>waiting where we left him.

>>>INVISIBLE MAN
>>>Now then. We can talk
>>>as man to man.

>He gives a low chuckle
>and motions to a chair.

>>>-- sit down.

>Kemp obediently goes to a
>chair and sits down. The
>Invisible Man takes a quick
>glance round the room; at
>the drawn curtains - at
>the telephone. He goes to
>the windows - cautiously
>feels between the curtains
>with his gloved hands and
>thrusts up the bolt. He
>goes to the door and turns
>the key - Kemp watching ap-
>prehensively. There is a
>restless, hunted look about
>the strange figure. Then he
>comes forward and draws up
>a chair.
>CUT TO:

D-35   <u>INT. SITTING ROOM..EXTREME
CLOSE ON</u>

>The Invisible Man.

>>>INVISIBLE MAN
>>>One day I'll tell you
>>>everything. There's no
>>>time now. I began five
>>>years ago - in secret.
>>>Working - all night -
>>>every night - right into
>>>the dawn. A thousand
>>>experiments - a thousand
>>>failures -- and then at
>>>last the great, wonderful
>>>day!

>He pauses.

>CUT TO:

D-36   INT. SITTING ROOM
CLOSE UP ON..KEMP

> At last Kemp finds a
> choking, hysterical voice:

KEMP
> But - Griffin - it's -
> ghastly!

CUT TO:

D-37   INT. SITTING ROOM
MED. CLOSE...TWO-SHOT

> QUEER LOW ANGLE.
> The Invisible Man goes on
> as if he has not heard.

INVISIBLE MAN
> - the great, wonderful
> day! - the last little
> mixture of drugs. I could
> n't stay here any longer,
> Kemp. I couldn't let you
> see me slowly fading away.
> I packed up and went to a
> village for secrecy and
> quiet - to finish the ex-
> periment and complete the
> antidote - the way back to
> solid man again. I meant
> to come back just as I was
> when you saw me last - but
> the fools wouldn't let me
> work in peace. I had to
> teach them a lesson.

> He pauses - and chuckles
> at the memory. There is a
> horrid, unearthliness in
> his laugh.

KEMP
> But why! - why do it,
> Griffin!

CUT TO:

D-38   INT. SITTING ROOM
MED. SHOT ON...

> Vivid flash of the Invisible
> Man sitting up - but before
> he can speak...we...
> CUT TO:

D-39   INT. SITTING ROOM
BIG CLOSE UP ON...

> The Invisible man.

INVISIBLE MAN
> Just a scientific experi-
> ment - at first. That's
> all. To do something no
> other man in the world had
> done.
>> (he is quivering with
>> excitement - his
>> voice comes in a
>> hard, icy whisper)

(CONTINUED)

D-39   (CONTINUED)

                                    INVISIBLE MAN
                                        (continued)
                                    But there's more to it
                                    than that, Kemp - I know
                                    now - it came to me -
                                    suddenly - the drugs I
                                    took seemed to light up
                                    my brain. Suddenly I saw
                                    the power I held - the
                                    power to rule! To make
                                    the whole world grovel at
                                    my feet.
                                        (he laughs)
                                    We'll soon put the world
                                    right now, Kemp! You and
                                    I!

        CUT TO:

D-40   INT. SITTING ROOM
        CLOSE UP ON..KEMP

                            KEMP   (appalled)
                                I! You mean? -

        CUT TO:

D-41   INT. SITTING ROOM
        TWO-SHOT...MEDIUM

        On Kemp and the Invisible
        Man.
                                    INVISIBLE MAN
                                    I must have a partner: a
                                    visible partner - to help
                                    me in the little things -
                                    you're my partner - Kemp!

        CUT TO:

D-42   INT. SITTING ROOM
        MED. CLOSE ON...

        The Invisible Man as he
        points with finger
        (gloves?) at Kemp.
                                    INVISIBLE MAN
                                    We'll begin with a reign
                                    of terror - a few murders
                                    - here and there - murders
                                    of great men - and little
                                    men - to show we make no
                                    distinction: we may wreck
                                    a train or two -

        CUT TO:

D-43   INT. SITTING ROOM
        CLOSE SHOT ON...

        The Invisible Man as he
        leans forward - thrusts
        out his gloved hands and
        goes through the imaginary
        motions of strangling.
                                    INVISIBLE MAN
                                    Just these fingers - round
                                    a signal-man's throat,
                                    that's all.

        He laughs.
        CUT TO:

D-44   INT. SITTING ROOM
        MED. SHOT ON THE TWO
        _____

        Kemp springs from his
        chair with a cry:

                                        KEMP
                                    Griffin! For God's sake!

        The Invisible Man rises
        slowly and takes hold of
        the buttons of his dressing
        gown.

                                    INVISIBLE MAN
                                    You want me to - throw
                                    these off?

                                        KEMP
                                    No! - no!
                                            (in agony)

        CUT TO:

D-45   INT. SITTING ROOM
        CLOSER TWO-SHOT
        _____

        Favoring the Invisible Man.
        He chuckles and resumes
        his seat.

                                    INVISIBLE MAN
                                    Very well, then. We shall
                                    make our plans tomorrow.
                                    Tonight there's a small
                                    job to do. Go and get your
                                    car out, Kemp.

                                        KEMP
                                    Why? Where are we going?

                                    INVISIBLE MAN
                                    Back to the village I left
                                    this morning. I came away
                                    without my notebooks. They
                                    contain all the results of
                                    my experiments. I must
                                    have them here.

                                        KEMP
                                    But - it's past eight
                                    o'clock.

                                    INVISIBLE MAN
                                    It's only fifteen miles.
                                    Go now - quickly, and
                                    take a bag with you - for
                                    the books.

        CUT TO:

D-46   INT. SITTING ROOM
        LONG SHOT
        _____

        Keeping Kemp in the fore-
        ground - as he gets up and
        goes to the door, He seems
        completely under the spell of
        Invisible Man now - he moves
        as though hypnotized. The
        Invisible Man throws a final
        command as Kemp goes.

        (CONTINUED)

D-46   (CONTINUED)

                                    INVISIBLE MAN
                                        Put a warm rug in the car.
                                        It's cold outside - when
                                        you've got to go about
                                        naked.

          The Invisible Man rises
          as we...
          CUT TO:

D-47   MED. CLOSE ON...

          The Invisible Man begins
          to unwind the bandages off
          his head as the picture...

          DISSOLVES TO:

D-48   EXT. KEMP'S HOUSE
          LONG SHOT

          Kemp draws up in his car,
          gets out and goes up the
          steps to the front door -
          CAMERA PANS WITH HIM. - He
          opens the door and a voice
          says:
                                    INVISIBLE MAN
                                        All ready?

                                    KEMP
                                        Yes.
          Kemp turns and goes back
          to the car. He has a rug
          under his arm - he looks
          vaguely round - wondering
          where his invisible companion
          is, until suddenly he is star-
          tled by a voice that raps out
          beside the car...
                                    INVISIBLE MAN
                                        Come on ! - Get in.

          CUT TO:

D-49   EXT. HOUSE....AT CAR

          CLOSER SHOT OF DOOR.
          The door of the car jerks
          open; Kemp clambers hastily
          in - and the door slams behind
          him. The car starts and glides
          off into the night.
          CUT TO:

D-50   SHOT INSIDE THE CAR

          Kemp sits rigidly at the driv-
          ing wheel. Beside him sits the
          Invisible Man - only a blanket
          can be seen - wrapped round his
          shoulders.

          (CONTINUED)

D-50   (CONTINUED)

                                        INVISIBLE MAN
                                            We'll stop in a lane - a
                                            hundred yards from the Inn.
                                            I'll go in and give you the
                                            books through the window.

                                        KEMP
                                            But they'll have a guard!

                                        INVISIBLE MAN
                                                (with a laugh)
                                            A guard! - what can a guard
                                            do - you fool!
                                                (there is a pause)
                                            I must have those books,
                                            Kemp. I'll work in your
                                            laboratory till I've found
                                            the antidote. Then sometimes
                                            I'll make you invisible - to
                                            give me a rest.

              Kemp stares at the huddled
              blanket - shudders - but
              makes no reply.

              DISSOLVE TO:

D-51   INT. VILLAGE INN
         FULL SHOT...

              The Bar is arranged rather
              like a court. The enquiry
              is in full progress. Witnesses
              sit round on the benches. The
              Inspector, with his assistant
              beside him, is questioning the
              old man whose hat was thrown
              into the pond. (The old man -
              a farmer type; bald - with a
              beard and wearing a smock.)

                                        THE OLD MAN
                                            I was walking home to my
                                            lunch, sir - when all of a
                                            sudden something takes hold
                                            of my hat and throws it in
                                            the pond!

              CUT TO:

D-52   INT. SALOON
         MED. CLOSE TWO-SHOT

              On Inspector Bird and the
              old man.

                                        INSPECTOR BIRD
                                            How many drinks did you
                                            have on your way home?

                                        THE OLD MAN
                                            Only a couple - that's all,
                                            sir.

              (CONTINUED)

D-52   (CONTINUED)

g
h
r

                                          INSPECTOR BIRD
                                               A couple of drinks and a
                                               gust of wind - so much for
                                               you.
                                                    (he glares round)
                                               Now then - about the bi-
                                               cycle. Where's the owner
                                               of the bicycle?

          CUT TO:

D-53   INT. SALOON
         CLOSE SHOT ON...

         A man - another type.

                                          THE MAN
                                               Here, sir!

          CUT TO:

D-54   EXT. LANE...
         MED. LONG SHOT

         A lane - with high hedges.
         Kemp's car, travelling slowly,
         draws up in the shadows.
         CUT TO:

D-55   INT. CAR
         CLOSE SHOT
                                          INVISIBLE MAN
                                               Take your bag and walk
                                               straight down the street.
                                               I'll guide you. Wait out-
                                               side the window till the
                                               books come out. Put them
                                               in your bag and come back
                                               to the car. Then wait for
                                               me.

         CAMERA PANS as the blanket
         drops over the seat and the
         door of the car opens. Kemp
         takes his bag and gets out.
         CUT TO:

D-56   EXT. LANE
         FOLLOW SHOT ON...

         Kemp - he sets off down the
         lane - fearfully gazing to
         his side.
                                          INVISIBLE MAN
                                               Don't stare at me, you
                                               fool! Look in front of
                                               you.

          CUT TO:

D-57   EXT. LANE
          CLOSE SHOT ON KEMP

          He jerks his head round
          and looks straight in front
          of him with a fixed stare.
          CUT TO:

D-58   EXT. VILLAGE INN
          FULL SHOT

          Kemp comes down the street,
          carrying his bag. A man
          passes by, unconcerned. Kemp
          turns suddenly as if pushed,
          down a lane beside the Inn,
          until he comes beneath a win-
          dow.
          CUT TO:

D-59   EXT. VILLAGE INN
          MED. SHOT

          Kemp - under window.

                             INVISIBLE MAN
                             Here you are. Stroll up
                             and down - as though you
                             were waiting for someone.
                             Watch for the window to
                             open.

          Kemp stands still -
          rigidly. Then he whis-
          pers:

                         KEMP
                        Griffin! - Are you there!

          There is no reply.
          Kemp looks fearfully
          round.

          CUT TO:

CG   D-60   EXT. VILLAGE INN .MOVING SHOT

THE CAMERA moves slowly round
the Inn, as if following the
Invisible Man. It comes to the
front door. A few small boys, on
tiptoe, are trying to look into
the window, thru which the witnesses
can be seen standing. The Inn door
is seen.
CUT TO:

D-61   EXT. VILLAGE INN. CLOSE SHOT ON

The Inn door as it slowly opens.
CUT TO:

D-62   INT. SALOON..MED. LONG SHOT

Shooting towards the door. The
owner of the bicycle is still
giving his evidence.

                              THE BICYCLE OWNER
                              It was pulled clean out of
                              my hand, sir! Then it
                              went peddling off down the
                              street all by itself!

The door opens, papers blow
off the table.
                              INSPECTOR BIRD (seeing this)
                              Who's that -- opened the
                              door?

                              MRS. HALL
                              It's them boys again.

CAMERA PANS with her as she
goes to the door.
CUT TO:

D-63   EXT. VILLAGE INN. MEDIUM SHOT

Mrs. Hall peers angrily out
at the boys by the window.

                              MRS. HALL
                              Look 'ere - you leave this
                              door alone - it's private
                              see?

                              A BOY
                              We never touched it!

                              MRS. HALL
                              Yes you did! Go on! Hop it!

She makes a threatening
gesture and the boys run
away.

CUT TO:

CG   D-64   PASSAGE OUTSIDE THE SITTING
              ROOM

              Shot of door opening to passage
              as they are all looking at the
              other door.
              CUT TO:

      D-65   INT. SITTING ROOM...MEDIUM SHOT

              The door opens - CAMERA PANS to
              shelf, the notebooks lie on a
              shelf of the sideboard. After a
              moment they rise from the shelf
              and travel across to the table
              by the window.

              (NOTE: Invisible hands might
              tear up some obnoxious calender
              or smash a hideous ornament -
              or put portrait of landlady up-
              side down, or back to front.)

              CAMERA PANS to window - it slowly
              and softly opens; the books rise
              from the table and travel thru.
              They hover in mid-air.
              CUT TO:

      D-66   EXT. VILLAGE INN..AT WINDOW...
              MEDIUM CLOSE

              Kemp standing on box or old cart,
              we see him look up and to the books
              in mid-air - CAMERA PANS - he
              feverishly grabs the books and drops
              them into his case. He closes the
              case, and with a fearful glance
              round, makes for the main road.
              CUT TO:

      D-67   INT. SALOON..MEDIUM LONG SHOT

              HIGH CAMERA. The enquiry is over.
              The Inspector is sitting back,
              speaking to the villagers.

                                    INSPECTOR BIRD
                              Lies, that's all. Lies
                              from beginning to end. I've
                              a good mind to prosecute
                              the lot of you for con-
                              spiracy.
              CUT TO:

      D-68   INT. SALOON..CLOSER SHOT ON

              Inspector Bird continuing.

                                         I shall announce this eve-
                                         ning that the whole thing's
                                         a hoax - and you'll be the
                                         laughing stock of the whole
                                         country.

              He takes a last scowl round,
              and picks up his pen to sign
              his report.
              CUT TO:

D-69   INT. SALOON..CLOSE SHOT ON

    The Inkpot -- as Inspector Bird's
    hand reaches forward to dip the
    pen into the ink - but as he does
    so the inkpot gently moves away
    from him. He tries again and the
    inkpot dodges his pen. Then, slowly
    the inkpot rises from the table-
    hoves in mid-air and jerks the ink
    full into the Inspector's face.
    CAMERA PANS up to the Inspector as
    this happens.
    CUT TO:

D-70   INT. SALOON..LONG SHOT

    On the people. There is a moment
    of deathly stillness; everyone is
    hypnotized -- then comes a low,
    maniacal laugh -- and panic is let
    loose. There are shrieks and hoarse
    cries: Mrs. Hall screams.

                        MRS. HALL
                        He's here! The Invisible
                        Man!

    CUT TO:

D-71   INT. SALOON...SHOT OF BAR

    One after another a row pewter
    beer mugs rise from their places
    on the shelf and fly into the
    panic stricken crowd.
    CUT TO:

D-72   INT. SALOON...MEDIUM SHOT

    Someone smashes a window and
    leaps out - others dash for the
    door (old farmer man)
    CUT TO:

D-73   INT. SALOON....LONG SHOT

    Everyone rushing panic stricken
    out of the saloon. After a short,
    frantic struggle, everyone has gone,
    save the Inspector who lies on the
    floor, struggling with an invisible
    opponent who has him by the throat.
    CUT TO:

D-74   INT. SALOON..MED.CLOSE SHOT

    A horase, brutal voice breathes
    over the helpless Inspector.
                        INVISIBLE MAN
                        A hoax is it? -- all a hoax
                        all -- a -- hoax...!

                        (CONTINUED)

D-74   (CONTINUED)

          - The last three words are timed
            to the rise of a heavy stool--
            that hovers - and crashes into
            the Inspector's face on the last
            word - "hoax".
            CUT TO:

D-75   INT. SALOON..FULL SHOT

            The saloon bar is in silence.
            The Inspector lies crushed on
            the floor amidst indescribable
            wreckage left by the panic
            stricken crowd. Distant shout-
            ing can be heard from the streets
            outside.
            CUT TO:

D-76   EXT. LANE...PAN SHOT

            The corner of the land where
            the car stands. THE CAMERA picks
            up an empty scene, but there is
            the sound of padding, running
            feet and heavy breathing. CAMERA
            PANS past trees - dust, etc.
            FOLLOWING the sounds along the
            lane to the car, Kemp sits tensely
            inside. He starts as the door
            flies open and slams too.

                              INVISIBLE MAN
                                   All right. Off you go!

            CUT TO:

D-77   EXT. LANE..MEDIUM SHOT

            Kemp obediently starts up and
            the car moves off.
                              INVISIBLE MAN
                                   Go for your life too!

            The engine roars and the car
            jumps forward.
            CUT TO:

D-78   INT. CAR..MED. CLOSE SHOT...

            Kemp and the blanket, as the
            car sways and jolts on its
            journey thru the night.

            (NOTE: shoot so as to be able
            to cut this if necessary)

                              INVISIBLE MAN
                                   Did you hear some shout-
                                   ing and screaming?

                              KEMP
                                   What was that screaming?

          (CONTINUED)

E-3 EXT. STREET
   CLOSEUP ON..DR. CRANLEY

    The Doctor reads the
    great black headlines.
    The dreadful truth flashes
    to his brain. He stands
    for a moment rigid -
    horrified - the papers
    gripped stiffly beside
    him. The crowd around
    him are too absorbed in
    their papers to notice him.

    CUT TO:

E-4 EXT. STREET
   MED. CLOSE ON..

    Two men - a big man and a
    little man - exchanging
    opinions.

            BIG MAN
             Nasty business, this.

            LITTLE MAN
             It's a conjuring trick;
             that's what it is. I saw
             a feller make a peanut
             disappear once.

    THE CAMERA PANS TO
    Dr. Cranley - we see
    people reading the news-
    papers. The Doctor gazes
    up the steps of the police
    station - shudders, and
    turns away. He makes
    blindly for his home.

    DISSOLVE TO:

E-5 INT. BEDROOM - KEMPS' HOUSE
   MEDIUM SHOT. (NIGHT)

    The Invisible Man is sitting
    at a small table. Thrust to
    one side is a tray containing
    the remains of a meal. His
    hands lay palm downwards upon
    the two big notebooks which he
    rescued from the Inn. He is
    dressed as he was before
    leaving the house, Kemp stands
    opposite him. The first acute-
    ness of Kemp's fear has passed
    away. He looks utterly dejected
    and cowed. He carries out his
    orders as if under hypnotic
    influence.

            INVISIBLE MAN
             There are one or two things
             you must understand, Kemp.
             I must always remain in
             hiding for an hour after
             meals.

    CUT TO:

E-6   INT. KEMP'S BEDROOM
        CLOSE SHOT OF...

        Head drinking - and we
        hear -.....
                                        --/The food is visible inside
                                        me until it is digested. I can
        NOTE: During this scene   only work on fine, clear days.
        he could eat or walk
        about - The business
        of eating will have to
        keep this scene going
        as suggested in the
        following cuts:

E-7   INT. BEDROOM
        CLOSE SHOT OF..

        Gloved hands dealing
        with food.

        CUT TO:

E-8   INT. BEDROOM
        CLOSE SHOT OF...

        Hands breaking bread.

        CUT TO:

E-9   INT. BEDROOM
        CLOSEUP OF...

        The Invisible Man eating.

        CUT TO:

E-10   INT. BEDROOM
        CLOSE ON KEMP...

        Watching him - and
        listening. (He might
        smoke comfortably here)

        NOTE: (During the above
            cuts we hear:-
                                        INVISIBLE MAN
                                            If I work in the rain - the
                                        water can be seen on my
                                        head and shoulders. In a
                                        fog you can see me like a
                                        bubble. In smoky cities
                                        the soot settles on me
                                        until you can see a dark
                                        outline. You must always
                                        be near at hand to wipe
                                        off my feet. Even dirt
                                        between my fingernails
                                        would give me away.

        (Shoot CLOSEUP in case
        of cutting here.)

                                        It is difficult at first to
                                        walk downstairs. We are so
                                        accustomed to watching our
                                        feet. But they're trivial
                                        difficulties - we shall
                                        find ways of defeating
        CUT TO   everything.

223

E-11   INT. BEDROOM
        LONG SHOT...

                                        INVISIBLE MAN
                                            You will sleep in the room
                                            opposite and bring me some
                                            more food at eight o'clock.
                                            Good night.

        Kemp leaves the room
        without a word. The
        Invisible Man goes to
        the door and locks it.

        CUT TO:

E-12   INT. BEDROOM
        CLOSER PAN SHOT...

        The Invisible Man moves
        across to the dressing
        table and unwraps the
        bandages from his head.
        Then he takes off his
        dressing gown and gloves,
        and stands before the
        mirror - a headless,
        handless figure in
        pajamas. He goes to the
        bed and sits down.

        CUT TO:

E-13   INT. BEDROOM
        CLOSE SHOT....

        Of the Invisible Man's
        slippers being kicked off.

        CUT TO:

E-14   INT. BEDROOM
        MED. SHOT...

        He turns the covers of
        the bed down, - then
        gets into bed. Then,
        very wearily he pulls
        the clothes over him -
        switches off the light
        and lies still. The
        moon shines in upon
        the strange headless
        figure in bed.

        DISSOLVE TO:

E-15   INT. SALOON - IPING
        MED. SHOT (NIGHT)

        Two policemen stoop to
        a covered stretcher,
        raise it from the ground
        and bear the body of the
        dead Inspector from the
        room.

        CUT TO:

E-16   INT. SALOON
       FULL SHOT...

       High Camera. A group
       of Police Detectives
       watching in silence
       as the stretcher is
       borne away. Then the
       Chief Detective strides
       to the table where a
       large map is spread out.
       He gives orders to his
       staff like an Army Commander
       upon the eve of a battle.
       The others have gathered
       round the table.

                                CHIEF DETECTIVE
                              You understand my plan?
                              You are in charge of all
                              country east of here,
                              Thompson, for twenty
                              miles to the north of
                              the main road.

       QUICK CUT TO:

E-17   INT. SALOON
       CLOSE UP ON....

       Neville. Over this we
       hear the Chief Detective:

                                CHIEF DETECTIVE (off scene)
                              Neville takes the opposite
                              section to the south.

       CUT TO:

E-18   CLOSE UP ON..

       Stoddart - over this we
       hear the Chief Detective.

                              Stoddard takes charge of
                              the search in the hills and-

       QUICK CUT TO:

E-19   CLOSE UP ON...

       Hogan - we hear Detective
       off:

                              --Hogan takes all the
                              villages out to the river.

       CUT TO:

E-20   INT. SALOON
       MED. SHOT ON...

       The Chief Detective:

                              We shall comb the country
                              for twenty miles round.
                              We've got a terrible
                              responsibility. He's mad
                              and he's invisible. He
                              may be standing beside us
       (CONTINUED)   now.

E-20   (CONTINUED)

The Detectives shift
uneasily.

                                        -- But he's human - and we shall
                                        get him....

The scene darkens as the
Detective goes on with
his orders: and there comes
a series of scenes, dissolving quickly into each other -
revealing the great man-hunt
spreading throughout the
country; silent pictures,
over which comes the firm,
incisive voice of the
Detective.

CUT TO:

E-21   POLICE STATION
         LONG SHOT - HIGH CAMERA

A posse of motor cyclist
police sweep out of a
station yard and make in
different directions.   DETECTIVE
                                  ...We shall have a thousand
                                  men out tonight: tomorrow
                                  we shall have ten thousand
                                  volunteers to help them.

CUT TO:

E-22   EXT. ROAD
         LONG SHOT - LOW CAMERA

An open line of uniformed   There's a broadcast warn-
men - advancing stealth-   ing going out at ten o'
ily abreast of a road -   clock. At all costs we must
the line crosses the road,   avoid a panic spreading.
taking in a wide section   Get away to your districts
of the fields to either   at once and send me a note
side.   of your headquarters. Re-
                                 member he will leave tracks -
CUT TO: even if he's invisible...

E-23   SHOT OF...

A giant wireless mast
crackling its message
out into the night.

CUT TO:

E-24   SHOT OF

A fast police car - racing
down a main road.

CUT TO:

E-25   SHOT ON...

A part of police, beating
their way through a thick
copse of trees.
CUT TO:

E-26   SHOT ON...

> There comes a faint,
> darkened picture of
> the Invisible Man -
> asleep, aswe left him
> in the bed in Kemp's
> room.

THE PICTURE DISSOLVES TO:

E-27   INT. DANCE HALL
        LONG SHOT....

> A gay, brightly lit
> dancing hall. Couples
> glide round the room
> to the music of a large
> radio in a corner.
> Suddenly - without
> warning, the music fades.
> The dancers pause in
> surprise and look across
> at the radio.
>
> The voice of the Announcer
> comes clearly to the room.

                    ANNOUNCER
            I must interrupt the dance
            music for a moment. I have
            an urgent message from
            Police Headquarters. Earlier
            this evening we broadcast
            a report of an Invisible
            Man.

            CUT TO:

E-28   INT. DANCE HALL
        PAN SHOT...ON DOLLEY

> On the dancers reactions
> as this comes across -
> they instinctively be-
> come tense and anxious.
> CAMERA TRAVELS THRU THE
> dancers as the voice of
> the Announcer is heard:

                    ANNOUNCER
            The report has now been
            confirmed. It appears that
            an Unknown Man - by
            scientific means, has made
            himself invisible. He has
            attacked and killed a
            Police Inspector and is now
            at large...

> CAMERA ON DOLLEY has now
> reached the mouth of the
> radio, which is of the
> old-fashioned type horn,
> and it fills the screen-
> speaking directly out
> at the audience, as if
> appealing to them for
> their co-operation.
> (CONTINUED)

227

E-28   (CONTINUED)

-- The Chief of Police appeals
to the public for help and
assistance...Those willing
to co-operate in the search
are requested to report tomorrow
morning to their local station.

Out of the dark mouth
of the radio, there
comes a picture of...

--The Invisible Man works without
clothing. He will have to seek
shelter ...

An old man and woman
in a country cottage,
listening from a small,
primitive set - with
earphones to their
heads.

    DISSOLVE TO:

E-29   INT. ORPHANAGE
        MED. SHOT ON...

A room in an Orphanage.
The children, in uniform,
grouped round, listening
to a radio - excited and
awed. An older girl is
in charge.

..You are requested to look
every door and window -
and every out-building he
may use to hide in...

    DISSOLVE TO:

E-30   INT. OFFICE

A vacant, open-mouthed
night watchman in an office,
also listening in.

...The police will be glad
to receive any suggestions
that will help in captur-
ing the fugitive. Remember
he is solid - but cannot be
seen...

    DISSOLVE TO:

E-31   SHOT OF...

...A reward of $5000.00
will be given to any person
whose information leads to
his capture...

A stout farmer, who
rises upon news of the
reward - picks up his
hat and a large stick
and makes for the door.

    DISSOLVE TO:

E-32   INT. DANCE HALL
        DOLLEY SHOT...

CAMERA STARTS ON CLOSE SHOT
as the last words come from
the full, open mouth of the
original amplifier...

                ANNOUNCER
        .....The police appeal to
        the public to keep calm-
        and to admit uniformed
        search parties to all prop-
        erty.

(CONTINUED)

228

E-32 (continued)

  THE CAMERA PULLS BACK
  as the words of the
  Announcer die away -
  and after a moment of
  silence the dance music
  returns. A few couples
  begin to dance again-
  half-heartedly: others
  help their women on
  with their coats and
  go away quietly.

  A SERIES OF DISSOLVES.

E-33 TRICK SHOT...OF

  Hands shooting bolts -
  turning window clasps,
  locking doors - slamming
  down windows - anxious,
  fumbling hands super-
  imposed one upon the
  other.

  DISSOLVE TO:

E-34 INT. KEMP'S BEDROOM
  CLOSE SHOT ON...

  The Invisible Man -
  sleeping in his bed -
  the moon shining upon
  the round dent in the
  pillow where his head
  lies - the armless
  sleeve of his pajamas
  outside the blankets.

  The CAMERA MOVES across
  the room and past the
  locked door. It re-
  veals Kemp, standing in
  his dressing gown -
  listening with bated
  breath for any sound
  that might come to him
  from the room beyond.
  Very slowly he turns -
  and tiptoes downstairs.

  CUT TO:

E-35 CLOSE SHOT ON...

  Kemp going downstairs -
  several times he looks
  back and listens. His
  face is contorted in
  an agony of suspense
  and fear.

  CUT TO:

E-36 INT. PASSAGE
  MED. SHOT..

  We follow him, as swiftly and
  (CONTINUED)

silently he passes
down the passage and
enters his sitting
room.

CUT TO:

E-37   INT. SITTING ROOM
        MEDIUM SHOT...

Kemp locks the door. He
sways back against the
door, half fainting:
recovers himself and goes
to the telephone. He
feverishly fumbles with
it, removes the receiver
and dials a number.

CUT TO:

E-38   INT. LIBRARY-
        CRANLEY'S HOME - FULL SHOT

Dr. Cranley is pacing to and
fro. The 'phone bell rings
and he crosses to it.

CUT TO:

E-39   INT. SITTING ROOM
        CLOSE SHOT ON..

Kemp - waiting - his
eyes fixed on the door.
He quickly turns and
speaks in a fast, breath-
less undertone.

                                        KEMP
                                Doctor! - listen! - it's
                                something - ghastly - it's
                                Griffin - he's come back-
                                he's asleep in my room!
                                He's the Invisible Man!
                                he's mad - a raving lunatic-
                                he killed a man tonight...

His voice dies away;
he sits listening - his
eyes protrude his teeth
are chattering - an
abject picture of
terror.

CUT TO:

E-40   INT. LIBRARY
        CLOSE SHOT ON.

Dr. Cranley. The old
man is calm; he has only
heard what he had feared.

                                        DR. CRANLEY
                                Listen to me, Kemp. No one
                                but you and I know that it's
                                Griffin. I shall come in
        CUT QUICKLY TO   the morning.

E-41   INT. SITTING ROOM
        CLOSEUP ON...

        Kemp; very nervous.

                                        KEMP
                                    You must come now - I can't
                                    bear it!

        CUT BACK TO:

E-42   INT. CRANLEY'S LIBRARY
        MED. CLOSE SHOT ON...

        Dr. Cranley speaking into
        phone;

                                        DR. CRANLEY (firmly)
                                    I shall come in the morning-
                                    If I come now he'll be
                                    suspicious and escape. I
                                    shall come as though I know
                                    nothing; you must keep him
                                    calm and quiet till nine
                                    o'clock - we must take him
                                    together and bind him -
                                    it's our only hope - then
                                    we must work to find the
                                    antidote. I trust you,
                                    Kemp - that's all.

        Dr. Cranley replaces the
        receiver - and looks
        toward the door with
        a start of surprise.

        CUT TO:

E-43   INT. CRANLEY'S LIBRARY
        MED. LONG SHOT

        Flora is discovered stand-
        ing in the doorway - in
        her dressing gown.

                                        FLORA
                                    Who was that, father?

                                        DR. CRANLEY
                                    It was Kemp.

                                        FLORA   (coming down to him)
                                    It was about Jack - I know.
                                    What is it - tell me!

        Dr. Cranley sits in
        chair and covers his face
        with his hands.

                                        DR. CRANLEY
                                    Leave me alone, Flora -
                                    please!

        Flora comes slowly forward,
        conscious of tragedy, but
        fighting to keep calm as
        we...

        CUT TO:

E-44   INT. CRANLEY'S LIBRARY
          MED. CLOSE TWO SHOT.

    Flora sits on arm of
    chair by her father's
    side - quite resolute.

                    FLORA
                    I'm not afraid. Tell me.

    The old man looks up
    at his daughter. It is
    useless to conceal the
    news from her.

                    DR. CRANLEY
                    Jack Griffin's come back,
                    Flora. He's at Dr. Kemp's
                    house..Jack Griffin is
                    the Invisible Man.

    CUT TO:

E-45   INT. LIBRARY
          CLOSE UP ON .. FLORA

    She sits quite rigidly
    as the picture...

    DISSOLVES TO:

E-46   INT. PHONE BOOTH
          MEDIUM SHOT ON...

    A cranky, excited looking
    man 'phoning.

                    THE MAN
                    Say! - that the police?
                    Is that $5000. O. K.? Well
                    listen! I got a way to
                    catch him! The paper says
                    he threw some ink at the
                    man he killed.

    CUT TO:

E-47   INT. PHONE BOOTH
          CLOSEUP ON.....

                    THE MAN   (continuing)
                    Well, you get your own
                    back and squirt ink about
                    with a hose pipe till you
                    hit him. The ink'll stick
                    on him, see? - then you
                    can shoot him!

    CUT TO:

E-48   SHOT OF...

Another mild little man
phoning the police.

                                THE MAN
                            Is that the police? I want
                            to tell you how to catch
                            the Invisible Man! The
                            paper says it's going to be
                            frosty in a day or two. Well,
                            you watch out when it's
                            frosty and you'll see his
                            breath.

        CUT TO:

E-49   INT. SITTING ROOM (KEMP'S)
        FULL SHOT...

        Kemp is sitting as we left
        him - beside the telephone -
        in blank despair and misery.
        He rises - paces the room,
        turns and looks over at
        the telephone. It seems to
        be drawing him to it.
        Finally he makes up his mind.
        He comes forward into CAMERA
        to the telphone and takes
        off the receiver.

                                KEMP (in a low, stifled voice)

                                    Police! Quickly!
                                    (he pauses a moment)

                                    Is that the police? This
                                    is Dr. Kemp. The Invisible
                                    Man is in my house -
                                    asleep upstairs. For
                                    God's sake come at once!

        CUT TO:

E-50   INT. LOCAL POLICE STATION
        AT PORT STOWE

        A sergeant is at the telephone,
        sitting with his feet up on the
        table. He is very happy - and
        slow. An Inspector is standing
        beside him. The sergeant looks
        up.

                                SERGEANT
                                    It's Dr. Kemp. He's a
                                    sensible chap. He's not
                                    likely to imagine things.

                                INSPECTOR
                                    Ask for particulars.

                                SERGEANT (officiously)
                                    Are you there, Dr. Kemp?
                                    Can you tell me some
                                    particulars? What?
                                        (he looks up at the
                                        Inspector)
                                    He says he can't say any
                                    more - his life's in
        CUT TO: danger.

nn E-51   INT POLICE STATION
            MED CLOSE ONL..

    The Inspector as he sprawls
    over the table andtakes the
    receiver. - CAMERA PANNING
    with him.

                        INSPECTOR (lying on table)
                            Listen, Doctor. There's
                            only five men here. We
                            want a hundred to sur-
                            round the house. I'll
                            get them down as soon as
                            possible.

    He puts on the receiver
    and turns to the sergeant.

                        INSPECTOR
                            Call up Headquarters at
                            once.

    He rolls off the table.

    CUT TO:

E-52   INT. CRANLEY'S LIBRARY
        MED CLOSE SHOT

    The Doctor is sitting at the
    table. Flora is sitting
    opposite him. Both are calm
    and thoughtful.

                      DR. CRANLEY
                            That's all there is to
                            tell, Flora.

    She lowers her head,
    and makes no reply.
    He continues:

                        You know everything now.
                        You must leave it to me
                        and Dr. Kemp. We shall
                        take means to keep him
                        in the house. We shall
                        work day and night to
                        undo this terrible ex-
                        periment.

    Flora raises her head.

    CUT TO:

E-53   INT. CRANLEY'S LIBRARY
        CLOSE SHOT ON...

    Flora - SHOOTING OVER
    Dr. Cranley's shoulder.

    CONTINUED

FLORA
>You must let me go to
>him!

DR. CRANLEY   (in sudden fear)
>Only when he's well again.

FLORA   (rising)
>No! Now! - I can do far
>more with Jack than you or
>Dr. Kemp!

DR. CRANLEY
>But, Flora - he's not
>normal! His mind's un-
>hinged - at present he's
>mad!

CUT TO:

E-54   <u>INT. CRANLEY'S LIBRARY
FULL SHOT</u>

Flora and Dr. Cranley in
foreground.

FLORA
>I can persuade him to help
>you! You're powerless
>unless he helps you! Get
>your coat, father! I'll
>be ready in five minutes.

DR. CRANLEY
>But it's gone midnight! -
>wait till the morning.

FLORA
>It's life or death, father!
>You know it! - I'll go
>alone, then! -

DR. CRANLEY
>Flora! - wait! -

He leaps up - but
Flora has gone.

CUT TO:

INT. KEMP ... SITTING ROOM.
FULL SHOT
_____

    Kemp, lying in his chair in the
    sitting room, waiting in agony
-   for the police. He rises -goes
    stealthily to the window and
    peers between the blinds. Sud-
    denly he wheels round with a
    choking cry. A soft knock has
    come at the sitting room door.
    CUT TO:

E-56   INT. SITTING ROOM..CLOSE SHOT
       ON...
       _____

                            KEMP
                  Who's that!!.

    There is no answer. Kemp
    screams hysterically.

                  Who's that?

    The voice of the Invisible
    Man comes from outside..

                  INVISIBLE MAN (offscene)
                  Unlock the door, Kemp.
                  Let me in.
    CUT TO:

E-57   INT..SITTING ROOM..CLOSE SHOT
       ON...
       _____

    The door handle rattling.
    CUT TO:

E-58   INT. SITTING RCOM...?MEDIUM
       LONG SHOT
       _____

    Kemp is powerless, hypnotized.
    He goes slowly to the door,
    unlocks it, and throws it open.
    The Invisible Man stands on the
    threshold, in his dressing gown
    and pajamas. He has thrown the
    bandages round his head once
    more, and wears the great blue
    goggles. He stands in the door..

                  INVISIBLE MAN
                  What are you doin g here,
                  Kemp?
    CUT TO:

E-59   INT. SITTING ROOM..AT DOOR.
       MEDIUM SHOT..HIGH CAMERA
       _____

                  KEMP
                  I - I couldn't sleep -- I-
                  I had to get up and come
                  down.
                  INVISIBLE MAN
                  Why did you lock the door?

    (CONTINUED)

                                          KEMP
                              I - I was afraid.
                                   (he pauses, then
                                    feebly blusters)
                              Wouldn't you be afraid -
                              if I were - invisible
                              like you?

          The Invisible Man gives a
          soft laugh - he is flattered.
          CUT TO:

E-60   INT. SITTING ROOM...CLOSE TWO
        SHOT

                                          INVISIBLE MAN
                              There's no need to be
                              afraid, Kemp -- we're
                              partners -bosom friends.

          He stretches out his hand and
          lays it on Kemp's shoulders.
          Kemp shudders away. The In-
          visible man laughs again.
                                              We've a busy day ahead -
                                              you must sleep.

          CU T TO:

E-61   INT. HALL...FULL SHOT

          The Invisible Man is standing
          by the door. Kemp meekly comes
          out of the sitting room, and the
          Invisible man follows him upstairs.
          CUT TO:

E-62   INT. LANDING ... MEDIUM SHOT

          The landing outside the bedroom
          doors; the two men are passing
          a large moonlit window that looks
          out upon the drive. Suddenly
          the Invisible Man becomes tense
          and watchful; his eyes are star-
          ing out into the night. Kemp,
          fascinated, stands beside him.
          THE CAMERA MOVES FORWARD - to
          shoot out of the window - a
          small car swings into the drive
          and comes to a halt beside the
          front door.
          CUT TO:

E-63   AT LANDING CLOSE TWO SHOT

          LOW CAMERA. The Invisible Man
          turns slowly to Kemp and speaks
          in a low icy voice.

                              (CONTINUED)

                                        INVISIBLE MAN
                                            I see, Kemp. You've told
                                            the police -- that was why
                                            you went downstairs?

For a moment the Invisible
Man towers over his abject
companion; it seems as if
he is about to spring and
wring the life out of him,
when Kem suddenly shouts
hysterically.
                                        KEMP
                                            No, I didn't -- I swear
                                            I didn't ! Look! It's
                                            not the police -- it's
                                            Dr. Cranley - and Flora!

        CUT TO:

E-64   LANDING...CLOSEUP ON...

        Slowly the Invisible Man
        draws back; he seems to
        relax, and soften -- his
        eyes are thoughtfully
        upon the window. Kemp's
        words have sent something
        echoing back into the
        mind of the Invisible Man;
        they awaken a forgotten
        memory. He looks down at
        Dr. Cranley and Flora as
        they come slowly up the
        steps to the door, as if
        they are two biological
        specimens to be analyzed.
        He speaks very softly
        in awakened surprise.

                                        INVISIBLE MAN
                                            Why, yes - of course-
                                            Flora -
                                                (he repeats the word
                                                slowly as if it
                                                vaguely pleases him)
                                            Flora --

        CUT TO:

E- 65   ON LANDIND..CLOSE SHOT

     Kem- quickly notices the change that
     has come over the Invisible Man and seizes
     his chance.
                              KEMP
                         I had to tell them you were
                         back, Griffin! Flora was
                         nearly mad with anxiety.
                         You must let them join us!
                         Let them help us!

     CUT TO:

E-66   ON LANDING..TWO SHOT

     The Invisible Man nods quietly to
     himself. There is almost a
     tenderness in his voice.
                              INVISIBLE MAN
                         Flora. How could I forget?

     He looks puzzled and unhappy.
     The front door bell rings--
     very quietly. Kemp looks up
     at the Invisible Man.
                              KEMP
                         Shall I--let them in?

     CUT TO:

E-67   ON LANDING..BIG C.U. ON

     The Invisible Man.
                              INVISIBLE MAN (speaking as if
                                       in a dream)
                         Yes, of course you must let
                         them in. I shall go and
                         prepare myself--in my room.
                         I shall see Flora--alone.

     CUT TO:

E-68   ON LANDING..FULL SHOT

     The Invisible Man turns and goes
     silently into his room. Kemp looks
     wonderingly after him, then turns
     and goes down stairs. SWIFT PAN ON
     stairs with Kemp.

     CUT TO:

E-69   INT. HALL..MEDIUM SHOT

     Kemp opens the door. Dr. Cranley
     and Flora step into the hall. No
     word is spoken for a moment. Then
     Kemp speaks quickly in a whisper.

                              KEMP
                         He knows you are here--

                              DR. CRANLEY (with a start)
                         You said he was asleep.

                              KEMP
                         He saw you from the window.
                         He wants to see Flora--alone.

     CUT TO:

E-70   INT. HALL..CLOSE SHOT ON FLORA

Flora steps eagerly forward.
Dr. Cranley restrains her.

                    DR. CRANLEY   (offscene)
                        No, Flora! -- Don't--

                    KEMP   (off scene)
                        He's calm now--and quiet.

                    FLORA   (with a trace of scorn)
                        Do you think Jack would do
                        me any harm?

        CUT TO:

E-71   INT. HALL..THREE SHOT..ON

Dr. Cranley, Kemp and Flora.

                    DR. CRANLEY   (in agony)
                        I tell you--he's insane--
                        It's for us to cure him--
                        Kemp and I--keep away, Flora.

                    FLORA
                        I must go to him!--leave me
                        alone!

She shakes off her father's
restraining hand and goes to
the stairs--CAMERA PANS as
Dr. Cranley and Kemp follow her
over.

        CUT TO:

E-72   ON STAIRS..LONG SHOT

Flora goes up to the dark staircase.

        CUT TO:

E-73   INT. HALL.MEDIUM CLOSE TWO SHOT

HIGH CAMERA. Dr. Cranley looks
helplessly after her. Kemp takes
his arm and speaks with passionate
anxiety.

                    KEMP
                        Listen, Doctor! He was a
                        different man when he saw
                        Flora leave the car. He
                        won't hurt her!--we must
                        play for time.

                    DR. CRANLEY   (suddenly suspicious)
                        Why for time?

                    KEMP   (floundering)
                        We--we must prepare things--
                        if we try and bind him he'll
                        throw us off--and escape.
                        We must take him when he's
                        asleep and chloroform him!

        (CONTINUED)

240

                                          DR. CRANLEY
                                              We must be near Flora--
                                              come on!

        CUT TO:

E-74   ON STAIRS..PAN SHOT OF FLORA

        Flora, ascending the stairs. She
        is wearing an old mackintosh coat
        over a tweed walking suit. Outwardly
        she is calm and composed: only by the
        way her knuckles whiten as she grips
        the balustrade and by her tense,
        determined face can we detect the
        terrible call she is making upon her
        will power. She reaches the landing--
        hesitates before the several doors and
        turns to Kemp for guidance.

        CUT TO:

E-75   ON STAIRS. MEDIUM SHOT

        Kemp, halfway up the stairs, indicates
        the door behind which the Invisible
        Man is waiting.

        CUT TO:

E-76   ON LANDING..CLOSE SHOT ON FLORA

        Watching Kemp--she then turns the
        handle of the door and goes in--
        CAMERA FOLLOWS HER IN. She stands
        by the door and looks.

        CUT TO:

E-77   INT. BEDROOM..MED. SHOT ON

        The Invisible Man--he is seated at the
        small table near his bed. His hands
        lying downwards upon the two thick note-
        books. He slowly rises as the girl
        appears on the threshold. He is in
        pajamas and dressing gown, slippers, and
        the thin, skin-tight scientists' gloves.
        His bulbous, band aged head and great
        staring goggles are even more terrible
        in calmness than in his moments of
        maniacal anger.

        CUT TO:

E- 78   INT. BEDROOM..CLOSEUP ON FLORA

        For one moment the girl's nerve almost
        breaks: she struggles for control--and
        to aid her struggle comes a voice--not
        of the Invisible Man--but of her lover
        of happier days. A strong voice, but
        soft and very tender, the voice of a
        man of culture--of humanity and charm.

                                              (CONTINUED)

E-78   CONTINUED

        -A voice that brings infinite pathos:

                                INVISIBLE MAN
                                Flora--my darling--
        CUT TO:

E-79   INT. BEDROOM..MED. CLOSE ON

        The Invisible Man--a repulsive,
        unearthly figure by the table, as
        it slowly and gropingly advances
        towards the girl. Timidly, almost
        he stretches forward his gloved hands.

        CAMERA PANS TO INCLUDE flora--as she
        fights down the shudder that comes to
        her, and gently places her hands in his.

                                FLORA
                                Thank God you are home, Jack.

        The Invisible Man seems to smile.

                                INVISIBLE MAN
                                I would have come to you
                                at once, Flora--but--for
                                this.

        He raises his gloved hand to his
        head with a little awkward laugh.
        For a moment he seems just a big,
        confused boy, apologizing for some
        trivial graze that has disfigured
        him.

        CAMERA PULLS BACK as he leads her to
        a couch under the window, and sinks
        down beside her.
                                INVISIBLE MAN
                                How wonderful it is to see
                                you.

        The little bedside lamp illuminates
        part of the room--the moon shines
        brilliantly upon the strange couple
        by the window.

        CUT TO:

E-80   INT. BEDROOM..CLOSE SHOT ON..FLORA

        Flora sitting in the window seat.
        (Note: Romantic light)
                                INVISIBLE MAN´ (offscene)
                                How beautiful you look.
                                     (he is silent for a
                                     moment then softly 1
                                     laughs)
                                That funny little hat I
                                always liked...you've been
                                crying, Flora.

        The girl looks quickly away--
        then up at him imploringly.

                                     (CONTINUED)

                                242

E-80   CONTINUED

                          FLORA
                              Jack!--I want to help you!
                                   (she struggles to find
                                    words)
                              Why did you--do this?

                          INVISIBLE MAN (offscene)
                              For you, Flora.

                          FLORA (scarcely above a whisper)
                              For--me?

        CUT TO:

E-81   INT. BEDROOM..MED. CLOSE ON

    The Invisible Man.

                          INVISIBLE MAN
                              Yes--for you--my darling.
                              I wanted to do something--
                              tremendous--to achieve
                              what men of science have
                              dreamt of since the world
                              began--to gain wealth and
                              fame--and honor--to write
                              my name above the greatest
                              scientists of all time--
                                   (he lowers his head)
                              I was so pitifully poor--I
                              had nothing to offer you,
                              Flora. Iwas just a poor,
                              struggling chemist.

    He pauses as he sees:

        CUT TO:

E-82   INT. BEDROOM..CLOSE TWO SHOT

        ...how her eyes rove over his
        featureless head, white and ghastly
        in the light of the moon. He goes
        quickly on.
                          INVISIBLE MAN
                              ...I shall come back to you,
                              Flora...very soon now. The
                              secret of invisibility lies
                              there in my books. I shall
                              work in Kemp's laboratory
                              till I find the way back--
                                   (fiercely)
                              There is a way back, Flora.
                                   (softly)
                              --and then I shall come to
                              you--I shall offer my secret
                              to the world--with all its
                              terrible power--the Nations
                              of the world will bid for it
                              --thousands--millions--the
                              Nation that wins my secret
                              can sweep the world with
                              invisible armies!

    Suddenly a terrible change begins
    to work upon his calmness and control.

        CUT TO:

E-83   INT. BEDROOM..BIG CLOSEUP ON

The Invisible Man--the drug of madness--
the Monocane is fighting to regain its
power. His hands begin to twitch and
tremble; his mouth falls open--a horrible,
empty hole amidst the bandages that cover
his head. Again and again he passes his
gloved hand across his face--he clutches
at it--he struggles to keep the sanity
that has come to him for a fleeting moment.

CUT TO:

E-84   INT. BEDROOM..MED. CLOSE ON FLORA

The girl watches--helpless and dismayed.
She takes hold of both his hands, and
presses them.

                    FLORA
                Jack!--I want you to let my
                father help you. You know
                how clever he is. He'll
                work with you, night and
                day--until you find the
                second secret--the one
                that'll bring you back to us.
                Then we shall have those
                lovely, peaceful days again
                --out under those trees--
                after your work--in the
                evenings.

CUT TO:

E-85   INT. BEDROOM..MED. CLOSE ON

LOW CAMERA. The Invisible Man.
The change has come: the drug has
won its victory. The Invisible Man
sits bolt upright--stiff and rigid:
he is no longer a human being. He
stares at the girl before him. His
voice comes, sharp and gratingly.

                    INVISIBLE MAN
                Your father? -- clever!
                    (his head goes back
                    with a stiff jerk and
                    a high pitched, jagged
                    laugh)
                You think he can help me!
                He's got the brain of a
                tapeworm!--a maggot! beside
                mine! Don't you see what
                it means--Power!--power to
                rule--to make the world
                grovel at my feet!

CUT TO:

E-86   INT. BEDROOM..MED. TWO SHOT

The girl grips hold of his restless,
struggling hands.
                    FLORA
                Jack! Listen to me! Listen!

(CONTINUED)

E-86   CONTINUED

    The fierceness of her appeal for the
    moment silences him. He stares at
    her dumbly. He draws himself slowly
    and stiffly up, but does not speak.

    CUT TO:

E-87   INT. BEDROOM..CLOSE SHOT ON

    Flora, pleading earnestly.

                                    FLORA
                            My father found a note in
                            your room! He knows some-
                            thing about Monocane that
                            even you don't know. It
                            alters you--changes you,
                            Jack--makes you feel
                            differently. Father be-
                            lieves the power of it will
                            go if you know what you're
                            fighting. Come and stay
                            with us--let's fight it out
                            together--
    CUT TO:

E-88   INT. BEDROOM..MED. SHOT

    The Invisible Man releases his
    hands from the girl's grasp, and
    rises to his feet. Her imploring
    eyes follow him. It is clear that
    he has neither heard nor understood.

    CUT TO:

E-89   INT. BEDROOM..CLOSE SHOT ON INVISIBLE MAN

    LOW CAMERA. He looks down at her and
    speaks in a low, trembling voice that
    is bursting with exultation and
    excitement.
                                    INVISIBLE MAN
                            Power, I said--power to walk
                            into the gold vaults of the
                            Nations--into the secrets of
                            Kings--into the Holy of
                            Holies. Power to make
                            multitudes run squealing in
                            terror at the touch of my
                            little, invisible finger!
                                (he raises his head to
                                the window)
                            Even the moon's frightened
                            of me--frightened to death!
                            --the whole world's frighten-
                            ed to death!
    CUT TO:

E-90   INT. BEDROOM..MED. SHOT

> - He lowers his eyes from the sky and
> gloats over the silver-lit garden of
> lawns and trees beneath him. The
> CAMERA MOVES to take in what he sees
> below.
>
> Stealthy figures are gathering in dark
> groups amongst the shrubberies; uniformed
> men who come creeping forward from the
> fences they are scaling--creeping into
> the shelter of the trees.
>
> CUT TO:

E-91   INT. BEDROOM..MED. LONG SHOT

> CAMERA PANS ACROSS ROOM as swiftly
> and silently the Invisible Man crosses
> to a small window that looks out upon
> another side of the garden. The same
> scene greets his eyes:
>
> CUT TO:

E-92   EXT. GARDEN..LONG SHOT

> As the Invisible Man sees. Dark
> figures are forming into line in a
> flecked shadow of a rose pergola.
> A wall of men is steadily, relentlessly
> surrounding the house.
>
> CUT BACK TO:

E-93   INT. BEDROOM..MED. SHOT

> For a moment the Invisible Man stands
> watching--calmly, almost thoughtfully.
> Then he turns, and with his hands behind
> him, walks slowly to the little table.
> There is dignity in his bearing as he comes
> to a halt beside it. He looks across at
> the girl.
>
> CUT TO:

E-94   INT. BEDROOM..MED.CLOSE ON.INVISIBLE MAN

                              INVISIBLE MAN
                    So. I see. Kemp couldn't
                    sleep. He had to go down-
                    stairs. He was frightened.
                    I put my trust in Kemp: I
                    told him my secret and he
                    gave me his word of honor.
                         (he pauses for a moment)
                    You must go now, Flora.

CUT TO:

E-95   INT. BEDROOM..MED. SHOT

Flora rises and crosses to him.
CAMERA PANS with her. She too,
has seen the encroaching men below.

                              FLORA
                    I want to help you, Jack!
                    Tell me what I can do!

The impending peril has brought
a shadow of sanity to the
Invisible Man. He speaks to the
girl almost as softly as when she
first came to him.

                              INVISIBLE MAN
                    There's nothing for you to
                    do,my dear--except to go.
                    I shall come back to you--
                    I swear I shall come back--
                    because I shall defeat them.

He is standing close by her.
He tenderly takes her hand and
kisses it.

                              INVISIBLE MAN
                    Go now--my dear--

                              FLORA
                    No! I want to stay! You
                    must hide, Jack!

He shyly lays his hand upon her
shoulder and gives a soft laugh.

                              INVISIBLE MAN
                    Don't worry! The whole
                    world's my hiding place.
                    I can stand out there
                    amongst them--in the day
                    or night--and laugh at them.

CAMERA FOLLOWS THEM as gently
but firmly he turns her to the
door. He closes it, and with a
lightning movement tears at the
belt of his dressing gown as the
scene darkens.

CUT TO:

E-96   EXT. GARDENT.FULL SHOT

A corner of the moonlit garden. A
police Inspector is giving orders
in a quiet, urgent undertone.

                              INSPECTOR LANE
                    Pass down word to link hands
                    -- all round the house!

The stolid men in front of him
raise their arms and take each
other's hands.
                              VOICES
                    Link hands!--lind hands!

(CONTINUED)

247

                                    INSPECTOR LANE
                                        Keep close together--or
                                        he'll slip under your arm.!

    - CUT TO:

E-97   EXT. GARDEN..CLOSEUPS

       There is a fantastic series of
       trick shots of big hands linking
       one with the other, and then:

       CUT TO:

E-98   EXT. GARDEN..LONG SHOT

       HIGH CRANE SHOT. Of the men slowly
       advancing in a ring towards the house.

       CUT TO:

E-99   INT. HALL..KEMP'S MED.LONG SHOT

       The hall of the house, at the bottom
       of the stairs; Dr. Cranley and Kemp
       stand eagerly looking up as Flora comes
       down. The strain has done its work.
       The reaction has come--Flora sways and
       falls sobbing into her father's arms.

       CUT TO:

E-100 INT. HALL..MED. CLOSE ON FLORA

                                    FLORA
                                        Father! Save him!

       Her body becomes limp; she has
       fainted. CAMERA PULLS BACK as
       Dr. Cranley gently carries her to
       a chair. Kemp has turned.

       CUT TO:

E-101 INT. HALL..LONG SHOT

       CAMERA ON DOLLEY RECEDES Kemp as he
       gropes with staring eyes down the
       passage into the sitting room. He swiftly
       crosses to the window--throws back the
       curtains and feverishly fumbles with the
       latch. He throws open the doors and
       stands panting--gazing out onto the
       moonlit lawn. Some fifty yards away can
       be seen the line of policemen--very slowly
       and hesitantly advancing.

       CUT TO:

E-102 INT. SITTING ROOM..MEDIUM SHOT

       But as Kemp stands gazing out--a low
       chuckle comes close to his shoulder--
       and then the voice of the Invisible Man.

                                            (CONTINUED)

E- 102 CONTINUED

                              INVISIBLE MAN
                          Thank you, Kemp--for
                          opening the windows.

Kemp starts back with a low gasp
of horror. The voice goes calmly on,
gently chiding.

                              . . . You were a true friend,
                          Kemp; a man to trust. I've
                          no time now, but, believe
                          me, Kemp--as surely as the
                          moon will set and the sun
                          will rise--I shall kill you
                          tomorrow night. I shall
                          kill you even if you hide
                          in the deepest cave of the
                          earth--at ten o'clock
                          tomorrow night I shall kill
                          you.

The voice dies away. Kemp stands
paralysed; his mouth is working--
his eyes staring.

CUT TO:

E-103   INT. SITTING ROOM..SHOT OF

The curtains of the window moves with
a little rustle. The door opens a
little wider.

CUT TO:

E-104   INT. SITTING ROOM..MED CLOSE ON KEMP

There is a moment of silence before
Kemp gives a piercing scream.

                              KEMP K
                          Help!--help!--he's here L
                          --he's here!

He shrinks back against the wall,
gasping for breath.

CUT TO:

E-105   EXT. GARDEN..MED. CLOSE ON

Inspector Lane standing on the lawn--
shouting to his men. Several other
policemen included in this shot.

                              INSPECTOR LANE
                          Steady there! Stand where
                          you are!--Keep your arms
                          down!
CUT TO:

E-106   EXT. GARDEN..LONG SHOT

    VERY HIGH SHOT ON CRANE of the
    policemen who have circled the house--
    standing rigidly still. Showing the
    almost superstitious dread and tension
    on their faces--roving eyes--drawn
    features in the brilliant moonlight.

    QUICK TO:

E-107   MEDIUM SHOT..FLASH OF

    A policeman--very nervous and frightened.

    QICK CUT TO:

E-108   EXT. GARDEN..CLOSEUP OF

    Another policeman--very tense--waiting.
    CAMERA PULLSBACK A LITTLE GETTING MED.
    CLOSE SHOT - PANS along with the police-
    men--there comes a sharp smack and one of
    the men jerks back his head with a cry.

                 INSPECTOR LANE (hurrying forward)
                 What is it?

                 THE MAN (in a terrified voice)
                 Something--smacked my face!

    There comes a low laugh from the
    air. The Inspector wheels round
    as the voice of the Invisible Man
    says:
                 INVISIBLE MAN
                 Naughty boy!

    CUT TO:

E-109   EXT. GARDEN..CLOSE SHOT OF

    Another policeman in a different part
    of the ring. His face is suddenly
    pulled forward: his eyes roll as he
    lets out a howl.
                 POLICEMAN
                 Ow !--Ow !--

    CUT TO:

E-110   EXT. GARDEN.MED. PAN SHOT

    The flurried Inspector comes running
    forward. CAMERA MOVES INTO MED. CLOSE
    as he reaches the policeman.
                 INSPECTOR LANE
                 What's the matter?

                 POLICEMAN
                 He-he twisted my nose!

                 INSPECTOR
                 Keep steady,boys ! Keep
                 closed tightly up! We've
                 got him all right this time!

            (CONTINUED)

E-110 CONTINUED)

As he speaks his helmet shoots sideways
off his head onto the ground. CAMERA
PANS DOWN as he darts to pick it up, but
with a thud it soars away over the heads
of the policemen--CAMERA PANNING WITH IT.
The Invisible Man's laugh bursts out nearby.

                    INVISIBLE MAN
                Good shot ! Goal to me !
                One nil !

CUT TO:

E-111 EXT. GARDEN..MEDIUM SHOT

There is a quick shot of the
Inspector as an invisible foot
smartly kicks him backside,

                    INSPECTOR LANE
                Now then, boys--advance
                slowly--it's all right.
                He's unarmed ! You've got
                him easily !

The policemen begin stealthily
to advance once more. There are
several shots of the slowly
contracting circle.

CUT TO:

E-112 EXT. GARDEN..LONG SHOT

HIGH CAMERA ON CRANE...of the
different parts of the garden
showing the contracting circle.
Then the CAMERA CONCENTRATES upon
a part of the line where a policeman smaller than the rest is stationed.
Suddenly with a cry, his legs disappear
from beneath him and he hangs in mid-air.

CUT TO:

E-113 EXT. GARDEN..MEDIUM SHOT

The policemen to either side grasping his
out-stretched hands, his legs floating
helplessly out behind him where they are
help by the Invisible Man, who has run
between the little man's legs and picked
up his feet.

CUT TO:

E-114 EXT. GARDEN..CLOSE SHOT OF

The three heads. The policemen are too
bewildered and amazed to do anything but
stare openmouthed at their floating
companion.

CUT TO:

E-115 EXT. GARDEN..CRANE SHOT

    The men to either side hang grimly
onto his hands, but the little
policeman is pulled outwards and outwards, kicking and squealing until the
line breaks--the policemen to either
side of him leave go of his hands; he
falls tothe ground with a thud and goes
sliding and bumping away from them
across the lawn, on his chest.

    CUT TO:

E-116 EXT. GARDEN (ON DOLLEY) MED. CLOSE
       SHOT..POLICEMAN

    His outstretched hands grasping at the
grass--his face looking beseechingly
at his receding companions, his feet in
the air, where they are firmly held and
drawn along by the Invisible Man.

    He proceeds a considerable distance in
this remarkable manner--squealing and
gibbering with terror.

    CUT TO:

E-117 EXT. GARDEN..FULL SHOT

    Of the gap in the line. The policemen--
stolid, slow thinking, unimaginative men--
are completely bewildered; they stand looking
after the little man in helpless amazement.

    CUT TO:

E-118 EXT. GARDEN..CLOSEUP ON

    Two large astonished faces looking
at each other.
                POLICEMAN
             Who taught him to do that?

    CUT TO:

E-119 EXT. GARDEN..MED. SHOT..LONG

    Inspector Lane recovers from his
astonishment and springs to activity.

                INSPECTOR LANE
             It's the Invisible Man--got
             him by the feet! After him,
             boys, quick!

    The policemen pelt after their
unfortunate comrade, who has now reached
a further side of the lawn.

    But before they reach him a still more
remarkable thing occurs. The little man
stops sliding, and executes a strange
circular swing on the grass.

    CUT TO:

E-120   EXT. GARDEN..MED. SHOT OF

-   The whirlwind policeman. The Invisible
    Man--in the manner of an acrobatic dancer
    begins to swing the little policeman in a
    circle; the policeman leaves the ground
    and swings round, head outwards, feet
    inwards, a foot or two from the ground.
    Once, twice, three times he circles--and
    then there is the sound of bursting braces.
    The little policeman flies out of his
    trousers.

    CUT TO:

E-121   EXT. GARDEN.. SHOT OF

    The policeman's trousers which remain in
    the hands of the Invisible Man.

    CUT TO:

E-122   EXT. GARDEN..MED. SHOT OF GROUP

    The trousers describes a circls in the
    air and lands with a thud, full in the
    midst of the pursuing policemen. They
    collapse in a heap on the lawn: the little
    man, in tunic and wollen pants, on top.
    There are cries of anger, groans of pain,
    and chaos.

    CUT TO:

E-123   EXT. COUNTRY LANE..MED. SHOT

    An old woman, dashing headlong down a
    lane, shrieking for help.

    A moment later the policeman's trousers come
    into view, walking griskly and jauntily along
    the lane behind her. A cheerful tune is being
    whistled from the emptiness above the
    marching trousers.

    THE PICTURE FADES.

                            END OF SEQUENCE "E"

SEQUENCE "F"

FADE IN:

F-1   INT. KEMP'S SITTING ROOM
       FULL SHOT (DAY)

       Converted by the Police
       into an informal Court of
       Inquiry. The Chief of Police
       is seated at the table. Dr.
       Kemp, Dr. Cranley and Flora
       are present. A strong police
       guard is stationed at the doors
       and windows. Kemp is leaning
       forward, begging for protection.
       CUT TO:

F-2   INT. SITTING ROOM
       MED. CLOSE ON...KEMP

                      KEMP
            He threatened to kill me! -
            at ten o'clock tonight! - You
            must lock me up! - put me in
            prison! -

       CUT TO:

F-3   INT. SITTING ROOM
       MEDIUM SHOT OF...

       The group. The Chief of
       Police thinly disguising
       his contempt.

                  CHIEF OF POLICE
            You are not the only one in
            danger, Dr. Kemp. I'll see
            that you have protection.
              (he turns to Dr. Cranley)
            Now, Dr. Cranley:
              (he pauses, and looks very
              keenly at the old doctor)
            You are concealing something
            from me.

       CUT TO:

F-4   INT. SITTING ROOM
       CLOSEUP ON...

       The unhappy old Doctor makes
       a gesture to speak, but the
       Officer curtly silences him.
       CUT TO:

F-5   INT. SITTING ROOM
       MED. SHOT...GROUP

                  CHIEF OF POLICE
            ....One moment! I want you
            to explain why you and your
            daughter were in this house
            at two o'clock this morning.

      (continued)

F-5   (CONTINUED)

                                        DR. CRANLEY
                                            Dr. Kemp rang me up. He told
                                            me the man was here. He wanted
                                            my help.

                                        CHIEF OF POLICE
                                            Why did he ring you before the
                                            police? Why did your daughter
                                            come, too?

                                        DR. CRANLEY
                                            She came to - to drive the
                                            car.

              There is a pause. The
              Chief of Police looks
              very sternly at the
              old Doctor.
                                        CHIEF OF POLICE
                                            You know who the Invisible
              CUT TO: Man is, Doctor.

F-6   INT. SITTING ROOM
         CLOSEUP...DR. CRANLEY

              Dr. Cranley lowers his
              head, but makes no reply.
              CUT TO:

F-7   INT. SITTING ROOM
         MED. TWO SHOT...

              On the Chief of Police and
              Dr. Cranley - The Chief goes
              on - sharply and decisively.

                                        CHIEF OF POLICE
                                            You realize you are conceal-
                                            ing a murderer? You realize
                                            that your silence may be re-
              A Sergeant whispers a   sponsible for other murders?
              word to the Chief of
              Police - who nods, and
              addresses Dr. Cranley
              again.
              CUT TO:

F-8   INT. SITTING ROOM
         CLOSE SHOT ON...

              The Chief of Police.
                                        CHIEF OF POLICE
                                            I understand you have another
                                            assistant, besides Dr. Kemp.
                                            A Dr. Griffin. Where is Dr.
                                            Griffin?
              CAMERA PANS TO Dr.
              Cranley.
                                        DR. CRANLEY (in a low voice)
              CUT TO: He's - gone away.

F-9   INT. SITTING ROOM
        FULL SHOT...

        There is silence - sudden-
        ly broken by Kemp's loud,
        trembling voice.

                                KEMP
                    It is Griffin! What's the
                    good of concealing it! It's
                    Griffin - and he's threaten-
                    ed to murder me! He may be
                    here now, beside us! - or in
                    the garden - looking in that
                    window - or - or in a corner
                    of my bedroom waiting for me !-
                    waiting to kill me! - and you
                    just sit there ! - doing noth-
                    ing!

        The scene darkens, and
        ....DISSOLVES TO:

F-10   INT. POLICE STATION
        FULL SHOT....

        The Chief Detective is
        sitting at the table.
        Inspector Lane comes in
        and salutes.

                                INSPECTOR LANE
                    We've doubled the search
                    party ten miles round Kemp's
                    house. There's nothing to
                    report, sir. The policeman's
                    trousers were found in a
                    ditch, a mile away, that's
                    all. We found naked foot-
                    prints in the dust - they go
                    into a field and disappear.

        There is silence. The
        Detective lies back in
        his chair; he looks tired
        and ill.

                                CHIEF DETECTIVE
                    It's beaten me. I'll give ten
                    thousand dollars for a prac-
                    tical idea. He's roaming
                    the country at will - a mad-
                    man!

        DISSOLVE TO:

F-11   EXT. WOODS
        LONG SHOT...

        A search party - beating
        through a wood.
        CUT TO:

F-12   EXT. WOODS
        MED. SHOT...

        One man separated from the
        rest, suddenly throws up his
        hands and gives a cry. He
        struggles with an unseen
        opponent who has him by the
        throat. He is dragged through

        (continued)

F-12   (CONTINUED)

    the undergrowth, CAMERA
    PANNING WITH HIM - and
    disappears with a cry of
    terror into a deep chalk
    pit.
    CUT TO:

F-13   EXT. WOODS
        FULL SHOT...

    Men come running vaguely and
    helplessly to the brink.
    Another man is given a vio-
    lent push by the unseen hands
    and follows his companion into
    the depths below. One of the
    search party yells out.
                        ONE OF SEARCH PARTY
                    Stand away! - keep back!

    The men get back.
    CUT TO:

F-14   INT. SIGNAL'S BOX
        FULL SHOT...

    A signalman's box on a rail-
    road. The signalman is quiet-
    ly working his signals, smoking
    his pipe, when the door opens.
    He looks up surprised. A heavy
    lamp rises from the table and
    crashes down on his head. He
    falls unconscious.
    QUICK CUT TO:

F-15   A FLASH...OF...

    A signal lever is seen to be
    drawn back.
    QUICK CUT TO:

F-16   FLASH OF...LONG SHOT...

    A train roaring by.
    QUICK CUT TO:

F-17   FLASH OF...LONG SHOT...

    Another train coming in the
    opposite direction.
    QUICK CUT TO:

F-18   RAILROAD

    The trains rushing to their
    destruction - a terrible crash -
    bursting flames - (Miniature or
    newsreel)
    CUT TO:

F-19   INT. BANK
<u>LONG SHOT...</u>

The clerks busily at work -
customers standing at the
rails - people moving to and
fro. CAMERA DOLLEYS UP TO a
Bank Clerk attending a customer - examining a check.
The drawer beside him slowly
opens, comes right out of its
recess and floats in the air.
CAMERA PULLS BACK - the clerk
gazes in amazement. The drawer
floats away - through the door
leading into the public area,
and out of the main entrance.
CUT TO:

F-20   INT. BANK
<u>MED. SHOT ON...</u>

The people as they gather in
astonished groups and gaze
after the drawer.
CUT TO:

F-21   EXT. BANK
<u>FULL SHOT...</u>

The drawer hangs in the air a
few feet above the pavement.
Suddenly handfuls of notes rise
out of it and fly amongst the
crowd - handfuls of coins follow
it - the people have rushed out
of the bank. A voice rings out
of the air.

              INVISIBLE MAN
              There you are! A present
              from the Invisible Man! -
              Presents for everybody!

There is a shout of
laughter from the empti-
ness above the drawer,
and mad confusion in the
street. Some people turn
and run - others fight and
scramble for the money.
CUT TO:

F-22   EXT. BANK...STREET
<u>MED. CLOSE ON...</u>

A policeman makes towards the
floating drawer. It gives a
jerk, and shoots a shower of
money in his fafe. The empty
drawer comes down with a crash
upon his head and stuns him.
<u>DISSOLVE TO:</u>

F-23   INT. OFFICE AT POLICE
         STATION...FULL SHOT...

         The Chief Detective - in his
         office. The room is filled
         with reporters with open
         notebooks. He is address-
         ing them.

                            CHIEF DETECTIVE
                     I tell you in confidence that
                     twenty men of the search
                     parties have been killed -
                     and a hundred in the train
                     disaster. But I appeal to
                     you, gentlemen, to keep all
                     the news of these disasters
                     from your papers.

         CUT TO:

F-24   INT. OFFICE
         PAN SHOT OF...

         The reporters notebooks
         rapidly writing.
         CUT TO:

F-25   INT. OFFICE
         MED. CLOSE ON GROUP...

         of reporters.

                        CHIEF DETECTIVE (continues)
                     The public are naturally in
                     a very nervous condition -
                     all manner of rumors are
                     flying around. The Invisible
                     Man has been reported in a
                     hundred different places. I
                     appeal to you to help us keep
                     the public calm.

         CUT TO:

F-26   INT. OFFICE
         CLOSE SHOT ON...

         One of the reporters.

                        REPORTER
                     Can you tell us what plans
                     you've got for capturing him?

         CUT TO:

F-27   INT. OFFICE
         TWO SHOT ON...

         Chief Detective and a
         reporter.

                        CHIEF DETECTIVE
                     A hundred thousand men are
                     searching - and watching.

                        REPORTER
                     But have you any special
                     secret means of getting him?

         (continued)

F-27   (CONTINUED)

                                    CHIEF DETECTIVE
                                    The police have offered twen-
                                    ty thousand dollars for the
                                    first effective means.

                                    REPORTER
                                    Why not bloodhounds?

                                    CHIEF DETECTIVE
                                    The bloodhounds have lost the
                                    scent.

                                    REPORTER
                                    Why not put wet tar on all
                                    the roads? - then chase the
                                    black soles of his feet?

        CUT TO:

F-28   INT. OFFICE
        CLOSE SHOT ON...

        The Chief Detective.

                                    CHIEF DETECTIVE
                                    Because he's not a fool. He
                                    keeps to the open country.
                                        (he pauses - and goes on
                                         impressively)
                                    We've got one hope, gentle-
                                    men, - but I dare not say a
                                    word of it here. He may be
                                    standing there with you, lis-
                                    tening. I can only say that
                                    we expect to catch him - at
                                    ten o'clock tonight. If you
                                    come here at midnight I may
                                    have good news.

        DISSOLVE TO:

F-29   INT. KEMP'S SITTING ROOM
        FULL SHOT - HIGH CAMERA (NIGHT)

        The Chief Detective is stand-
        ing there, with several Police
        Officers. Dr. Cranley and
        Kemp are also present.

                                    CHIEF DETECTIVE
                                    Everything depends upon the
                                    way we carry out my plan.
                                    I'll tell you directly we've
                                    made certain he's not in this
                                    room.

        CUT TO:

F-30   INT. SITTING ROOM
        MEDIUM SHOT...

        The Chief Detective turns
        to two detectives who are
        holding a large net.

                                    CHIEF DETECTIVE
                                    Draw that net right across
                                    the room. Stand back, gentle-
                                    men, close against the wall.

        (continued)

F-30 (CONTINUED)

CAMERA PANS WITH the two
detectives as they take
their stand in opposite
corners upon the far side
of the room. They raise
the net as high as possible -
and keeping close to the wall,
bring the net straight across
the room, passing so close to
the men against the wall that
no invisible body could slip
by.
CUT TO:

F-31   INT. SITTING ROOM
         MED. CLOSE SHOT...

The operation finished, the
Detective turns with a slight
laugh.

                              CHIEF DETECTIVE
                         Well, we're safe in here at
                         last! Keep an eye on the
                         windows.

He leans forward - all
crowd round him as the
CAMERA MOVES IN CLOSER
GETTING SCREEN FULL of
heads close together in
conspiracy. He lowers
his voice, and speaks
tensely and clearly.

                         CHIEF DETECTIVE
                         Now listen carefully. We've
                         got a chance tonight that'll
                         never come again. He's threat-
                         ened to murder Dr. Kemp at
                         ten o'clock. For what we
                         know of him he'll do his ut-
                         most to carry that out. He
                         is certain to be watching
                         near this house for some
                         time beforehand. At half
                         past nine, Dr. Kemp, with
                         a bodyguard of police will
                         leave this house and walk
                         down to the Police Station.
                         It's a natural thing for Dr.
                         Kemp to seek protection. The
                         Invisible Man is certain to
                         be near - he is certain to
                         see what is happening.

         CUT TO:

F-32   INT. SITTING ROOM
         CLOSE TWO SHOT...

Kemp and the Chief
Detective.

                         KEMP (in a trembling voice)
                         You mean - you're going to
                         use me as a bait?

                         CHIEF DETECTIVE
                         Yes.

     (continued)

261

F-32   (CONTINUED)

                                        KEMP
                                            I can't.

                                        CHIEF DETECTIVE
                                            You must. You're perfectly
                                            safe.

        Kemp gives a hard, dry
        laugh...as we...
        CUT TO:

F-33   INT. SITTING ROOM
        MEDIUM SHOT ON...

        The group listening
        to Kemp.

                                        KEMP
                                            Safe! He's not human! - he
                                            can pass through anything -
                                            prison walls - everything!

                                        CHIEF DETECTIVE
                                            Don't be a fool!

                                        KEMP
                                            I tell you - I can't sit
                                            there in the station - wait-
                                            ing! - He'll kill you! - kill
                                            you all - then take the keys
                                            and come to me!

        The Detective is silent
        for a moment. He con-
        siders Kemp thoughtfully.
        CUT TO:

F-34   INT. SITTING ROOM
        CLOSEUP OF...

        The Chief Detective.

                                        CHIEF DETECTIVE
                                            Very well, then. If you're
                                            afraid of staying in the
                                            Police Station you can leave
                                            it - directly you are inside.
                                            There's a secret way out thru
                                            the Inspector's private house.
                                            We'll disguise you as a police-
                                            man. You can go out with
                                            other uniformed men and drive
                                            away. Even if he sees you go
                                            he won't recognize you - he'll
                                            most probably be in front -
                                            waiting to break in at ten
                                            o'clock.

        CUT TO:

F-35   INT. SITTING ROOM
        CLOSEUP ON...KEMP

                                        KEMP
                                            What happens to me then?

        CUT TO:

F-36   INT. SITTING ROOM
        TWO SHOT ON...

        The Chief Detective and
        Kemp.

                                    CHIEF DETECTIVE
                                I'll have you driven back to
                                this house - quietly - by the
                                back lanes. Get in your car
                                and drive away, miles away -
                                and stay in the country till
                                you hear we've got him. You
                                needn't fear. We shall get
                                him this time. I shall lay
                                traps that even an invisible
                                man can't pass.
                                    (he looks at his watch)
                                You've got an hour to get
                                ready. I shall send a dozen
                                policemen at half past nine.

        DISSOLVE TO:

F-37   EXT. COURTYARD OF PRISON
        LONG SHOT...(NIGHT)

        The Chief Detective, surround-
        ed by uniformed men, is de-
        monstrating his plan.   A
        large white sheet is nailed
        to one of the walls; before
        it stands a paint spraying
        machine - the type used for
        cellulosing cars. He presses
        a button - a spray of black
        paint covers the sheet ex-
        cept for the corners.

                                    CHIEF DETECTIVE
                                You see it covers a wide
                                range - even at close quarts.
                                I've got twenty of these
                                machines - a good man to
                                each. One splash of this
                                on his skin - and you've
                                got something to follow at
                                last.

            CUT TO:

F-38   EXT. COURTYARD
        CLOSER GROUP SHOT...

                                    A SERGEANT
                                Why not paint the top of the
                                wall?

                                    CHIEF DETECTIVE
                                Because he would smell it.
                                I've got a better plan. I'm
                                laying a thin layer of loose
                                earth along the top. The
                                slightest touch will disturb
                                it....and we've got something
                                to follow at last.

        DISSOLVE TO:

                            263

F-39   INT. FLORA'S BEDROOM
        FULL SHOT...(NIGHT)

        She is seated in her dress-
        ing gown. Dr. Cranley is
        by her side. It is clear
        that the terrible events of
        the day have brought her to
        the verge of collapse.
        CAMERA ON DOLLEY MOVES IN
        CLOSER as Dr. Cranley leans
        over her and speaks kindly.
                        DR. CRANLEY
                Try and sleep now, my dear.
                There's nothing you can do.
                We must just pray that the
                police can take him without
                harming him.

        He leans over her, and
        kisses her, then quietly
        leaves the room. She sits
        wearily in her chair. Be-
        fore her on a little table,
        stands a photograph. She
        draws it towards her - gazes
        at it - (but we do not see
        the face). Her head falls
        between her hands. Her
        shoulders tremble as she
        tries to stifle the con-
        vulsive agony within her.
        DISSOLVE TO:

F-40   EXT. KEMP'S HOUSE
        FULL SHOT...(NIGHT)

        The front door of Kemp's house.
        A squad of uniformed men are
        waiting. Kemp emerges - takes
        his place in their centre, and
        the little group moves out into
        the moonlit lane. CAMERA PANS
        WITH THEM - The last policeman
        closes the gate behind him.
        CUT TO:

F-41   CLOSE SHOT ON...
        GATE

        The gate stands closed for a
        moment - then the latch clicks
        up; the gate opens and closes
        as the Invisible Man steps out
        to follow Kemp and his bodyguard.
        CUT TO:

F-42   EXT. POLICE STATION
        LONG SHOT...

        CAMERA PANS with the group going
        down the street and entering the
        police station. It is a forbidding,
        prison-like building, standing iso-
        lated from other habitation. A stone
        wall, about six feet high, surrounds
        all sides.
        CUT TO:

F-43   INT. COURTYARD
        FULL SHOT...(NIGHT)

        The Chief Detective is in the
        courtyard as the party enters -
        in a solid block to prevent all
        possibility of an invisible body
        slipping through beside them.
        Policemen are stationed round
        the walls, each with a spraying
        machine beside him. The Chief
        Detective is standing by.
                            CHIEF DETECTIVE (in a low voice)
                                All right? Go straight
                                ahead!
        Kemp and his bodyguard
        enter the station. The
        door closes behind them.
        DISSOLVE TO:

F-44   INT. POLICE STATION
        MEDIUM SHOT...(NIGHT)

        Kemp is feverishly buttoning
        a police greatcoat up to his
        chin. Several uniformed men
        stand by.
        CUT TO:

F-45   EXT. BACK OF STATION
        MED. LONG SHOT...(NIGHT)

        The secret, back entrance to
        the Station. It is simply the
        door to the Inspector's house.
        A car draws up. A Sergeant and
        a policeman get out - go up to
        the door, knock and gain ad-
        mittance.
        CUT TO:

F-46   PASSAGE INSIDE THE HOUSE
        MED. SHOT...

        Kemp stands waiting. The
        Inspector curtly says:
                            INSPECTOR
                                Come on.
        Kemp swiftly leaves the
        house with the Inspector.
        CUT TO:

F-47   EXT. BACK OF STATION
        MED. LONG SHOT...

        Kemp and Inspector comes out
        of the house and enter the car,
        which drives off into the night.
        CUT TO:

265

F-48   EXT. COURTYARD
        FULL SHOT...

        The guards tensely on the
        alert. The Chief Detective
        looks at his watch.

                            CHIEF DETECTIVE (softly)
                        Twenty minutes to ten.
                        Keep your eyes open now,
                        boys.

        There is a shot of various
        policemen standing by their
        strange weapons - their eyes
        fixed on the wall.
        CUT TO:

F-49   EXT. COURTYARD
        MED. TWO SHOT...

        One policeman suddenly grows
        excited - he whispers to the
        Chief Detective who is passing.

                            POLICEMAN
                        Here! Quick, sir!

        The Detective crosses
        to the man.
                            I heard footsteps outside -
                            soft footsteps, like naked
                            feet!

        CUT TO:

F-50   EXT. COURTYARD
        CLOSEUP OF...

        The two heads - as the
        Chief Detective and the
        policeman stand tensely
        listening and watching.
        CUT TO:

F-51   EXT LAND (NIGHT)
       MED LONG SHOT ON...

-   the police car - drawing up
    in a dark narrow lane behind
    Kemp's house.

F-52   INT CAR. CLOSE TWO SHOT

Kemp leans forward to the
driver.

> DRIVER
> Where are you going to?

> KEMP
> Up in the mountains - a
> hundred miles away!
> This'll do - drop me here!

The car halts. Kemp
quickly gets out and makes
off through the darkness.
DISSOLVE TO:

F-53   INT KEMP'S GARAGE
       FULL SHOT ON...

Kemp climbing into his car
in his garage.

F-54   EXT COURTYARD. MED TWO SHOT

The Chief Detective is anxiously
looking at his watch. The Sergeant is standing beside him.
Both are obviously in a state
of great nervous tension.

> CHIEF DETECTIVE
> It only wants ten minutes
> to ten. He's bound to do
> something in a minute.

CAMERA PANS to show the
guards in their positions round
the walls; it pauses by the
heavily barred front gate.

F-55   EXT COURTYARD. CLOSE SHOT

The Chief Detective and the
Sergeant.

> SERGEANT
> Those certainly were steps
> outside - like naked feet.
> (he pauses)
> D'you suppose he'll try
> getting in through the
> house?

> CHIEF DETECTIVE
> Every door and window's
> barred - with a couple of
> guards on each. He'll try
> the wall right enough -

CUT BACK TO:

F-56   EXT COURTYARD. CLOSEUP ON..

       one of the guards - anxiously
       listening.

F-57   OUTSIDE PRISON WALLS
       MED CLOSE ON...

       a white cat, strolling round
       outside the prison walls.
       QUICK CUT TO:

F-58   EXT COURTYARD. CLOSEUP ON..

       the guard, who has heard a
       faint sound, and is acutely
       on the alert.

F-59   OUTSIDE PRISON WALL
       MED SHOT ON..

       The cat, jumping up from
       the outside, onto the wall.

F-60   EXT COURTYARD. MED CLOSE SHOT

       opposite side of wall. A little
       shower of loose earth is dis-
       turbed as the cat's paws alight
       on it. The guard gives a shout
       of excitement and lets fly with
       his spray of black paint.

F-61   EXT COURTYARD. FULL SHOT

       Shouts of warning - the Chief
       Detective runs excitedly about.

                              CHIEF DETECTIVE
                             Keep to your stations!
                             Watch the wall there!

       CAMERA MOVES to a fat,
       goggle-eyed policeman,
       shouting to the Chief
       Detective.

                         POLICEMAN
                             He's over the wall! - I
                             felt breathing! - Down my
                             neck!

F-62   EXT COURTYARD. MED SHOT

    The cat - now a completely
    black one - galloping madly
    off in the moonlight.

F-63   EXT ROAD IN MOUNTAINS..
          FULL SHOT ON...

    Kemp - alone in his car, crouch-
    ing over his driving wheel, tear-
    ing furiously through the night.
    He is up in the mountains now -
    we can see the forbidding moonlit
    crests and the ominous ravines
    beside the road. The car flies
    through a little wayside village.
    The Church clock is slowly strik-
    ing ten.

F-64   INT CAR. MED CLOSE ON...

    Kemp - listens and throws back
    his head in exultation.

                            KEMP
                  Ten o'clock - at ten
                  o'clock he wanted to murder
                  me!

    He laughs loudly and
    triumphantly, bends to
    the wheel and flies on
    through the night - a grim
    smile of victory on his face -
    up and up the winding mountain
    road - into the desolation.
    Slowly CAMERA PANS from his set
    profile and concentrates upon
    the empty back seat of the car.
    CAMERA REMAINS FIXED upon the
    bare seat for a few seconds -
    until a calm voice comes from
    the emptiness; the voice of the
    Invisible Man.

                      INVISIBLE MAN
                  I think this'll do nicely,
                  Kemp. We'll stop here.

F-65   INT CAR. TWO SHOT

    Kemp is too astonished and
    horrified to utter a sound.

                      INVISIBLE MAN
                  It's ten o'clock. I came
                  with you to keep my promise.

    The car has come to a
    halt.

F-66   INT CAR. CLOSEUP ON

Kemp, suddenly finds his voice -
hoarse and unreal though it
sounds.

KEMP
No - it's all a mistake,
Griffin! I swear I never
told the police! I want
to help you - let me be
your partner!

The voice of the Invisible
Man comes calmly and relent-
lessly..

INVISIBLE MAN
I've had a cold and uncom-
fortable journey - just to
keep my promise at ten
o'clock.

F-67   INT CAR. MED SHOT

The Invisible Man pauses, then
continues, Kemp listening in
terror.

INVISIBLE MAN
...I went into the Police
Station with you, Kemp.
I stood by while you changed into that coat. - I rode
on the running board of
the car that took you home
again --

Kemp makes a sudden dive for
the door - a thick scarf that
he is wearing suddenly jerks
back and nearly throttles him.

F-68   INT CAR. CLOSEUP ON

Kemp - strangling. His head
is pulled back over the driving
seat - he gives a strangled cry.
There follows a fierce struggle -
Kemp snarling and groaning like
a beast at bay. But he is powerless
against his stronger opponent -
hopelessly out-pointed by his opponent's dreadful advantage.

F-69   EXT ROAD. MED SHOT

Kemp is dragged by invisible hands
from the car to the grass verge
of the road - his hands are lashed
behind him by a piece of rope -
his feet are bound together.

F-70   EXT ROAD. CLOSE SHOT ON

    Invisible hands tying Kemp's
    hands and binding his feet.

F-71   EXT ROAD. MED SHOT ON KEMP

    Powerless and impotent he rises
    from the ground - hovers in a
    sitting position and sails slowly
    back into the car - into the front
    seat beside the driver. In a moment
    the car starts up, the steering
    wheel moves.

F-72   INT CAR. CLOSE SHOT ON

    The gear handle slips into
    connection - the accelerator -
    and the brake.

F-73   EXT MOUNTAIN ROAD. LONG SHOT

    The car moves off apparently by
    itself - climbing up the mountain
    road.

F-74   INT CAR. MED CLOSE KEMP

    His eyes roll around in agony
    to the empty seat beside him. Once
    more the voice comes - from the
    emptiness above the wheel.

                INVISIBLE MAN
                I hope your car's
                insured, Kemp. I'm
                afraid there's going
                to be a nasty accident
                in a minute.

F-75   EXT MOUNTAIN ROAD. FULL SHOT

    The car has climbed to a great
    height upon the winding mountain
    road. Slowly it pulls up and
    steers into a little piece of
    slightly sloping ground - the kind
    of clear space used by picnicers
    to get the magnificent view beneath
    them. A little flimsy white rail-
    ing marks the further end of the
    space - beyond that the mountain
    steepens into the dreadful, boulder-
    strewn descent of the ravine.

                INVISIBLE MAN
                ---a very nasty accident.

F-76   INT CAR. MED CLOSE ON

    Kemp - as he cries out in
    terror..

                    KEMP
           Griffin! - I'll do any-
           thing! - everything you ask
           me!

                  INVISIBLE MAN
           You will? - that's fine.
           Just sit where you are.

F-77   EXT MOUNTAIN ROAD
        MED SHOT

    Kemp, sitting in the car,
    terrified.

                  INVISIBLE MAN
           I'll get out and take the
           hand brake off, and give
           you a little shove to help
           you on. You'll run gently
           down - and through the
           railings. Then you'll have
           a big thrill for a hundred
           yards or so - till you hit
           a boulder. Then you'll do
           a somersault and probably
           break your arms - then a
           grand finish up with a
           broken neck.

    There is a moment of
    silence. The driver's
    door opens and closes.

F-78   INT CAR. CLOSE SHOT ON

    Kemp - frantic with fear.
    The voice comes again from
    outside.

                  INVISIBLE MAN
           Well, goodbye, Kemp. I
           always said you were a
           dirty little coward. You're
           a dirty, sneaking little
           rat as well. Goodbye.

    Kemp's terrified eyes are
    on the hand brake - the catch
    rises and the lever moves for-
    ward - slowly the car begins
    to move as we... CUT TO:

F-79   EXT MOUNTAIN ROAD. MED LONG SHOT

    The car quickens its pace as
    strong, invisible hands assist
    it from the behind. It comes to
    the railings.

F-80   MED SHOT

>   As the car breaks through
and breaks the railings and
begins its terrible descent
into the ravine.

F-81   EXT RAVINE. FULL SHOT

of the falling car.

F-82   MED SHOT. OF THE RAILINGS

The railings are broken. We
hear the low, maniacal laughter
of the Invisible Man as if he
were standing by the railings
watching the car go to its destruction.

F-83   BOTTOM OF RAVINE. LONG SHOT

A shot of the shapeless, blazing
wreck at the bottom of the ravine.
Off stage we hear again the low,
maniacal laughter of the Invisible
Man.

FADE OUT

END OF SEQUENCE "F"

SEQUENCE "G"

FADE IN:

G-1   INT. CONFERENCE ROOM
       DOLLEY SHOT. DAY

    At general Police Headquarters.
    A sternly furnished, lofty apart-
    ment with a long table down the
    center. A conference is in pro-
    gress. The Chief of Police is
    at the head of the table; seated
    round are the senior Detectives
    and Officers concerned in the man-
    hunt. The Chief of Police is
    summarizing the case. CAMERA STARTS
    ON MED. CLOSE on the Chief of Police
    and PULL BACK to a FULL SHOT show-
    ing the stupid, formal arrangement.

                  CHIEF OF POLICE
             A thousand replies have
             come to my appeal for sug-
             gesting ways of catching
             the Invisible Man. Some
             are clever - some are
             stupid - all are impos-
             sible. Most of them sug-
             gest laying tar, or other
             substances that would
             stick to his feet. Some
             suggest getting together
             all the blind people in
             the country - to track him
             with their acute instinct-
             ive senses. That's no
             good. Crowds of searchers
             are a waste of time - he
             can slip through with
             absolute ease.

G-2   INT. CONFERENCE ROOM
       CLOSE SHOT ON..

    A very stupid, sleepy-
    looking Police Officer.

                  POLICE OFFICER
             But he's got to sleep.
             They might catch him
             asleep.

    CUT TO:

G-3   INT. CONFERENCE ROOM
       CLOSE SHOT ON..

    Another one of the Police
    Officers.
                  2ND POLICE OFFICER
             He's got to eat and drink.

    CUT TO:

nn   G-4   INT. CONFERENCE ROOM
             MEDIUM SHOT..

> The Chief of Police is sitting
> at the head of the table - the
> others in their respective
> places.

                              CHIEF OF POLICE
                                   A cafe was robbed last
                              night in Manton - but
                              it's no proof. There are
                              robberies every night -
                              by ordinary burglars -

> As the Chief of Police is
> speaking, the picture
> DISSOLVES TO:

      G-5   EXT. FIELDS..LONG SHOT..

> showing an old barn, stand-
> ing isolated upon some flat,
> bare fields.
> CUT TO:

      G-6   CLOSE SHOTON...THE DOOR

> The door of the barn opens
> with a rusty grating sound -
> and gently closes.
> CUT TO:

      G-7   INT. BARN...DAY...MED LONG SHOT

> A remarkable old place: a few
> farming implements along the
> walls - a pile of straw in one
> of the corners - CAMERA PANS
> over to the straw and we see
> evidences of feet disturbing hay,
> etc. Slowly the straw is pulled
> back: it forms itself into all
> kinds of weird heaps as the
> Invisible Man prepares for him-
> self a resting place. Then some
> of the straw forms itself into a
> little mound. The Invisible Man
> has pulled it over his tired
> body. The straw becomes still.
> All we hear is a long drawn sigh -
> and weary, rhythmic breathing.
> CUT BACK TO:

      G-8   INT. CONFERENCE ROOM
             MED SHOT..HIGH CAMERA   .

> The Chief of Police is summing
> up the Conference.

                              CHIEF OF POLICE
                                   There's only one thing to
                              do. We must wait until
                              we hear of him again.

                              POLICE OFFICER
                                   You mean - another murder?

            CONTINUED

G-8   CONTINUED

                                           CHIEF OF POLICE
                                      If necessary we must wait
                                      for another murder.
                                      Directly the news comes
                                      we must race every man we
                                      have - by lorry and car
                                      and cycle and aeroplane -
                                      five hundred police and
                                      ten thousand soldiers
                                      will surround the area -
                                      not one deep but five
                                      deep - and close in until
                                      we take him. I've with-
                                      drawn all the search
                                      parties: they are standing
                                      by - waiting for the
                                      signal.

        DISSOLVE TO:

G-9   EXT. BARN...LONG SHOT..DAY

        The barn in the bare fields.
        The sky is overcast. Snow
        is lightly floating down in
        the still sky. An old farmer
        comes slowly along with a rake
        over his shoulder.
        CUT TO:

G-10   EXT. BARN
        CLOSER SHOT...ON

        The old farmer as he goes up
        to the door - opens it and
        goes in.

G-11   INT. BARN...MED SHOT ON...

        He leans his rake against the
        wall and picks up a little straw
        to clean his hands. As he
        wipes them, a faint sound at-
        tracts his attention. He pauses
        to listen.
        CUT TO:

G-12   INT. BARN...MED CLOSE SHOT..

        On the straw - there comes the
        heavy, rhythimic breathing of a
        sleeping man - now and then a
        faint snore.
        CUT TO:

G-13   INT. BARN...MED PAN SHOT...

        The old farmer looks surprised,
        and glances round, expecting to
        find a tramp. He looks still more
        surprised when he sees nobody.
        CAMERA PANS as he approaches the
        sound of the snoring and sees the
        strangely piled heap of straw which
        covers the Invisible Man.
        CUT TO:

G-14   INT. BARN...CLOSE SHOT ON...

          The old farmer as he listens
          again. There is no mistaking
          the position of the heavy
          breathing - or the faint rise
          and fall of the straw that
          accompanies it.
          CUT TO:

G-15   INT. BARN...MED LONG SHOT...

          He very stealthily examines the
          straw - and his jaw drops in
          astonishment when the straw moves
          more definitely as the Invisible
          Man stirs in his sleep, and gives
          a deeper snore. The farmer backs
          very stealthily away. He gets to
          the door, slips out, and runs off
          as fast as he can through the
          snow. THE CAMERA PANS with him
          and we see him running away.

          The snow is falling more heavily
          now. It is beginning to whiten
          the ground.
          CUT TO:

G-16   INT. CONFERENCE ROOM...LONG SHOT

          The Committee are rising from
          the table.

                              CHIEF OF POLICE
                         Go back to your stations
                         now - and stand by for
                         orders.

          As the men turn from the
          table, one of them looks
          towards the window and
          sees the snow. The significance
          of it flashes to his mind.
          He turns excitedly to the
          Chief of Police and points
          to the window.

                              DETECTIVE
                         Look there! - We wanted
                         help! There it is!

          The Chief looks out
          upon the street. Already
          it is powdered white. He
          turns to the waiting man
          and they all go to the
          window.
          CUT TO:

G-17   INT. CONFERENCE ROOM...MED
          SHOT ON...

          The group at the window looking
          out into the street at the snow.

                              CHIEF OF POLICE
                         It's now or never. Snow
                         won't lie long this time
                         of year. It may be gone
                         in a few hours.

          CONTINUED

CHIEF OF POLICE (contd)
(he turns briskly to
his lieutenant)
Norton! Find out if the
snow's general over the
country - get a broadcast
message out! He can't
stay out in this bitter
cold - he'll seek shelter--
every barn and building
must be searched - every
field and wood and road
must be watched for bare
foot-prints - quick! Get
ahead!

As the men start to
leave the window we ...
CUT TO:

G-18   EXT. VILLAGE STREET
EXTREME LONG SHOT...DAY

The old farmer, lumbering as
quickly as he can down the
street of a small village.
The snow is falling heavily.
He reaches the local Police
Station and runs in.
CUT TO:

G-19   INT. POLICE STATION...MED.
SHOT...DAY

A Police Officer looks up in
astonishment at the excited,
panting old farmer.
CUT TO:

G-20   INT. POLICE STATION...TWO SHOT...

FARMER   (between gasps for
breath)
Excuse me, sir - there's
breathing in my barn.

POLICEMAN
What d'you mean? - breathing in your barn?

FARMER
The - Invisible - Man!

The Policeman sits up,
as the Farmer continues:

-Sure as I stand here!
(he gasps)
Went to put my rake away-
and there he was - asleep
in the straw! - snoring,
sir!

The Policeman eyes the
Farmer thoughtfully.

POLICEMAN
Where is the barn?

FARMER
The one down in Five-acre
Field! - 'bout a mile from
'ere - on the main road!

CONTINUED

The Policeman picks up
his telephone.

       POLICEMAN
        Give me Headquarters -
        quickly!

CUT TO:

G-21 INT. CHIEF DETECTIVE'S OFFICE..
    MED SHOT...DAY

Chief of Police - speaking to
the Chief Detective in his office:
other officers standing eagerly
round - all together like sheep.

       CHIEF OF POLICE
        The farmer may have im-
        agined it! - but we can't
        leave anything to chance.
        Surround the barn - it's
        no good trying to take
        him inside - force him
        out into the snow! - take
        a pile of wood and some
        gasoline - and set fire to
        it.

CUT TO:

G-22 EXT. POLICE STATION...
    MED LONG SHOT...DAY

The policemen running out -
all in rows.
QUICK CUT TO:

G-23 EXT. ROAD...FULL LONG SHOT

Lorries full of soldiers swing
out of some barracks and roar
off down a road.
QUICK CUT TO:

G-24 EXT. ROAD...FULL SHOT...

Mobile Police on fast cycles -
moving quickly down a straight
road.
QUICK CUT TO:

G-25 EXT. POLICE STATION...FULL SHOT

The Chief of Police - and the
Chief Detective with his Staff -
coming out of Headquarters and
quickly climbing into a large
car.
DISSOLVE TO:

G-26 EXT. FIELD...FULL SHOT...

The Police car is drawn up - a
Chauffeur at the wheel. The
Chief of police sitting in car.

The barn can be seen - half a
mile away, across the fields.
The snow is still falling, but
somewhat lighter now. The ground
CONTINUED

is covered about half an
inch deep. The roof of the
barn is as white as the ground
surrounding it, but the dark,
rough timbered walls stand
starkly in their isolation.
CUT TO:

G-27   MED CLOSE ON

The old Farmer and the Chief
of Police.

> FARMER   (pointing)
> That's it, sir! He's in
> there! - under a pile of
> straw!

> CHIEF OF POLICE
> Are there any windows he
> can watch from?

> FARMER
> No, sir, there's only the
> door.

The Chief of Police stands
for a moment, looking at the
barn: his keen eyes take in
the surrounding country.
CUT TO:

G-28   INT. BARN...FULL SHOT...DAY

The straw lies as it was when
the Farmer left it. The peaceful
breathing of the sleeping man comes,
as before, from the dim corner
of his refuge. CAMERA DOLLEYS UP
TO CLOSE SHOT on the Invisible Man.
CUT BACK TO:

G-29   EXT. ROAD...FULL SHOT...

The Chief of Police and the Farmer
are standing up in the car. The Chief
of Police, completing his survey.
He turns to the Farmer.

> CHIEF OF POLICE
> Thank you. There's a re-
> ward of one thousand
> pounds waiting for you if
> we're successful.

The CAMERA MOVES to the
Farmer's dazed face, then
follows the Chief of Police
down the lane to where it
branches from the main
thoroughfare. A line of
lorries, filled with soldiers,
stands waiting. The Military
Officer in charge of the party
is standing beside the leading
lorry, and comes eagerly to the
Chief of Police.
CUT TO:

                              CHIEF OF POLICE (indicating the
                                        barn)
                              That's the place. We're
                              lucky to have the open
                              country. Take your men
                              over to that line of trees
                              and cover the country
                              from the road to the top
                              of the hill.

The Military Officer
salutes, and swings
himself onto the seat
beside the driver of the
leading lorry. The lorries
move off down the road.
CUT TO:

G-31   EXT. FIELD...FULL SHOT...

The Chief of Police, Chief
Detective and other important
officials, standing together
beside a fence. The barn lies
below them - a few hundred yards
away.

                              CHIEF DETECTIVE
                              There's no time to lose.
                              We can't wait till he
                              comes out to search for
                              food. We must fire the
                              barn at once and drive
                              him out into the snow.

He turns. The CAMERA PANS
to a line of policemen standing nearby. Each has a pile
of dry wood stacked under his
arm. The Detective gives his
orders.

                              CHIEF DETECTIVE
                              Keep in a single file - we
                              don't want a lot of your
                              footprints round the hut -
                              we want the snow left for
                              his feet alone.

CUT TO:

G-32   EXT. FIELD...MED SHOT

He nods abruptly to the men,
who make off stealthily - in
single file - about five of
them in all. The last carries
a can of paraffin.
CUT TO:

G-33   EXT. BARN...LONG SHOT...

The men - their approach softened
by the snow, reach the wall, and
stack the wood against its side.
CUT TO:

G-34   EXT. FIELD...MED.SHOT...

Quick shot of a line of soldiers,
standing waiting behind the trees.
CUT TO:

nn   G-35   EXT. ROAD...MED SHOT...

               Policemen, lining the hedge
               alongside the road.
               CUT TO:

     G-36   EXT. LANE...MED CLOSE SHOT ON...

               The old Farmer - stolidly watch-
               ing in the bye lane.
               CUT BACK TO:

     G-37   EXT. BARN...MED SHOT...

               The men beside the hut. The
               fuel is laid. The man with the
               can of paraffin comes forward
               and empties its contents over
               the wood and upon the wall of
               the hut.

     G-38   EXT. BARN...CLOSER SHOT...

               One man strikes a match and
               applies it to the wood. There
               is a sheet of flame - the men back
               away from its heat and retire the
               way they came.
               CUT TO:

     G-39   EXT. FIELD...MED SHOT....

               The Chief Detective, standing with
               his staff - binoculars to his eyes.
               CUT TO:

     G-40   A BINOCULAR VIEW...CLOSE UP...

               Of the door of the burning hut.
               The door remains closed.
               CUT TO:

     G-41   INT. BARN...FULL SHOT...

               The interior of the hut. Smoke
               begins to wreath the ceiling
               and creep round the pile of straw -
               suddenly the straw heaves, and a
               way is broken between it.
               CUT BACK TO:

     G-42   EXT. FIELD...MED SHOT...CLOSE

               The Chief Detective - standing
               rigidly with the glasses to his
               eyes - THE CAMERA MOVES FORWARD
               getting medium shot of the barn.
               Although the snow has naturally
               melted upon the ground to the side
               where the fire is blazing, it still
               lies thickly up to the door of the
               barn on the opposite side. The snow
               has ceased to fall now: the air is
               bright and clear. Suddenly the door
               is flung open. Nothing happens
               for a moment. It is as if the In-
               visible Man has thrown the door
               open and now stands looking out from
               the threshold - dismayed at the sight
               CONTINUED

of the thick snow in front of
him. But the fire has now got
the barn firmly in its ravenous
grip - a swirl of dark smoke
eddies from the thatch above the
door.
CUT TO:

G-43   EXT. BARN...MED CLOSE SHOT...

Slow, furtive footsteps appear in
the snow as the Invisible Man is
forced to advance across the bitter,
desolate field.
CUT TO:

G-44   EXT. FIELD...TWO SHOT...

The Chief Detective, who has
lowered the binoculars and is
excitedly holding the arm of the
Sergeant beside him

                    CHIEF DETECTIVE
                      He's out! Look!

He hands the binoculars
to the Sergeant, who scans
the scene fascinated.
CUT TO:

G-45   SHOT OF...

The blazing barn through the
binoculars. The Chief Detective's
voice comes over the picture.

                    CHIEF DETECTIVE
                      The fire's got hold all
                      right - he'll never get
                      back now.

CUT TO:

G-46   EXT. BARN...MED SHOT...

PAN SHOT of the trail of footsteps advancing from the hut -
the Invisible Man has not yet
seen the hidden watchers around
him.
CUT TO:

G-47   EXT. FIELD...MED SHOT...

The Chief Detective and his
group. He turns to the
Sergeant.

                    CHIEF DETECTIVE
                      Give the signal to
                      advance.

The Sergeant raises his
revolver and fires into the
air. The sound echoes over
the silent meadows.
CUT TO:

nn   G-48   EXT. FIELD...LONG SHOT...

HIGH CAMERA. The soldiers,
leaving the shelter of the
trees advancing in close line.
CUT TO:

G-49   EXT. LANE...LONG SHOT...

HIGH CAMERA. The police, rising
from the hedgerows of the lane.
CUT TO:

G-50   EXT. FIELD...LONG SHOT...

The Chief Detective, advancing
with his staff - a line of
police behind them.

G-51   EXT. BARN...MED SHOT...

The footprints in the snow. The
trail has stopped dead, upon the
sound of the revolver. The Invisible Man is standing quite
still: we feel that he is gazing
round - taking in the scene around
him - the waves of men - inexorably
closing upon him from every side.
Behind him the blazing barn sends a
pall of dark smoke into the sky.

THE CAMERA HOLDS the smooth surface of the snow - the trail of
footsteps ending in two prints side
by side, where the Invisible Man
stands waiting.
CUT TO:

G-52   EXT. FIELD...LONGER SHOT...

Suddenly they move forward again -
turn abruptly to the left and widen
as the Invisible Man runs - straight
towards the line commanded by the
Chief Detective. There are medleyed,
excited shouts.
CUT TO:

G-53   EXT. FELD...MED CLOSE ON...

                              CHIEF DETECTIVE
                        Look out - there he goes.

CUT TO:

G-54   EXT. FIELD...MED LONG SHOT...

The Chief Detective, the Sergeant
beside him. They watch, fascinated
as the deep, clear footprints come
towards them.
CUT TO:

nn   G-55   EXT. FIELD...CLOSE SHOT ON..

        The Chief Detective raises his
        revolver - takes careful aim
        and fires into the emptiness
        above the advancing steps.
        CUT TC:

      G-56   EXT. FIELD...MED SHOT...LONG

        The steps halt - there is a
        moment of stillness - and then
        the snow-white space is churned
        by the falling body. Slowly -
        fascinated the Chief Detective
        comes forward and kneels beside
        the roughened dented surface.
        His hands steal forward -
        searching - feeling over the
        invisible, wounded body. Other
        men come forward and stand
        silently around. Someone says:

                                    "Is he dead?"

        CUT TO:

      G-57   EXT. FIELD...MED CLOSE ON...

        The Detective makes no reply.

        FADE OUT

FADE IN:

H-1   A SMALL WAITING ROOM
        IN A HOSPITAL - FULL SHOT.
        ────────────────────────────

        Two policemen stand on guard
        to either side of a door that
        leads into a private ward.

        The Chief Detective is slowly
        pacing the room. Dr. Cranley
        stands waiting by the windows.
        Presently the door from the
        private ward is softly opened,
        and a white-coated Doctor enters.
        The Chief Detective quickly turns.

                                    DOCTOR   (to Chief Detective)
                                        I don't think your guard
                                        will be needed any longer.
                                            (there is a moment
                                            of silence before
                                            the Doctor speaks
                                            again)

                                        He's very near the end.
                                            (he turns to the old
                                            Doctor)
                                        Are you Dr. Cranley?

                                    DR. CRANLEY
                                        Yes. I had a message - to
                                        come immediately.

                                    DOCTOR
                                        Towards dawn this morning
                                        he grew quiet. He called
                                        the name of a girl. I
                                        understand - your daughter,
                                        Dr. Cranley.

                                    DR. CRANLEY (with a slight nod)
                                        She's waiting below.
                                            (he pauses)
                                        Is there - any chance?

        CUT TO:

H-2   INT. WAITING ROOM
        CLOSE TWO SHOT...
        ─────────────────────

        The Doctor shakes his
        head.

                                    DOCTOR
                                        The bullet passed through
                                        both lungs. It's impossible
                                        to treat the wound. Do
                                        you think your daughter -
                                        could bear to go to him?
                                        I'm afraid the end may be
                                        - rather terrible. The
                                        effect of the drugs will
                                        die with him; his body
                                        will become visible as
                                        life goes.

        (CONTINUED)

286

H-2   (CONTINUED)

        Dr. Cranley faces the
        Doctor in silence for
        a moment, then turns
        to the door.

                    DR. CRANLEY
                I'll bring her now.

DISSOLVE SLOWLY TO:

H-3   INT. HOSPITAL ROOM.
      FULL SHOT...

        Where the Invisible
        Man lies dying. A small
        plainly furnished private
        ward. A nurse moves away
        as the Doctor comes for-
        ward and looks down at
        the empty bed. The
        clothes are tucked
        round as they would cover
        the body of a still, pros-
        trate form. They rise and
        fall very slightly to the
        shallow breathing of the
        dying.man. A weak, urgent
        voice comes up to the
        waiting Doctor.

                    INVISIBLE MAN
                - is - Flora there?

        The Doctor bends down a
        little.
                    DOCTOR
                She is coming - now.

        CUT TO:

H-4   INT. HOSPITAL ROOM
      MEDIUM SHOT...

        The door opens, and
        Dr. Cranley enters. He
        stands aside to make way
        for the girl, who crosses
        quietly to the bed. The
        Doctor draws up a chair
        and motions to the girl
        to approach. He withdraws
        to a far corner of the room
        with Dr. Cranley, and the
        two men stand waiting in
        silence. The girl sits be-
        side the bed.

        CUT TO:

H-5   INT. HOSPITAL ROOM
      CLOSE SHOT OF...

        The pillows. There is no
        sound until the tired,
        weak voice rises from
        the empty pillows.

        (CONTINUED)

H-5   (CONTINUED)

                                    INVISIBLE MAN
                                         I - knew you would -
                                         come to me, Flora.

        CUT TO:

H-6   INT. HOSPITAL ROOM
        CLOSE SHOT ON....
        _____

        Flora - she raises
        her hand and gently
        feels along the side
        of the bed until she
        grasps the hand of the
        dying man. He speaks again -
        scarcely above a whisper.

                                    INVISIBLE MAN
                                         I wanted to come back to
                                         you - my darling, I failed.
                                         I meddled in things that
                                         man - must leave alone...

        His last words die
        away.

        CUT TO:

H-7   INT. HOSPITAL ROOM
        MED. CLOSE ON FLORA
        _____

        The girl sits with his
        invisible hand in hers -
        she is helpless to do
        more than comfort him
        in this little way. At
        last she speaks, alarmed
        at his silence.

                                    FLORA
                                         - Jack! -

        CUT TO:

H-8   INT. HOSPITAL ROOM
        MED. FULL...
        _____

        The clothes around the
        body no longer rise and
        fall with the faint breath-
        ing. Without moving her
        hand, she turns to her
        father and calls -

        CUT TO:

H-9   INT. HOSPITAL ROOM
        CLOSE UP ON..FLORA.
        _____

        Calling to her father
        in a low, urgent voice:

                                    FLORA
                                         Father - come quickly!

        CUT TO:

H-10   INT. HOSPITAL ROOM
        MEDIUM SHOT...

        Dr. Cranley and the
        hospital Doctor
        turning and approach-
        ing the bed.

        CUT TO:

H-11   INT. HOSPITAL ROOM
        MED. CLOSE ON.....

        The bed - the dented
        pillow - and tucked in
        clothes. Very slowly -
        from the emptiness -
        begins to gather a thin
        grey mist. Gradually
        it takes form - a human
        head and shoulders -
        as transparent as glass -
        that slowly gathers a
        thin opaqueness, that
        deepens and hardens into
        shadows and substance -
        until at last there lies
        upon the pillows a human
        face. A strong, handsome
        face - dark and very
        peaceful in death.

        THE PICTURE FADES.

                        THE   END

                          ***

CPSIA information can be obtained at www.ICGtesting.com
Printed in the USA
LVOW090817011212

309646LV00001B/331/P